Where a g[...]
concerned, it wouldn't do to
trust any man…especially one as
undeniably charming as Mr. Anders.

His sincere-sounding compliments, combined with the
devilishly appealing trait he had of seeming to focus his
entire attention on what one said, made him very hard to
resist.

Adding that to the handsomeness of his person—for a
moment she allowed the image of that tall, upright figure,
the handsome face and arresting green eyes to play through
her mind again—made him a vastly attractive gentleman.

She'd had a potent lesson on the terrace in just how easy it
was to fall under his spell. Tantalizing as she—still, alas—
found the notion of kissing him, it would be dangerously
easy to be lured into improper behavior.

So she would just *have* to resist him. Upon that firm
conclusion, she entered the parlor to find papa finishing his
sherry. Beside his chair, sipping a sherry of his own, stood
Mr. Anders.

And another of those annoying thrills rippled through her.

* * *

Society's Most Disreputable Gentleman
Harlequin® Historical #1028—February 2011

Praise for
Julia Justiss

From Waif to Gentleman's Wife
"An enjoyable read with absorbing characters
and a slice of English history."
—Debbie Macomber, *New York Times* bestselling author

A Most Unconventional Match
"Justiss captures the true essence of the Regency period…
The characters come to life with all the proper mannerisms
and dialogue as they waltz around each other
in a 'most unconventional' courtship."
—*RT Book Reviews*

The Untamed Heiress
"Justiss rivals Georgette Heyer in the beloved
The Grand Sophy (1972) by creating a riveting
young woman of character and good humor…
The horrific nature of Helena's childhood adds complexity and
depth to this historical romance, and unexpected plot twists
and layers also increase the reader's enjoyment."
—*Booklist*

The Courtesan
"With its intelligent, compelling characters, this is
a very well-written, emotional and intensely charged read."
—*RT Book Reviews*, Top Pick

My Lady's Trust
"With this exceptional Regency-era romance,
Justiss adds another fine feather to her writing cap."
—*Publishers Weekly*

SOCIETY'S MOST
DISREPUTABLE GENTLEMAN

JULIA JUSTISS

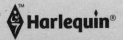

TORONTO NEW YORK LONDON
AMSTERDAM PARIS SYDNEY HAMBURG
STOCKHOLM ATHENS TOKYO MILAN MADRID
PRAGUE WARSAW BUDAPEST AUCKLAND

Recycling programs
for this product may
not exist in your area.

ISBN-13: 978-0-373-29628-6

SOCIETY'S MOST DISREPUTABLE GENTLEMAN

Copyright © 2011 by Janet Justiss

**Available from Harlequin® Historical and
JULIA JUSTISS**

The Wedding Gamble #464
A Scandalous Proposal #532
The Proper Wife #567
My Lady's Trust #591
My Lady's Pleasure #611
My Lady's Honor #629
A Most Unconventional Match #905
One Candlelit Christmas #919
"Christmas Wedding Wish"
From Waif to Gentleman's Wife #964
†*The Smuggler and the Society Bride* #1004
Society's Most Disreputable Gentleman #1028

*linked by character
†*Silk & Scandal* miniseries

**Also available from
Harlequin® Books**

The Officer's Bride
"An Honest Bargain"
Wicked Wager
Forbidden Stranger
"Seductive Stranger"

**Also available from
HQN™ Books**

Christmas Keepsakes
"The Three Gifts"
The Courtesan
The Untamed Heiress
Rogue's Lady

In Memory of my Mother
Who read all my books and proudly displayed them
on her shelves
And who taught me a woman can do anything

Chapter One

A shake to his bad shoulder brought Greville Anders awake with a gasp. Through the stab of sensation radiating down his arm, he dimly heard the coachman say, 'Here we be, now, sir. At ycr destination. Ashton Grove.'

Trying to master a pain-induced nausea, Greville struggled to surface a mind he'd submerged in soothing clouds of laudanum to ease the agony of a long, jolting coach journey. The late-winter air spilling through the door held ajar by a man in footman's livery helped dissipate the mental fog.

England. He must be back in England. No place else on earth had this combination of chilly mist and a scent of damp earth.

Like a tacking sail that suddenly catches the wind, his vacant mind filled. Yes, he was in England, at Ashton Grove, the home of Lord Bronning. The manor where, at the intervention of his noble cousin, the Marquess of Englemere, he was to stay after being transferred from his berth on the *Illustrious* to the Coastal Brigade, while the Admiralty sorted out the matter of his—illegal—impressment. And he finished healing.

Unfortunately, that also meant he must now attempt to convince his unsteady limbs to carry him from the vehicle into the manor, hopefully without having his still-roiling stomach disgrace him. Taking a deep breath, he staggered into the early evening dimness, then proceeded at a limping gait up to the entry and through a door held open by the butler.

Perspiration beading his forehead from the effort, he was congratulating himself on his success at reaching the stately entry hall when an older, balding gentleman walked forwards and bowed. 'Mr Anders,' the man said, giving him a strained smile. 'Delighted to welcome you to Ashton Grove.'

The gentleman's expression was so far from delighted that Greville bit back a smile before the unmistakable, swishing sound of skirts trailing over polished stone prompted him to carefully angle his head left.

That uncomfortable manoeuvre was rewarded by a vision lovely enough to raise a red-blooded sailor from the dead. A category into which, after the *Illustrious*'s action with that Algerian pirate vessel off the coast of Tunis, he'd very nearly fallen, he thought wryly before giving mind and senses over to the sorely missed pleasure of gazing at a beautiful woman.

For the first time in a long while, parts of his body tingled pleasantly as he took in an angelic vision of golden hair and a petite form wrapped in a flattering gown, just a hint of décolletage tempting one to peek down at an admirably rounded bosom. As he raised his gaze to the perfect oval of her face, large blue eyes stared back at him over a small, pert nose and plump rosebud-pink lips that were currently pursed. She frowned.

Greville suppressed a sigh. Angels generally did frown at him.

Long-inbred habits of gentility prompted him to attempt a bow, awkward as it was with the thick bandage still binding his chest and the fact that his equilibrium hadn't yet adjusted to having a surface beneath his feet that remained firmly horizontal. 'Lord Bronning, isn't it?' he asked. 'And…?'

'My daughter, Miss Neville. Welcome to our home. I trust Lord Englemere made your journey as comfortable as possible—under the circumstances, of course,' Bronning said, casting him a troubled glance.

The lovely daughter merely inclined her head, her frown deepening. Greville hadn't seen his own face in a glass for months, but in his ragtag sailor's gear, with an unkempt beard and what he supposed must be the pallor induced by his lingering fever, doubtless he looked nothing like the sort of gentleman Miss Neville was accustomed to receiving in her father's grand hall.

'Miss Neville, my lord,' he replied, acknowledging the introductions. 'Yes, Lord Englemere did…all that was necessary.' Given his already disreputable appearance, he thought it best not to mention that his passage from Spithead through Portsmouth and thence by coach to Ashton Grove had passed in such a laudanum haze that he had little memory of it. 'I thank you, Lord Bronning, for receiving one so completely unknown to you.'

'Not at all,' Bronning replied quickly. 'I'm happy to oblige Lord Englemere—and your sister, Lady Greaves, of course. Her husband, Sir Edward, is a valued acquaintance. But we won't keep you standing here with the evening chill coming on! You must be exhausted from your travels. Sands will have a footman show you to your room.'

His room. A real chamber with a bed that didn't sway with the roll of the ship, doubtless located in a private space he wouldn't share with a score of noisy, tar-begrimed, sweating sailors.

Heaven.

'I should like that, thank you,' he said, summoning his

waning strength for the task of climbing the forbiddingly tall stairway towards which a footman was leading him.

'And, Mr Anders,' Bronning called after him, 'please don't feel obliged to join us for dinner. Cook will be happy to prepare you a tray, if you'd prefer to remain in your chamber to rest and repose yourself after your long journey.'

Rest and repose. He clung to the notion as a drowning man clutches at a spar after a shipwreck. Rest to finish healing his battered body, repose in which to put his fever-dulled wits to examining the implications of his abrupt transition from deckhand on a man-of-war to guest at an elegant English estate.

'Thank you, my lord, I may do that,' he said, reflecting as he tackled the stairs upon the irony of greeting the notion of solitude with such pleasure, he who not so very long ago would have done almost anything to avoid the boredom of having only himself for company.

Gritting his teeth in determination, Greville made his way upwards, Miss Neville's soft floral fragrance still teasing his nose.

Amanda Neville felt disappointment and an entirely illogical sense of being ill-used replace her initial shock, as she stared after the newcomer hobbling up the stairs behind the footman.

Ever since Papa had told her they were to house a relation of the Marquess of Englemere, she'd been bubbling over with anticipation, hoping he would be someone she could meet again in London this spring when she made her long-delayed come-out—mayhap even a handsome young man who might be a potential suitor. She'd had Mrs Pepys prepare the best guest bedchamber and instructed Cook to create a sumptuous meal for the night of his arrival.

Stunned into silence by the appearance of the man who'd limped over their doorstep, she'd barely been able to nod a greeting. That grimy, battered man dressed like a common sailor was their *guest*? she thought again, still aghast and scarcely able to comprehend such a conundrum. Whatever had Papa been thinking, to agree to house such a person?

Before she could utter a word, however, her father grabbed her arm and steered her down the hallway towards his study. 'Don't give me that look, puss, until I can explain,' he said under his breath. 'That will be all for now, Sands,' he added, dismissing the butler who trailed after them, interest bright in his eyes.

'Really, Papa, I know better than to gossip before the servants,' she protested after he'd shut the study door behind them. 'But when you told me you were to host Lord Englemere's relative—why, he's a Stanhope, head of one of the most prominent families in England! Are you sure this…sailor is truly his cousin?'

'He gave the name "Anders" and arrived in a private coach, as I was led to expect, so he must be. Though I confess, I was as shocked by his appearance as you.'

After depositing her on the sofa, her father took an agitated turn about the room. 'Now that I think on it, though naturally I assumed so, the note from his lordship's secretary never precisely said Mr Anders was an officer.'

'He looks more like a—a ruffian!' Amanda exclaimed, still feeling affronted. 'A drunken one, at that! How are we to go about entertaining such a person? Is he to dine with us, be presented to our acquaintances?'

Lord Bronning's troubled frown deepened. 'Dear me, I hope I haven't made a terrible mistake, allowing him to come…' His voice trailed off and he grimaced.

'Now, Papa, you mustn't upset yourself and bring on one of your spells,' Amanda said quickly, concern for her father, who had not been in the best of health of late, quickly overshadowing her irritation and chagrin. 'Come, sit, and let me pour you some wine,' she urged, hopping up to guide her father to a chair and then fetch him a glass of port. 'What precisely did his lordship's note say?'

'Only that Mr Anders had been serving on a warship and was being furloughed back to England after being wounded during a skirmish with privateers,' her father replied, easing back into the cushions. 'Apparently naval men injured too severely to perform their duties are sometimes posted to the Coastal Brigade while they heal. Having learned that Ashton Grove was not far from one of their stations, the marquess begged me to offer his cousin accommodations while he recuperated. Naturally, one does not say "no" to a marquess, especially one who writes so politely.'

Amanda bit her lip. 'Nor, after installing this "Mr Anders" in the best guest bedchamber, will it be easy to move him elsewhere. In any event, he didn't seem fit enough to appear in company, so for dining and entertaining, I suppose we shall wait and see.'

'That would be best, I expect. Besides, he is also brother to the wife of Sir Edward Greaves, and after that unfortunate incident last spring, I should not wish to do anything that might offend Sir Edward.'

Amanda felt her face flush. 'I am sorry about that, Papa.'

Smiling fondly, her father patted her arm. 'Never you mind, puss. You can't help that you are just naturally too lovely and charming for any sensible gentleman to resist.'

Though Amanda felt a pang of guilt, she didn't correct her papa. The truth was, she had quite deliberately sought to be at her most enticing when, after last year's agricultural meeting at Holkham Hall, Papa had brought home to visit a man he'd often mentioned as being one of the most forward-thinking gentlemen farmers in the realm. She'd only thought to flirt a bit, seizing one of the few opportunities that came her way to practise her wiles on a single gentleman of noble birth.

Who could have imagined the quiet, rather stodgy Sir

Edward, who had barely spoken to her of anything beyond a boring narration about crops and fields, would have possessed sufficient sensibility to become smitten?

She'd been surprised—and a bit ashamed—when Papa told her, after Sir Edward's sudden departure, that the baronet had made him an offer for her hand. Thankfully, knowing well that the very last thing she wanted was to buckle herself to some gentleman farmer and spend the rest of her years immured in rural obscurity, Papa had spared her the embarrassing necessity of refusing him.

However, she reassured herself pragmatically, since Sir Edward had married within six months of his departure from Ashton Grove, she could not have wounded his heart too severely.

Still, she could not help but regret that her flirtation had put a rub in her father's friendship with the man.

'Of course, Papa, I'm as anxious as you to make amends to Sir Edward and dispel any lingering…awkwardness. Have you any idea how long Mr Anders is to be our guest? And… surely I am not called upon to nurse him?'

'Of course not!' her father assured her. 'Even if it were not most improper, I would never ask you to do something so expressly designed to bring back…unfortunate memories.'

Abruptly, they both fell silent. Despite her papa's hope to avoid it, she found her thoughts sucked inexorably back to the terrible spring and summer just past. Nightmarish visions chased across her mind: Mama's cheeks flushed with fever; Aunt Felicia thrashing in delirium; both faces fixed in the still, cold pallor of death.

Shaking her head to dislodge the images, she turned to Papa and saw, from the stricken look on his face, that he must be remembering, too. Anxiety instantly replaced grief; Papa's own health had nearly broken under the strain of losing both wife and sister, and he was still, she feared, far from recovered.

Before she could hit upon some remark that might distract him, Papa said, 'Of course, Mr Anders is welcome to stay as long as he may need. Should it turn out that he requires further care, I shall consult with Dr Wendell in the village to obtain a suitable practitioner. But do not worry, puss…' he reached out to pat her hand '…however long our visitor tarries, I promised your dear mama I would let nothing else delay the Season for which you've waited so long and so patiently.'

Amanda smiled her thanks and tried to refocus her mind on that happy event. London, this spring! Dare she even hope this time that it would finally happen? The Season, which she and her mama had planned and anticipated for so long, had been delayed by such a series of unfortunate events that sometimes it seemed Fate itself was conspiring to prevent her having any opportunity to realise her dreams.

Still, with her last breath, Mama had made Amanda promise that she *would* go this year, come what may. So perhaps the visit would take place after all.

Oh, to finally be in London, that greatest of English cities, where she would not have to pore over accounts of events already days or weeks old by the time the newspapers reached them. London, where her future husband, a man of substance and influence in his party, would sit in the Lords and help direct the affairs of the nation. Supported, of course, by his lovely wife, whose dinners, soirées and balls would bring together all the influential people of the realm, where policy would be discussed and settled over brandy and whispered about behind fans.

If no further disaster occurred to prevent it, in a few short weeks, she would be there. She could hardly wait.

Suddenly the study door opened on a draught of cold air and her cousin Althea dashed in. 'Is he here yet? Have I missed him?' she demanded.

Amanda swallowed the sharp words springing to her lips

about the decorum a young lady should employ when entering a room. As she'd learned all too swiftly after Althea joined them at Ashton last spring just before the death of her mother, Amanda's Aunt Felicia, the cousin who had once followed her about like an adoring puppy now seemed to resent every word she uttered.

Ignoring, as usual, the girl's rudeness, Papa only said mildly, 'Missed who, my dear?'

His own bereavement had made him more indulgent than was good for the girl, Amanda thought a tad resentfully. Papa never offered her tempestuous cousin the least reproof, no matter how deplorable her speech or actions, though he was perhaps the only one who might be able to correct her highly deficient behaviour.

'Why, Mr Anders, the Navy man, of course!' Althea replied. 'He has arrived, hasn't he? I saw a rum fine coach being driven round to the stables, one done up to a cow's thumb!'

The girl must have been hanging about the stables herself, to have picked up that bit of cant. Swallowing a reproof on that point, Amanda said, 'I fear you've missed him. Mr Anders did indeed arrive and has just gone up to his room.'

'Fiddlesticks!' Althea exclaimed. 'I suppose I shall have to wait to meet him at dinner.'

A sudden foreboding filled Amanda, sweeping away her more trivial concern over their genteel neighbours' probable reaction to having Mr Anders thrust among them. What if Althea, who already seemed eager to seize upon anything of which Amanda disapproved, decided to befriend this low sailor? Considering her current behaviour, it seemed exactly the sort of thing she would do.

Though normally she would never wish anyone ill, Amanda couldn't help being thankful that, for tonight at least, Mr Anders appeared to be in no condition to join them for dinner.

'I don't think he will be coming down to dine. He appeared much fatigued from his journey.'

'Fatigued—from riding in a coach? What a plumper!' Althea replied roundly. 'Not a Navy man! I'll wager Mr Anders has steered his ship for hours in a driving gale and survived for months on hardtack and biscuits! More likely, he'll be sharp-set enough to eat us out of table.'

While Amanda gritted her teeth anew at Althea's vocabulary, Papa replied, 'Perhaps, but he was wounded and is still recovering.'

'Wounded in battle?' Althea demanded, her eyes brightening even further. 'Oh, excellent! Where? When?'

'I believe it was off the Barbary coast, some weeks ago,' Papa responded.

'How exciting! He must be veritable hero! I cannot wait to have him tell us all about it. What a joy it will be to speak with a truly interesting person, someone who's had real adventures, who doesn't natter on and on about gowns and shops and *London*!' she declared with a defiant glance at Amanda—just in case she was too dim to understand the jab, Amanda thought, struggling to hang on to her temper.

'Uncle James, have you any books in your library about the Navy?' she said, turning to Lord Bronning. 'Oh, never mind, I shall go directly myself and look!'

At that, with as little ceremony as she'd displayed upon her precipitate arrival, Althea bolted from the room.

In the wake of her departure, Amanda sent her father an appealing look. 'Papa, you must warn her off Mr Anders. If we're not careful, she'll be painting him as another Lord Nelson!'

'And doubtless urging him to recite details of shipboard life in language not fit for a lady's ears,' Papa agreed ruefully.

'I know you feel for her, having lost her mama so soon after her papa, but truly, you must counsel her about this. Heaven knows, I don't dare say anything for fear she will immediately take that as a challenge to parade with him about the neighbourhood.'

Papa nodded. 'She does seem to take umbrage at everything you say. Which I find most odd, since during Felicia's visits when you girls were younger, Althea used to hang on your every word and copy everything you did.'

Amanda sighed. A smaller but no less stinging wound to her heart this last year was the, to her, inexplicable hostility with which her cousin now seemed to view her. 'Truly, Papa, I have tried to be understanding. I don't know why she seems to resent me so. Perhaps I did criticise her conduct overmuch when she first arrived—I really can't recall—but with Aunt Felicia so ill and the house in such an uproar, and then Mama falling sick—'

'There now, you mustn't be blaming yourself,' Papa said, patting her arm. 'You were a marvel through that trying time, taking over the household so your dear mama need concern herself only with Felicia…' His breath hitched and his eyes grew moist before he continued, 'So strong and capable, I couldn't be prouder of you. But Althea is young, and perhaps chafed at authority being assumed by one she'd considered almost a peer. She was distraught, and bereft, and grieving—not a felicitous combination for any of us.'

Amanda blinked the tears back from her eyes. 'Indeed not, Papa.' Papa might think her strong, but in truth she had barely managed to hold the household together and was still trying to recover her spirits. Oh, how she yearned to escape Ashton Grove, all its problems and sad memories, and lose herself in the distractions of London!

Though her younger brother had lately arrived to add to her anxieties, Althea remained the most acute of her burdens. Her own feelings depressed and raw after Mama's death, Amanda couldn't help wishing she might be rid of the troublesome girl—a desire Althea probably sensed, which did nothing to ease the tensions between them.

All her life, she reflected with another pang of grief, she'd been wrapped in a protective cocoon of love and affection spun by her mother and grandmother, buoyed along the floodtide of events by a happiness and security she'd taken for granted until the catastrophes of the last two years—losing first Grandmama, then Aunt Felicia, then Mama—had stripped it from her. Her longing for supportive female company had been sharpened by her difficult relations with her cousin, the only female relative left to her.

Small wonder she yearned to reach London, where she would be staying with Lady Parnell, her mother's dear friend whom she'd had known since childhood. Perhaps the affection of this companion from Mama's own début Season might ease her grief and fill some part of the void left by the last two years' devastating losses.

'So you will speak to Althea?' she pleaded, hoping against hope Papa might be able to head off this new complication. ''Tis for her own good, you know. What would Aunt Felicia say if she knew we'd allowed Althea to pursue a most unsuitable friendship with a common sailor?'

'Yes, I know I must reprimand her, and I will—gently, though.'

Her chest squeezing in a surge of love for her kindly sire, Amanda couldn't help smiling. 'I only ask that you try to *guide* her, Papa. You know as well as I you haven't the heart to reprimand anyone, no matter how much she might need it!'

'I suppose I have been too indulgent. But you're quite right—it is my responsibility to my dear sister to protect her daughter and counsel her as best I can.'

'Perhaps you could chat without my being present. She'd probably be more inclined to accept instruction if I'm not looking on. Well, I suppose I must go inform Cook about the changes in the dinner plans.'

'I'll escort you out,' Bronning said, rising and coming to take her hand. 'One of my prize mares is about to foal. I think I'll take myself down to the barn and check on her.'

Accepting her father's arm, Amanda walked back down the long hall to the marble entryway with him, her concern about Althea somewhat mollified. Given her cousin's contemptuous disregard of her, there wasn't much else she could do but leave the matter in Papa's hands.

They had just reached the grand entry when the front door was thrown back so violently it banged against the wall. Staggering across the threshold, Amanda's brother George stumbled into the room, waving off the footman who sprinted over to take his coat.

Her father stopped abruptly and eyed his only son with alarm. 'George, what's amiss? Have you suffered an injury?'

With his red face and bleary eyes, hair in disarray, neckcloth coming undone and his waistcoat misbuttoned, George did indeed look as if he might have been in an altercation—a fear Amanda initially shared, before a strong odour of spirits wafted to her.

Her initial concern turned swiftly to irritation as she recalled her brother had not appeared at dinner last evening. Most likely he'd not returned home at all and had instead spent yesterday afternoon, evening and today gaming—or wenching—at some low tavern.

A glance at her father's face confirmed he had just reached the same conclusion. His expression of alarm turned to chagrin and a pained sadness, and unconsciously he raised a hand to press against his chest.

Fury swept through her and she could have cheerfully throttled her brother. How could George be so stupid and thoughtless as to make his dramatic entrance in such a deplorable condition? It was almost as if he expressly desired to agitate and disappoint his already sorely troubled father!

'Papa, why don't you head out to the stables and check on your mare? I'll see George to his room. Come along, now,' she said to her brother, pleased she'd managed to keep her tone even when what she really wished to do was shriek her displeasure into her feckless brother's ears.

Contenting herself with giving George's arm a sharp pinch as she took it, she steered him towards the stairs. Nodding over her shoulder to Papa, who hesitated before finally approaching the butler for his coat, she began half-pushing, half-pulling her brother upwards.

'I hope I shall not contract some nasty disease from having to haul you about,' she snapped as she finally succeeded in wrestling him up the stairs and into his room. 'How can you still be so drunk at this hour of the afternoon?'

'Not drunk,' he slurred, stumbling past her towards the bed. 'Just…trifle disguised.'

'Was it not enough that you had to distress Papa by getting yourself sent down from Cambridge for some stupid prank?' she said, unable to hold her tongue any longer. 'Must you embarrass him before the servants in his own home? Can you never think of anything beyond your own reckless pleasure?'

George put his hands over his ears and winced, as if her strident tone pained his head. She hoped it did.

'God's blood, Manda, Allie's right. You've become a shrew. Better sweeten up a little. No gentleman's goin' to wanna shackle himself to a female who's always jaw'n at 'm.'

A pang pierced her righteous anger. Was that indeed how Althea saw her—as a shrill-voiced harpy always ordering her about? But she'd tried so hard to avoid being just that.

Before she could decide what to reply, George groaned and clutched his abdomen. Amanda barely had time to snatch the pan from beneath the bed before her brother leaned over it, noisily casting up his accounts. Wrinkling her nose in distaste, Amanda retreated to the far corner of the room.

After a moment, George righted himself and sat on the bed, wiping his mouth. 'Ah, that's better. Ring for Richards, won't you? I believe I'll have a beefsteak and some ale.'

Amanda couldn't help grimacing. 'George, you are disgusting!'

'Shrew,' he retorted with an amiable grin—which, despite her irritation and anger, she had to admit was full of charm, even in his present dishevelled condition. This brother of hers was going to cause some lady a great deal of heartache.

But she didn't intend it to be her—not for much longer, anyway.

'If you must debauch yourself, at least have the courtesy to come in through the back stairs, so that Papa won't see you. Can't you tell he's still far from recovered from Mama's death?

'Are any of us recovered?' he flashed back, a bleak look passing briefly over his face before the grin returned. 'What d'ya expect, Manda? There's dam—dashed little to do in this abyss of rural tranquillity but drink and game at the one or two taverns within a ten-mile ride. I'd take myself off where my reprehensible behaviour wouldn't offend you, but Papa won't allow me to go to London while I wait for the beginning of next term.'

'London, where you might spend even more on drink and wagering? I should think not! You'd do better to spend some time studying, so as to not be so far behind when you do return.'

George made a disgusted noise, as if such a suggestion were beneath reply. 'Lord, how did I tolerate living in this dull place for years? Nothing but fields and cows and crops and fields for miles in every direction! It's almost enough to make those stupid books look appealing.'

'Fields and crops in prime condition, thanks to Papa's care, that fund your expensive sojourns at Cambridge. And if you'd paid more attention to those "stupid books" and less to carousing with your fellows, you wouldn't be marooned in this "dull place" to begin with.'

George squinted up at her through bloodshot eyes. 'When did you become such a disapproving spoilsport?'

'When will you become a man worthy of the Neville name?' she retorted, her heart aching for her father's disappointment while her anger smouldered at how George's thoughtlessness was adding to the already-heavy burden of care her father carried. 'Start showing some interest in the estate Papa has so carefully tended to hand on to you, instead of staying out all night, consorting with ruffians and getting into who-knows-what mischief.'

Anger flushing his face, George opened his lips to reply before closing them abruptly. 'Maybe I'm not ready for that steak after all,' he mumbled, reaching for the basin.

Realising he was about to be sick again, Amanda shook her head in disgust. There was probably no point in trying to talk with George now. 'I'll send Richards in,' she said, swallowing her ire and willing herself to calm as she tugged on the bell pull and left the chamber.

She met the valet in the hall, where he must have been hovering, having no doubt been informed by the butler of her brother's return—and condition. 'I'm afraid he's disguised again and feeling quite ill. You'd better bring up some hot water and strip him down.'

Feeling a pang of sympathy for the long-suffering servant, Amanda headed for the stairs. She paused on the landing, pressing her fingers against the temples that had begun to throb.

Between her irresponsible brother and her sullen cousin and having to watch Papa drift around the halls and fields, a wraith-like imitation of his former hale and hearty self, was it any wonder she longed to leave Ashton and throw herself into the frivolity of London? There the most difficult dilemma would be choosing what gown to wear, her most pressing problem fitting into her social schedule all the events to which she'd be invited. Her day would be so full, she'd tumble into bed and immediately into sleep, never lie awake aching and alone, yearning for the love and security so abruptly ripped from her.

Oh, that she might swiftly make a brilliant début, acquire a husband to pamper and adore her and settle into the busy life of a London political wife, seldom to visit the country again.

She only hoped, as she went to search out Cook and rear-range dinner, that their unwanted guest would not make the last few weeks before she could set her plans in motion even more difficult.

Chapter Two

With a bestial roar, the crewman tossed the boarding nets over the side of the pirate vessel. Fear, acrid in his throat, along with a wave of excitement, carried Greville over the side and on to its prow, into the mass of slashing cutlasses, firing pistols and thrusting pikes. Blood already coated the decks, thick and slippery, when he saw the pirate charging at the captain, curved sword raised and teeth bared...

Abruptly, Greville came awake, his heart pounding as the shriek of wind, boom of musket fire and howls of fighting men slowly faded to the quiet tick of a clock in a room where warm sunlight pooled on the floor beneath the windows.

Morning sun, judging by the hue, he thought, trying to get his bearings. Brighter than light through a porthole.

About the moment Greville realised he was in a proper bedchamber—a vast, elegant bedchamber—in Lord Bronning's home at Ashton Grove, Devonshire, praise-the-Lord-England, he heard a discreet cough. Turning towards the sound, he spied a young man in footman's livery standing inside the doorway, bearing a laden tray.

'Morning, sir,' the lad said, bowing. 'Sands sent me up with something from the kitchen, thinking you'd likely be right sharp-set after so many hours.'

'Have I been asleep long?' Greville asked, still trying to recapture a sense of place and time.

'Aye,' the young man replied. 'All the first night, the next day and now 'tis almost noon of the next. Some of the staff was worried you was about to stick your spoon in the wall. But Mrs Pepys—that's the housekeeper, sir—she's done some nursing and she said as long as you was breathing deep and regular, there weren't no danger of you dying and that you'd feel much the better for the rest.'

He did feel much better, Greville thought. Moreover, he realised suddenly, for the first time since his wounding over a month ago, he hadn't awakened to the slow, strength-sapping burn of fever.

He was also, he discovered, truly starving. Contemplating what might lie beneath the plate cover on the tray, his mouth began to water.

'You are right, I am very hungry,' he told the footman.

'Shall I put the tray on the bed here for you, sir?'

'Yes, that would be fine. Thank you…' He hesitated.

'Luke, sir,' the footman supplied. 'Sands says I'm to assist you with dressing and such, if'n you need any help.'

'I'd like a bath after I've eaten, if you would arrange that. I'll be better able to ascertain how much assistance I'll require then. Oh—and if you please, ask that housekeeper for some linen bandages. I've a wound I'll have to rebind.'

'Very good, sir,' the footman said, depositing the tray in front of him. 'I'll go see about your bath. By the by, there's a chest by the fireplace and a note sent by your sister, Lady Greaves.'

Greaves? He did not even know which of his sisters had married into that name.

After being gone so long from England, his time spent at

hard labour in a job for which he'd had no preparation or train-ing, the idea that he was part of a family beyond the wooden walls of the *Illustrious* seemed disorienting. Not that he'd paid a good deal of attention to his closest kin before his involuntary removal from British soil.

A *frisson* of guilt passed through him. Truth be told, he'd seldom troubled himself to think at all about the family that had pampered and sheltered him for the first sixteen years of his life, before his father and sisters departed for India, leaving him at Cambridge. He'd contacted Papa only when he needed him to call upon his Army contacts to arrange Greville's ser-vice with the commissariat during the Waterloo campaign. And afterwards, wanting for some sort of position to support himself, he'd solicited his cousin the marquess's help in provid-ing one.

He shifted uncomfortably. He still had much to atone for in rectifying how that latter situation had turned out.

'Let me have the letter before you go,' he told the footman. 'I'll deal with the trunk later.'

After passing him the folded missive, the footman bowed himself out of the room. Greville's growling stomach reminded him it had been many hours since he'd last eaten—he had only a dim memory of wolfing down some sort of stew sent up the night of his arrival. He put the letter aside, content to wait to discover which of his sisters was the mysterious 'Lady Greaves' until after he'd taken the edge off his hunger.

As he removed the cover from the plate, the wonderful odour of eggs, bacon, beef, potatoes, ham and kippers wafted up, along with the sharp aroma of hot coffee and the pungent tang of ale. Inhaling with rapture, he abandoned himself to the pleasure of consuming the first full hot meal he'd had since leaving England eight months ago.

The food tasted better than any breakfast he could remem-ber. Of course, after months at sea on a diet that consisted mostly of hardtack, boiled beef and an occasional plum duff, it wouldn't take much for Lord Bronning's cook to impress him.

A short time later, his happy stomach replete, Greville broke the seal on the note and, still sipping the delicious ambrosia of hot coffee, rapidly scanned it.

The signature, 'Joanna', indicated his benefactress must be his widowed elder sister, who had obviously remarried. He vaguely recalled that she'd sent him word of her first husband's death just after he'd taken over as manager at Blenhem Hill. Greville scanned his memory, but could not place any gentleman with the family name 'Greaves'. Still, by adding 'Lady' to her name this time—more dignity than had been due her after wedding a mere younger son from the prominent Merrill family—she must have married well.

She might even rank higher now than some of the former in-laws who had snubbed her. Greville hoped so.

If Papa and the rest of the family were still in India—and he had no reason to suppose they had returned—it must have been Joanna who'd pieced together the mystery of his disappearance, then entreated his exalted cousin Lord Englemere to search for him.

Having dismissed Greville from the job he'd solicited as estate manager at Blenhem Hill for incompetence and embezzlement—the first charge deserved, the second not—Englemere himself was unlikely to have been concerned about, or even aware of, Greville's precipitous and unwilling departure from England.

That Englemere had intervened, he was certain. Only a man with the influence and the prestige of a marquess, one who had the ear of the Admiralty board, could have effected his transfer, for the commanding officer of the *Illustrious* had categorically refused such a request.

He wondered how Joanna—assuming it was Jo—had

discovered his abduction. The note didn't say and his sister indicating only her relief that he was safely back in England, her hope that he would find the trunk of clothes she'd sent useful.

He felt another pang; absorbed in his own interests, it had never occurred to him to use the close acquaintances with young gentlemen of the nobility, acquired during his university days among them, to try to smooth his sister's way with her first husband's family. He was touched, and humbled, that though he'd been oblivious to her plight, she had learned about and concerned herself with his.

It would be good to visit her, he decided, a curious sense of anticipation stirring at the thought. Maybe the new Greville would learn to value family as his sister obviously did—even such a curmudgeon black sheep as himself.

He was distracted from his musings by a scratch at the door, which opened to reveal Luke and two other footmen hefting a large copper tub. They deposited it before the hearth, several others following in their wake to fill it with bucketfuls of hot water.

Greville eyed the steam rising from the tub with as much anticipation as if a naked mermaid might emerge from the mists.

Well, maybe not quite that much. Still, anxious as he was to redress that lack in his life and much as the spirit was willing, his still-feeble body probably would make better use of the hot water minus a hot-blooded, willing wench.

'Does you need help climbing in, sir?' Luke asked.

'I think I can manage. Is there someone who could trim my hair and beard after?'

'I'm a dab hand at that, sir,' Luke replied. 'I reckon I could help you.'

Greville smiled to himself. Lord Bronning undoubtedly possessed a valet, but such an elevated gentleman's gentleman would probably disdain to offer his services to as unprepossessing a specimen as Greville had appeared when he'd limped over the threshold at Ashton Grove.

After a moment spent wondering what his own valet had thought months ago, when he failed to meet the man at their lodgings in London as arranged upon leaving Blenhem Hill, Greville said, 'Thank you, Luke. I'll ring for you when I'm ready.'

The footmen dismissed, Greville climbed carefully out of the bed, shed the nightshirt into which someone had thoughtfully changed him the night of his arrival, unwound the binding at his chest and eased himself into the steaming water. Leaning his head back against the rim, he sighed in ecstasy.

For long delicious minutes he let his mind simply drift, finally returning to conscious thought with the resolution that never again would he go through life oblivious to the simple delights of hot water and nourishing food. After living for months at the brute edge of existence, he would savour every moment of comfort.

And every delight, he thought, bringing back to mind the lovely but disapproving face of his host's daughter.

The one pleasure he had probably missed most during his involuntary sojourn at sea was the company of women. Tall, short, slim, rounded, coy, sweet, even sharp-tongued, he appreciated them all. Though he prized most, of course, the deep euphoria of the ultimate intimate embrace, he also enjoyed the simple pleasure of feminine company.

Even with a talkative miss who was chattering her teeth off, Greville could tune out the soft voice and observe instead the rise and fall of a bosom animated by a lively discourse. Caress with his gaze the lady's smooth skin, sparkling eyes and plump, kissable lips. Trace with his eyes the enticing curve of breast and hip. Breathe in her unique womanly scent.

Was Miss Neville a chatterer? he wondered, grinning at the

notion. Somehow, he didn't think so. No, Lady Bronning had greeted him in the hall—so Miss Neville must be her father's hostess and chatelaine of his household. That would explain the proprietary, managing air he'd sensed during his one quick glimpse of her.

My, how perspicacious he'd become during the last eight months, he thought with rueful humour. Transitioning abruptly from being served to the one doing the serving—with swift and severe penalties for unsatisfactory performance—taught a man with amazing speed how to discern how much authority an individual possessed.

How much more pleasant to employ that new skill in contemplating a lady! Especially a female as lovely as Miss Neville, Greville thought, running the image of her through his mind again.

So slender and petite was she, the golden curls of her coiffure would probably fit just under his chin. He could readily imagine pulling her close, filling his nostrils with the sweet fragrance of warm woman and floral perfume. Smoothing one hand around that enticing round of derrière while cupping the plump weight of a breast in the other

His palms itched with longing and his long-quiescent member rose stiffly in water, reminding him with a surge of urgency exactly how long he'd been without a woman.

Pleased as he was at this evidence that his body was finally recovering, still it would be best not to let his thoughts drift in this direction. Though in the past he'd not been above seducing a willing miss, this particular miss was gently born and his host's daughter to boot. He didn't debauch innocents.

Well, not often. And anyway, that part of his life was over. The new Greville, the better Greville he'd promised the Lord to become if he survived his time at sea, didn't intend to indulge in debauchery at all. No, sir.

Now, if there happened to be a willing widow in the neighbourhood…

He hardened further at that arousing possibility. Then Greville pulled his clean, refreshed body out of the rapidly chilling water. Wrapping a towel about his naked hips, he took a few experimental turns about the chamber.

He could feel a pull to his wound as he paced, as though the lacerated muscles of his chest were somehow directly connected to his legs, but the discomfort was not as severe as the last time he'd attempted walking. Pausing in the strong light before the window, he inspected the cutlass slash, deep across his ribs where the ship's surgeon had stitched the edges together, shallower where the weapon's tip had caught his arm. The wound hadn't stung when he immersed it in water, he realised suddenly. Thank the Lord, it must finally have closed completely.

The stitched edges were still a deep pink, but no longer fiery red and pulsing with torment. He'd put on more of the salve the ship's surgeon had sent with him and had Luke help him bind it up again, but more to keep his garments from rubbing it this time than from a need to protect his clothing from its suppuration.

He moved from the window and took two turns about the room. He felt weak and light-headed—not surprising after having been fevered and confined to a hammock or cot for so long—but the knee he'd wrenched after he'd gone down in the fight was much improved, causing him barely to limp. All in all, he felt a sense of renewed vigour he'd not experienced in all the dark days since leaving England.

Stopping by the chair where Luke had deposited the trunk of clothes sent by his sister Joanna, he opened it and inspected the contents. The garments were new and of good quality, but hardly fashionable. As he removed each one and shook it out, he found himself grinning again.

Greville Anders had been famed since Cambridge for his sartorial flair. Possessed of impeccable taste, he sported the finest inexpressibles, wore immaculate linen and knotted the most complicated cravats at the neck of beautifully tailored coats that fit him like a second skin.

A year ago, he would have rejected everything in the chest with a disdainful sniff. But after months garbed in the cast-off gear from the sea trunks of deceased sailors, he'd become much less finicky.

And much more appreciative, he thought, sending his absent sister a mental thanks. Without Joanna's intervention, he'd have been forced to put back on the soiled, bloodstained tatters he'd worn off the ship, he thought, grimacing with distaste.

It was only then that he noticed the small pouch at the bottom of the chest. Snatching it up, he opened the loop to find winking back at him a small cache of coins: pence, shillings, pounds, even a few golden guineas.

Swallowing hard at such unexpected largesse, he vowed to send his sister a written note of thanks as soon as he could obtain pen and paper. Of course, he'd arrived here penniless, possessing not even the few coins the servants would expect as the vails normally given by a guest. The service that could be expected by one who neglected to bestow such small tokens of appreciation would be dismal—and the respect he was accorded even less.

Filled with a renewed appreciation for his sister, he slipped into the small clothes, breeches and shirt, then rang for Luke. Though he was reasonably sure he could put on the coat without assistance—one benefit of wearing one that did not fit like a second skin—he'd have to wait until after his shave to don it, and tying the cravat was problematic. He feared his left arm would still be too tender to lift high enough to manage it.

Luke arrived a moment later. Though Greville had been initially dubious about the servant's claim of expertise, the footman showed himself to be quite skilled with both razor and scissors and possessed a deft hand with the cravat.

When he complimented the man, Luke told him he hoped to be a valet some day, and cast him a lingering glance, as if implying he thought Greville might be able to assist him in that desire.

Might he? Greville wondered. His immediate goals not extending beyond mastering stairs and having the stamina to walk further than three circuits about the room, he wasn't sure yet what the future would hold for himself, much less for the ambitious Luke.

The first step towards that discovery couldn't be taken until after he presented himself to the Coastal Brigade office. Though he intended to make an appearance downstairs in the parlour today, he knew he wasn't recovered enough to tolerate a several-mile jolting drive.

Luke offered him a mirror so he might inspect his new haircut in the glass. His reflection when he first glanced into a mirror before his bath had shocked him so much he marvelled that Lord Bronning had not taken one look at him and immediately had the coachman heave him back into the coach and spring the horses, dispensing with rubbish as quickly as the cook's assistant tossing the crew's refuse overboard.

Looking at himself now, he could not help being pleased at the improvement. Oh, he was still but a shadow of his former handsome self, he thought wryly. But with the beard gone, his auburn hair washed and trimmed, and wearing the clothing Joanna had sent, loose on his emaciated tall frame but quite respectable, he looked much more the sort of gentleman who might be invited as the guest of a rural baron.

Another thought struck him then, prompting another rueful smile. A year ago, he would never have considered accepting an invitation to a Devonshire estate that, from his hazy recollection, was rather remote, unless said estate came fully stocked with game for shooting, spirits for drinking and willing wenches for amusement.

Even his former meticulous self couldn't have faulted the elegant appointments of this room, though, he acknowledged, giving the vast chamber an admiring glance. Bronning might be merely a baron, but he was clearly a rich one.

How would he find the rest of the estate? Probably a good deal better managed than the one that had been given into his charge, he reflected with another painful flash of honesty.

Greville's lofty opinion of his own worth had taken as much of a beating during his time at sea as that pirate ship the *Illustrious* had boarded. He'd had months marooned within the small confines of a naval vessel with nothing to do but reflect, as the grit he holystoned over the deck cut into his knees or he took his turn hoisting sail or cranking the bilge pumps.

Those eight months had carved a divide as wide and deep as the cutlass gash in his chest between Greville Anders, pampered only son of minor gentry and distant cousin of a great peer, and the man he was now.

Along with his status as 'gentleman', the sea wind and grinding labour had worn away his former opinions, attitudes and values to such an extent that the face now gazing back at him belonged to a wholly different individual. One who'd gone from fury at his fate, to resignation, to a growing sense of pride as, with hard work and dogged persistence, he proved his worth to a sceptical crew…and to himself.

Not that he was sure yet what he'd do next, once Lord Englemere persuaded the Admiralty to release him from duty as a landsman with the Royal Navy. He did know, however, having lived among men who pledged their efforts and their very lives to a cause greater than themselves, that he could never stomach being idle again. He could not drift from estate to estate of his wealthy university friends, as he had after leaving Cambridge, his company valued as an amusing fribble who enlivened every party with his wit, his expertise at the gaming table and his ability to charm the ladies.

In addition to consulting Englemere about a new position, he had assurances from Captain Harrington that his former commanding officer would enquire about a place for him with his contacts in the Admiralty. On this fever-free, sunny English morning, Greville felt confident he'd find some honourable employment suitable for a gentleman's son.

Exactly *what* was a puzzle he didn't need to solve this moment, he thought with an echo of the insouciance with which he used to dismiss *all* problems. His only task now was to discern his true level of recovery by exiting this chamber and investigating his temporary residence.

'What is the routine of the household?' he asked the still-hovering Luke. 'I should like to see Lord Bronning and apologise for my rudeness in remaining two whole days in my chamber.'

'Don't expect that were a problem. I imagine his lordship was happy to have you stay put. And heal, I mean,' he added, the tips of his ears reddening.

Greville bit back a grin. Servants in a grand house being as fiercely proud of their master's home and status as the owner himself, the reception of a man who looked as much like gallows-bait as he had upon arrival had no doubt been greeted with as much disapproving speculation belowstairs as above. He'd wager his host—and hostess—were thankful he'd remained abed, sparing them the dilemma of what to do with him.

'It's past time for breakfast, I see,' he said with a nod towards the mantel clock. 'Do Lord Bronning and his family take nuncheon?'

'Lord B.'s off inspecting the estate, but Miss Neville and Miss Althea sometimes do. They'll be in breakfast room shortly if they are. I can have Cook send in something, whether the ladies be eating or not, if you're wishful.'

'Yes, I should like that. Please tell Cook how much I enjoyed the tray you brought earlier.'

The footman grinned. 'No need to say nothing. She saw the empty plate and was happy to see you're such a good trencherman! What with all the illness in the house, the master's sister and then the missus herself passing on last spring and summer, Lord B.'s been pecking at his food and Miss Neville no better. Be a right pleasure to cook for someone with a healthy man's appetite, she said. Breakfast room's on the main floor, to the left from the stairs.'

Greville thanked the footman, who bowed himself out with a promise to make sure there would be something waiting to tempt his appetite. Taking one last look in the glass to adjust the knot Luke had fashioned in his cravat, Greville carefully straightened and set forth for the breakfast room.

With his whole concentration the evening of his arrival focused on simply making it up the stairs to a bedchamber, the size and furnishing of Lord Bronning's house had made little impression. He soon discovered that the rest of the house was as luxurious and well appointed as his bedchamber.

Though related to the famous Stanhopes, the Anders family was not wealthy, Papa being merely a younger son of distinguished lineage. Like many younger sons, his father had been bundled off to the church, which he now served by ministering to the clerks and soldiers of the East India Company. But educated at Cambridge and having many friends among the wealthier of his class, Greville had visited enough elegant townhouses and grand country estates to recognise that Bronning's family was not only wealthy, but of ancient lineage.

Although his bedchamber had been decorated in cream-toned plasterwork with the classical pediments and pilasters of the Adams style, the hallway down which he was now walking boasted beautiful carving, which to his critical eye appeared to be of Renaissance origin. The floor beneath his feet was solid oak planking, polished to a high gleam. An array of portraits of men and ladies in Renaissance and Cavalier dress hung at intervals above the carved wainscoting.

He reached the landing, which overlooked a large stone-walled entry, its walls hung with tapestries and its huge front door flanked by suits of armour, indicating that the space must have originally been a medieval tower. After carefully descending a grand stairway of the same elegantly carved Renaissance oak—and leased to arrive at the bottom after a minimum of teeth-gritting discomfort—he was drawn to light emanating from under an archway beneath the stairs.

Walking through to what must be a later addition, he discovered a set of French doors opening on to a broad stone terrace that descended several steps to a second terrace of closely clipped lawn. Two brick wings in the Georgian style flanked the terraces to the left and right, their graceful tapered ends punctuated by a trio of Palladian windows. Beyond the grass terrace, steps descended to a rolling meadow leading in the distance to thick woods that climbed steeply uphill.

He had to laugh and grimaced at the pull to his wound. After viewing the hall and grounds, he was even more surprised Lord Bronning hadn't had him summarily carted back to his carriage upon arrival. No wonder Miss Neville had frowned at him!

Would she continue to frown today? he wondered. Though his entire view of the world and what made a man worthy had altered, Miss Neville doubtless shared the beliefs and values embraced by the majority of their class. According to these, any approval of the service he had rendered his country while aboard the *Illustrious* would be negated by the menial position he had occupied while serving there.

The old Greville had never met a lady he couldn't charm. Now that he looked more like that old self, despite her inclination to dismiss such a low person, would Miss Neville prove immune to his appeal? Though his plans most certainly did not include courting the daughter of a wealthy baron while he marked time here waiting for his future to begin, it might be amusing to find out.

At that conclusion, he returned his attention to calculating which doorway down the left of the impressively long hallway might lead him into the breakfast room. Wishing he'd asked Luke for more specific directions, he set off.

His satisfaction at finding the correct door turned to pleasure when, halting on the threshold, he discovered the space within already occupied by two young females. The glorious Miss Neville, looking like sunshine itself in a pale yellow morning gown that echoed her golden hair, sat across from a younger, plainly dressed female, who must be the Miss Althea the footman had mentioned.

He made them a bow, further cheered by how much easier that gesture was today than it had been a few days previous. 'Good day, ladies. May I join you?'

Chapter Three

Relieved to have company to break the tense silence that had fallen between her and her cousin Althea, Amanda was about to greet her father when she realised the deep masculine voice was not Papa's. As she looked up sharply, the vision that met her startled eyes made her catch her breath and sent her senses leaping like a colt loosed in a spring meadow.

A man stood in the doorway, smiling faintly. Despite his casual stance, the tall, lean body radiated an aura of such intense masculinity that everything female within her came instantly to the alert. A little thrill of anticipation zinged through her as she focused her gaze on the rugged, vaguely familiar face: handsome, if a bit lean and tanned, with vivid green eyes that seemed to gaze into one's soul and a beguiling smile playing about the lips.

That enticing smile coaxed forth an answering one before the truth of his identity struck her with force of a giant boulder, smashing her response at birth. The man wearing gentleman's garb and standing at ease on the threshold could only be their long-absent guest, Mr Anders.

Before she could order her disjointed thoughts to summon a suitable greeting, Althea bobbed up like a fishing cork after a pull on the line. 'Mr Anders, is it not!' she cried. 'How excellent to meet you at last! I'm so sorry I missed your arrival. You were ill, I'd heard, but are obviously better. Please, won't you help yourself at the sideboard and come sit by me? I cannot wait to converse with you.'

'How kind of you to solicit my company, Miss…?' He paused, raising a quizzical eyebrow.

'Holton—Althea Holton. No one of importance, as Amanda would tell you,' Althea said with a toss of her head in Amanda's direction. 'Lord Bronning is my uncle.'

'His lordship is doubly fortunate, then, to have both a handsome daughter and a lovely niece.'

'Prettily spoken, Mr Anders,' Amanda responded, finally collecting her wits. 'I, too, am glad to see you have recovered enough to join us.'

'Are you indeed, Miss Neville?' he replied, his dry tone and raised eyebrow telling her he doubted those polite words. 'I am heartily glad to be able to join you. I hope I shall be less trouble for the remainder of my sojourn here than I've been the last two days—however long that sojourn may be.'

'I do hope it will be extended!' Althea interjected. 'You are to report to the Coastal Brigade office, Uncle James said? What shall you do with them?'

'On that head, Miss Holton, I have no more information than you. I shall not discover the extent of my duties until I report in, which I intend to do as soon as I can manage the journey.'

'If you feel equal to the trip today, I can summon you a coach,' Amanda offered.

He showed her that quirk of eyebrow again, as if he thought her remark implied an eagerness to be rid of him. Though she hadn't intended to convey that impression—at least consciously—she supposed it was true.

A sudden shame heated her cheeks. She'd thought Anders too ill or cast-away to notice much upon his arrival—but had her less-than-enthusiastic reaction to his visit been so apparent? It must have, for he was treating her with an ironic courtesy that said he didn't believe a single one of her politenesses.

Chagrin deepened the burn. Though plain, Mr Anders's garments were undeniably those of a gentleman, and he wore them with the ease of long practice. His birth and connections were probably exactly as claimed, despite the low nature of his recent activities. Though she was still beset by problems and grieving, that didn't excuse her being uncivil or unwelcoming to one of Papa's guests—no matter how ill conceived she think the invitation.

'A kind offer, Miss Neville, but I don't believe I shall avail myself of it today,' he replied while incoherent words of apology churned around in her head. 'My emergence from the sickroom is so recent, I think it would be wiser to remain at Ashton Grove and try my luck exploring the house and grounds. From the few glimpses I had driving to the manor, both are magnificent.'

'Oh, they are indeed,' Althea chimed in. 'Would you like to tour the estate? I'd be happy to drive you—if you are up to it. I was told you'd been wounded, but have no idea of the severity. What happened? Oh, I mean if it is not too rude to enquire. It's just, I'm so fascinated by everything about the Navy!'

'Why don't we let Mr Anders eat before we press him to recount his history?' Amanda suggested, embarrassed by Althea's overly inquisitive behaviour.

Sparing Amanda only a quick dagger glance, Althea refocused her attention on Anders. 'Do try the ham and cheese, it's quite good,' she coaxed. 'Shall I assist you? Allow me to carry your plate.'

Goodness, Althea was acting as if their guest were an invalid or a child still in the nursery. Amanda's experience with gentleman was limited mostly to her brother, but she knew George would hate to be coddled in such a manner. 'Mr Anders probably prefers to fix his own plate, Althea,' she said in as light a tone as possible.

It didn't answer; the girl flashed her a resentful look. 'I know he's capable. I just want to help, if he wishes it.'

'That's most kind of you, Miss Holton, but I think I can manage,' Anders replied, tactfully forestalling any further exchange. 'I admit to being eager to try more of your cook's skill. If the exceptional breakfast sent up this morning is any indication, you keep a fine table, Miss Neville. That is, I understand you run the household yourself? And do so with admirable skill for a lady so young.'

'Yes, Amanda's a *paragon* of organisation, as anyone at Ashton Grove will tell you. An exemplary manager *and* a beauty! No doubt she'll have suitors lined up in the street when she makes her come-out in London this spring.' Though the words themselves were matter of fact, Althea's tone implied her disdain at such a goal.

Mr Anders either did not sense that, or chose to ignore it, merely replying, 'So you will go to London, then?'

'Yes, I hope to,' Amanda replied. At least one of the ladies present could be politely brief, she thought with annoyance.

'Indeed, Amanda can't wait to escape the country!' Althea exclaimed. 'Whereas I think Ashton Grove is wonderful, and so rich in history. The original part of the house dates from the late fourteenth century. I'd be delighted to show you around—when you are sufficiently rested, Mr Anders,' she added, directing another pointed look at Amanda.

'After I sample some of that ham and cheese, I may take you up on that kind offer, Miss Holton,' Anders said.

Althea insisted on walking to the sideboard with him, pointing out other dishes and offering to hold his plate or fetch him coffee. Amanda had to admit, Anders bore those ministrations with patience, tinged, if the wink he sent her over the girl's head was any indication, with good humour.

Returning to the table, he seated himself beside Althea as requested. Eating slowly, occasionally closing his eyes as if truly savouring the food, he continued to focus a flattering amount of attention on the girl.

Amanda couldn't fault his manners, and his conversation was skilful, too. With a few well-chosen phrases, he led Althea to describe Ashton Grove, the pleasant walks and rides to be had in the area, the fishing and hunting available, the route one took to reach the Devon coast, the beautiful red cliffs at Salcombe by the Coastal Brigade station at Salters Bay.

Probably he was Stanhope's cousin after all. She'd love to enquire about that relationship—when she could do so with more polite discretion than Althea was displaying.

Not required to add a syllable to the discussion, Amanda settled back to simply observing Anders. Which, she had to admit, was certainly no hardship.

The improvement in his looks from the bearded, grimy man she'd met in the entry two days ago was little short of amazing. Though the limp was gone, he walked a bit stiffly, testament to the fact that he was still not fully recovered. In spite of that impediment, there was a sinuous, almost feline quality to his movements.

Something about his rangy grace recalled to her mind the jungle cats she'd seen as a girl in the Royal Menagerie—sleek and feral. Despite the subtle signs of injury, Mr Anders still radiated a sense of self-confidence and power.

This was not a man to tangle with, that prowling stance said, but one who would protect what was his and hold his own in a fight. Free to roam about as the menagerie beasts were not, she suspected Mr Anders might prove even more dangerous.

From the deliberate way he was holding the fork in his left hand and the rigid angle of his arm, she surmised that his wound must be on that side. Speculating about the size and location of the injury hidden beneath the coat led her to imagining how his chest might look, stripped of clothing.

That image sparked such a strong, unsettling flash of sensation in her belly that she immediately shut down the thought. Taking a steadying breath, she turned her gaze instead to a covert study of his profile.

He possessed a straight, classical nose and the lips of a Greek sculpture. A determined chin, against which he was tapping one tanned finger, bronzed, no doubt, from performing all manner of tasks in heat and sun, as the calloused palm would also attest. At his brow and temples, a luxuriant curl of auburn hair, now cut and fashionably styled, inspired in her the oddest desire to run her fingers through it.

At the thought of him running one of *his* tanned hands through *her* unbound hair, she felt a little shiver. Despite the ravages worked upon him by his service at sea and his wounds, Mr Anders was still a strikingly well-made gentleman.

Unfortunately.

Though she had scarcely more acquaintance with personable gentlemen than her cousin, she was older and, she hoped, less impressionable than Althea, yet when Mr Anders had appeared on the threshold a few moments ago, he'd nearly stolen her breath. If Amanda didn't mistake the look on her cousin's face, now gazing up at their guest raptly, Althea had developed an instantaneous *tendre* for the man she'd already been predisposed to admire for his military connections.

How was Amanda going to prevent her impetuous cousin from hanging on Mr Anders's sleeve, chattering in his ear and trying to accompany him on every walk, stroll or ride he took on Ashton Grove land and elsewhere?

'Have I dripped egg on my coat, Miss Neville?'

Startled out of her reverie, Amanda realised Mr Anders's deep-green eyes were now focused on her, his amused expression announcing he'd caught her staring at him. Quickly she averted her gaze, while, to her added discomfort, she felt a blush mounting her cheeks.

'I don't think so,' Althea replied before she could respond. 'If you had, she would have told you so directly. Amanda is a stickler for propriety and proper behaviour.'

'Proper' meaning dull, Althea's tone said. Amanda suppressed a sigh and hoped her expression didn't betray her irritation. Althea's obvious attempt to disparage her in front of the object of her fascination might be humorous if it were not so annoying—and disquieting proof of just how mesmerised the girl already was.

'For a young lady about to make her début, being a stickler for propriety is an unfortunate necessity, or so I've been told,' came Mr Anders's surprising reply. 'It's quite unfair that gentleman are allowed great freedom of behaviour, while ladies, especially unmarried ones, are so restricted.'

Amanda risked a quick, covert glance at his face, which seemed serious rather than mocking. It was only polite of him to have so deftly deflected Althea's criticism, but could it be possible he really understood the truth of his remark?

Or was he just vastly experienced at leading young ladies astray? As of yet, she knew absolutely nothing about his character. Compellingly attractive as he was injured, she imagined his charm would be quite devastating when he was fully recovered. A rogue-in-sheep's clothing, who cloaked illicit designs in properly conventional speeches, would be as dangerous to Althea's heart and reputation as those jungle cats loosed among Ashton Grove cattle.

The idea of having to tangle wits with the gentleman to protect her cousin sent a sharp, and deeply disturbing, tingle of anticipation rippling through Amanda.

She struggled to suppress it, reminding herself that, alluring as he might be, even if Anders were the gentleman he seemed, his present circumstances rendered him entirely ineligible as a suitable companion for either her or Althea.

Meanwhile, her cousin eagerly latched on to his comment. 'Quite right!' she cried. 'When I was younger, I used to ride astride, in trousers, which is so much more practical and comfortable than going side-saddle in a tangle of skirts. But after... everything that happened last summer, Uncle James has forbidden me to follow the hunt. Indeed, he insists I maintain the most dull, dawdling pace when I do ride, though now more than ever I *need* a hard gallop. And you cannot even imagine the *dreariness* of the lady's academy they forced me to attend. Lecture after lecture about how a young lady must do this and mustn't do that, all those silly girls chattering of beaux and gowns and needlework until I thought I must scream. How glad I was to leave.

'And I'm not going back,' she announced with a mutinous glare at Amanda, whose shock at that pronouncement doubtless showed clearly on her face. 'I shall stay here at Ashton Grove and take care of Uncle James while Amanda goes to London.'

Though this was both a most unwelcome announcement and the first she'd heard of the decision, now in front of Mr Anders was hardly the place to debate the matter.

Unable to determine upon a reply that would not further inflame her cousin, Amanda was relieved when their guest smoothly continued, 'What would you study and do, Miss Holton, if you were permitted to choose?'

As good manners, it was an impeccable move. Even more surprising, Mr Anders appeared to genuinely be interested in the opinions of this shabbily behaved schoolgirl.

'I'd ride astride again. Learn to fence and shoot and hunt. Fish in my old clothes like I used to with Amanda, before she put off such "childish" things. Study politics and philosophy and...and *Greek* instead of china painting and deportment. Play billiards—and drink port and smoke cigars!' Althea finished defiantly.

If she'd tried to shock him, she'd failed. Their guest merely shook his head and laughed. 'I fear your relations would give you trouble, indeed, were you to embark on such an agenda. Though I should hardly wish for such a lovely girl to be miraculously transformed into a young man, it is a shame, for if you were on your way to university, you might indulge all those desires.'

'How I wish I might attend university,' Althea said wistfully—and Amanda suppressed a sigh of her own at virtually the only remark her cousin had made with which she agreed. How much more useful might a wife be to a husband with great responsibilities in government were she tutored as he had been in the intricacies of diplomacy and politics.

'How does one go about making a career of the sea?' Althea asked. 'When we walk along the beach, watching the ships, I always wonder what it would be like to be out there, sailing on one of the vessels skimming by the coast.'

'I am not making a career of the Navy, Miss Holton, although my short time in the service gave me a great admiration for those who do. Individuals who desire to rise to command must begin at a much earlier age. My captain, himself son of a commodore, went aboard his first ship as a "young gentleman" at the age of eleven.'

'Does it take so long, then?' Amanda asked, her interest piqued in spite of herself.

'It does—and the training is rigorous. A "young gentleman" must serve three years before he can become a midshipman, then at least another six as midshipman before he can take the exam for lieutenant. There are never enough commands to go around, and with the war finally over, even fewer will be available, although much important work remains for the Navy. The French no longer hamper British commerce, but despite the recent agreement signed with the Bey of Algiers to prevent dealing in, ah…the abduction of European citizens, piracy remains a serious threat.'

His momentary pause, and the slight tinge of colour in his face when he pronounced the last phrase, sparked Amanda to wonder if he were referring to the agreement to end the white slavery trade about which she'd read in the London papers last year. If so, no wonder he'd been embarrassed, almost mentioning such a shocking subject to young ladies of sensibility. The titillating notion of slave girls and seraglios sent a thrill of the forbidden through her.

Fortunately, the mention of pirates had apparently distracted Althea from noticing his hesitation. 'Was your ship engaged against the pirates?' she asked eagerly. 'Is that how you were injured?'

Suddenly, Anders's genial smile faded and his eyes took on a hard look. 'Yes, but it's probably best I not relate too much of that bloody encounter.'

'Oh, but I should love to hear about it!' Althea cried. 'Every cannon volley and thrust. It must have been so thrilling.'

While Anders's expression grew even more forbidding, her cousin opened her lips, looking as if she were about to entreat him again. 'Althea!' Amanda warned in a sharp undertone.

Finally sensing Mr Anders's reluctance, her cousin flushed. 'Excuse me,' she mumbled. 'Of course, I don't wish to tease you to talk about something you prefer not to discuss.'

'Should you like more coffee, Mr Anders?' Amanda intervened to cover the awkward moment.

Mr Anders's stern expression softened. 'No, I've had sufficient, Miss Neville. Perhaps a knife to pick my teeth?'

The room went suddenly silent. Shock and dismay must have blanched her face, but before she could form some reply, Anders chuckled.

'Belay that last,' he said with a grin. 'I believe I shall try a walk now. From what I observed from the French doors overlooking the terrace, a stroll through the gardens should be quite pleasant.'

Why, the…the wretch! Amanda fumed, feeling her face flame again. Not only had Anders obviously sensed her initial disdain for the man who'd stumbled across her threshold looking like the lowest of common sailors, he now had the audacity to tease her about it! Though as shabbily as she'd treated him as his hostess, she probably ought to tender him an apology… at some moment when her cousin wasn't looking on.

'Shall I show you?' Althea offered quickly. 'My Aunt Lydia's knot gardens are most ingenious—like a maze in miniature made of clipped herbs. Just give me long enough to fetch my pelisse.'

'That would be most pleasant, Miss Holton,' Anders said.

Damn and blast, Amanda thought, Althea's offer pulling her from her agitation to a more serious concern. It appeared her cousin did intend to dog the steps of their guest.

Except for that one remark about teeth-picking, Mr Anders had conducted himself like a gentleman. Polished behaviour, however, would be easy to affect by one who had grown up among the *ton*, as his lineage, if not his most recent associations, suggested. If he were a rogue, she was in for a difficult time, for judging by the adoring gaze Althea now had fixed upon the man, she would be deaf to any caution Amanda might utter about spending time alone in his company.

An even more dire possibility occurred to her. Despite her avowed interest in 'manly' pursuits, Althea was a girl hovering on the brink between child and young woman. If her adulation should turn in a flirtatious direction, the girl might throw herself at Anders's head. Possessed of a sizeable dowry herself, Althea would be a plump prize for a man who apparently possessed neither wealth nor property of his own.

One further glance at Althea's expression told Amanda that

any attempt to prevent her from escorting Mr Anders about was doomed to failure. The girl would simply disobey a direct order to refrain from his company; if Amanda tried to assign her some task that would prevent their meeting, Althea would likely find a way around it.

Desperately Amanda wished that Papa were present, removing from her shoulders the burden of protecting her cousin. But though she didn't wish to further offend their guest, she knew it simply was not safe for Althea to go waltzing about the estate with Mr Anders unchaperoned. And since her wily cousin was quite capable of fobbing off any maid or groom she tried to saddle with the task, the only person likely to successfully prevent that—was herself.

Reluctantly she forced the words through stiff lips. 'I believe I'd like to take the air as well. May I join you in your walk, Mr Anders?'

Though he might immediately guess her purpose, in his guise as a gentleman, Mr Anders could hardly refuse to accept her company if he'd already agreed to Althea's. Though the girl sent her a furious look for inserting herself where she was not wanted, Mr Anders replied with the only answer courtesy permitted.

'Of course, Miss Neville. If having the escort of one lovely lady is a delight, having two would be doubly so. Shall I meet you both at the entry in, say, ten minutes?'

After her polite and Althea's enthusiastic murmur of assent, the three rose from the table.

Amanda lingered in the breakfast room as the other two departed, fuming. With quarterly supplies to order, the household account books to review with Mrs Pepys, several ill tenants to visit and half-a-dozen other urgent tasks awaiting, the last thing she needed was to have to play unwilling chaperon to her equally unwilling cousin.

Amanda resisted a strong urge to hurl her unoffending coffee cup into the fireplace, merely to hear the satisfying crash.

There was no hope for it, though. Until she could transfer the responsibility for Althea's protection to Papa or work out a better way to separate the girl from the object of her fascination, Amanda would have to intervene.

The regrettable fact that a little stir of anticipation coursed through her at the idea of spending more time in Mr Anders's company only made her angrier.

Chapter Four

Some ten minutes later, Greville met the ladies in the down-stairs hallway before proceeding through the French doors on to the terrace. The pale February sun gave an illusion of warmth and cast a mellow light over the lichen-coated stone ornaments, balustrades, steps and the soft salmon brick of the Georgian wings. Ghostly trees rose out of the mist that still lingered over the lawns, while in the distance a dark wood climbed the hazy outlines of a slope.

Though the house and grounds had obviously been occupied for centuries, the alterations and additions had been made with care, the medieval tower and Elizabethan galleries flowing seamlessly into the Georgian wings.

'The prospect is delightful,' Greville said admiringly. 'The handsome buildings, the broad sweep of terrace, the lawn marching into the hills—all combine to give the impression of timeless serenity.'

Miss Neville glanced at him sharply, her cerulean-blue eyes narrowed. Apparently deciding he was sincere, for the first time, the carefully neutral expression she'd been maintaining brightened.

'Thank you, Mr Anders,' she said softly. 'It was the project of my mother's life to complete the wings and construct the terrace and gardens to unite the styles of many generations into one elegant whole.'

'She succeeded brilliantly,' Greville replied, pleased to see her face brighten further at the compliment.

'I find the medieval tower more interesting than the new additions,' Miss Holton broke in. 'Almost as fascinating as the remains of the original castle, which was built on a bluff overlooking the river. You must let me show you Neville Tour later, when you're feeling up to a drive. But now you must see Aunt Lydia's knot gardens, over there below the end of the terrace. These flagstones can be slippery in the damp. Here, let me assist you,' she said, reaching out to him. 'We wouldn't want you to fall and aggravate your injury!'

Dutifully offering the girl his arm, Greville suppressed a smile at Miss Holton's persistence in treating him like an invalid. But when he turned to share that amusement with Miss Neville, he saw the pleasant expression fade from her face as her cousin latched on to his sleeve. Her gaze fixed with obvious displeasure on the spot where Miss Holton's hand rested, Miss Neville fell into step behind them.

From whence did that disapproval arise? he wondered. Perhaps, as the reigning beauty of the area, she didn't take kindly to having her young cousin usurp the escort of the only gentleman present. Surely she couldn't imagine he had any designs upon Miss Holton, who looked as if she were barely old enough to have escaped the schoolroom.

'Have you visited Holkham, Mr Anders?' Miss Neville was asking.

'No, Miss Neville.' Though, having been given charge of an agricultural property, a task about which he'd known next to nothing, he probably should have. 'Regrettably, I haven't much knowledge of agriculture. I've heard of the yearly Clippings held at Coke of Norfolk's home, of course. I understand your father is also a skilful manager, which makes me even more eager to tour his estate.'

Progressing at the dawdling pace Miss Holton seemed to think necessary for a recovering invalid, they were nearing the garden end of the terrace when a groom sprinted towards them. Doffing his hat to the ladies, the man said, 'Miss Althea, will you be needing your horse? Harry has him saddled and ready.'

Miss Holton bit her lip, a frown creasing her brow. 'Oh, bother it, I completely forgot! I usually ride out after nuncheon when the weather allows,' she informed Greville.

'Should I tell Harry to walk him for you, miss, or…?' The groom's voice trailed off.

When Miss Holton hesitated, obviously torn between the pleasures of riding and her desire to show him around, Greville said, 'Please, Miss Holton, don't let me alter your plans. With the day promising clear, a ride should be most refreshing. I can view the gardens another day.'

'Are you sure you won't mind waiting? Amanda could show you, but I'm sure she needs to return to her many duties. If you prefer to continue now, I can always ride later.'

The girl obviously didn't want Miss Neville to take over her place as his escort. Not wishing to be responsible for any increase in the tension he sensed between the two girls, Greville replied, 'I believe I would prefer to wait. I'm a bit fatigued after walking this far and would just as soon return to the house. I shall count on you, Miss Holton, to show me around another time. You have such p— Ah, enthusiasm,' he substituted rapidly for 'passion', 'for Ashton Grove, it's a pleasure to have you as my guide.'

He'd only intended to deliver a pretty compliment to the

girl who seemed to resent her beautiful cousin—but even his milder phrase earned him a sharp look from Miss Neville.

Could she object to his using the word 'passion' with her cousin? Though the thoughts that word immediately conjured up did not feature Miss Holton.

No, the image erupting in his eager mind was of the infinitely desirable Miss Neville, drawn into his embrace. That small ripe body tucked under his chin, that soft, rounded bosom pressed against his hard chest… Heat washed through him as parts lower than his chest hardened.

Enough, he thought, dragging his mind back to the conversation at hand—schoolgirls, and words that might not be voiced in their company. Who knew a simple conversation could become so complicated?

'Very well, I suppose I shall ride as usual,' Miss Holton finally concluded. 'I shall see you at dinner, then, Mr Anders?'

'I certainly hope so,' Greville replied.

After informing the groom she would meet him at the stables as soon as she changed into her habit, Miss Holton, with obvious reluctance, set off for the house.

With equally obvious reluctance, Miss Neville remained. 'Shall we complete the circuit of this terrace before we go in, Mr Anders?'

Greville wondered why she wished to prolong a walk she seemed to have embarked upon so unwillingly. In addition to that idle curiosity, he had to admit to feeling a bit piqued that she *was* reluctant, given his strong attraction to her.

Had he been the Greville of a year ago, his hackles all too easily raised whenever he sensed he was being treated with disdain by one richer or more favoured by fortune, he might have tried to trade snub for snub. But the hot sun off North Africa seemed to have burned out of him any lingering resentment over the fact that a mere accident of birth had elevated his cousin Nicky to the rank of marquess, while he was only a younger son from a minor branch of the family, possessed of neither title nor wealth.

At present, he was more amused and curious than offended by her reticence. The new Greville could even concede, given his disreputable appearance upon arrival, that Miss Neville was probably justified in feeling time spent entertaining him could be better devoted to something else.

Mindful of that, Greville said, 'Your company would be a delight, but as Miss Holton pointed out, I imagine you have matters to attend that are of greater urgency than supervising a gimpy old sailor on a promenade over the terrace.'

To his surprise, another blush coloured her cheeks. So she'd understood his mild jab at her disinclination for his company.

'I should never wish to neglect a guest of Papa's,' she murmured.

'I shall not feel neglected, I assure you,' he replied. 'Miss Holton seems both capable and interested in showing me around later. Unless…it's my accompanying your cousin that disturbs you?' he guessed.

Her startled gaze shot back to his, confirming that suspicion.

Torn between amusement and indignation, Greville said drily, 'Though you may still feel it necessary to provide Miss Holton with a chaperon, I assure you, I have no intention of ravishing her in full view of the house—or anywhere else. I admit that the circumstances of my arrival may have given you good reason to doubt it, but I do in fact possess the morals of a gentleman.'

Nor was he yet physically up to the challenge of ravishing anyone. Though if the luscious Miss Neville were the prize, he might be forced to test the limits of his endurance.

But perhaps he'd been too blunt. He was thinking how he

might soften that bald statement when Miss Neville said, 'I fear I owe *you* an apology. If I appeared to give less credence to your scruples than you felt proper, please note that my cousin is in a delicate position, no longer a child, but still a year or more from her come-out. As you yourself remarked this morning, a young lady in such a position must take extreme care not to compromise her reputation. And so I feel I must protect her— whether she wishes me to or not.'

Greville nodded. 'Point taken. Though I confess, I have difficulty seeing Miss Holton, with her enthusiasm for fencing, shooting and cigars, as a young lady ready to embrace London society.'

Miss Neville gave a rueful grimace. 'Indeed! Unless something changes, I doubt she will be very enthusiastic about embracing it. But that's not all. Let me further confess that, distressed by your…appearance when you first arrived, I did not greet you with the warmth and hospitality due my father's guest. I do hope that, during the rest of your stay, you will allow me to make amends for that regrettable lapse.'

Of all the things she might have said, that apology was perhaps the most unexpected. In his observation, a Beauty was generally too complacent about her own worth and too absorbed by her own concerns to notice or care about the feelings of lesser beings.

Had some traumatic event—perhaps the tragic loss of her mother the previous summer?—spurred her to this unusual sensitivity? Whatever the cause, the perception and empathy she'd just displayed hinted at a character as sterling as her beauty.

A beautiful lady of gentle birth and sterling character who was already fully capable of managing a vast estate would be a prize indeed on the Marriage Mart this spring. The more discerning London gentlemen ought to fight each other to vie for her hand.

A pang of sadness flashed through him that in neither wealth nor title would he be considered worthy to enter that contest.

But then, he wasn't in the market for a wife, certainly not a wealthy, well-born one eager to plunge herself into the London society, he now disdained. Shrugging off that stab of regret, Greville said, 'Shall we exchange mutual apologies, then? I shall beg pardon for not initially appearing worthy of your hospitality.'

'Very well, mutual apologies it is,' she agreed with a smile.

Greville caught his breath. Frowning, Miss Neville had been lovely; uninterested, she was the handsomest woman he'd ever met, but with those tempting lips curved upwards, the smile adding a glow to her cheeks and an appealing softness to her countenance, she was magnificent.

The warmth of her expression flowed like molten honey over his cold heart, glazing it with sweetness. Smiling back, he glanced into her eyes and was captivated.

Ah, how mesmerising were the turquoise-blue depths, scintillating with highlights like a white-capped sea under a blustery fair sky! Greville could cast himself adrift in them for ever.

He felt almost dizzy, his equilibrium unexpectedly upended by a force too powerful to resist. He felt as if he'd been tossed to the deck by a 'wind shot', the blast of air from a passing cannon ball that could knock a man off his feet, though the ball itself never touched him.

The attraction was so strong, he instinctively wished to move closer, catching himself from doing so only at the last moment.

For several seconds they both remained motionless. Had the blast he felt affected her, too? he wondered. Certainly she had gone still and silent, her lips slightly parted but mute, her wide eyes staring back into his.

She *was* shaken, he concluded with a wild upswing of joy.

Every sense exulting, he felt the nearly irresistible urge to close the distance between them and kiss her.

Mercifully, good sense intervened. He stepped back, making himself recall why kissing the daughter of his host was not a good idea, even though other parts of his body enthusiastically endorsed such a course.

She broke the fraught silence then, saying something about returning to the house that his still-dazed ears were barely able to comprehend.

Pull yourself together, Greville. Though initially he'd merely thought to amuse himself, tweaking this pretty miss with her superior sense of worth, he now felt the strongest compulsion to discover more about her.

'Let me walk in with you,' he said, deliberately slowing his pace while he reassembled his scrambled wits to produce some suitable conversation to prolong their interlude. 'You'll be wanting to return to your duties, which, I understand, are considerable. Luke, the footman who acted as my valet this morning, told me about the sad losses your family has recently suffered. Please accept my condolences, Miss Neville. However brilliantly you handle the household—and in my observation, that is very competently indeed—taking over for your mama under such circumstances must have been very difficult.'

The smile faded—and somewhat to Greville's alarm, tears glistened in the corners of her eyes. 'Yes, it was…difficult.'

There was no reason the sadness on her face should pull at his heart—but somehow it did. Hoping to distract her from that reminder of her loss, he said, 'You are soon to depart to London for the Season, are you not?'

'Yes, but you mustn't think I mean to slight Mama's memory. I would remain here in mourning, but before she…left us, Mama made me promise I would go to London as planned. My Season has already been so often delayed that, compared to the other young ladies, I shall seem practically at my last prayers.'

Greville laughed at the sheer absurdity of such a notion. 'I assure you, Miss Neville, anyone meeting you will think only that you are one of the loveliest and most charming young ladies ever to grace London.'

Rather than preen coquettishly at his compliment, she blushed again and looked away, as if such gallantry made her uncomfortable. How wonderfully refreshing that a girl of her astounding beauty seemed to possess so little vanity! he thought, impressed despite himself.

Perhaps there were few personable or perceptive gentlemen in the vicinity of Ashton Grove, leaving her unaware of just what a Diamond she was—a circumstance that would certainly change once she reached London. She'd grow inured to flattery soon enough, he concluded with some regret.

'You are too kind, Mr Anders,' she said softly.

'No, ma'am, merely truthful. But, if you don't mind my asking, what has delayed your Season?'

She paused, a shadow passing over her face, and for a moment Greville thought she wouldn't answer. 'A succession of unfortunate events,' she said at length. 'Three years ago, Mama's best friend, with whom we were to stay, ended up at the last minute having to remain in the country due to complications after her daughter's lying-in. She and Mama had been bosom-bows during their own come-out year and had long planned to share mine; we preferred to delay a year rather than forgo her company. And practically speaking, by that late date, it would have been nearly impossible to find a suitable house to let, even if we'd wished to proceed alone.'

'And after that?' he prompted.

'Two winters ago,' she continued softly, a sorrowful note creeping into her tone, 'my grandmother, who had resided with us for years, fell ill with a fever that lingered on and on. Though she urged us to go to London without her, of course we refused. We lost her that summer. You've already heard what transpired this past year, when my aunt, the household and finally Mama fell ill.' She forced a smile. 'In sum, a rather dreary tale.'

So in the space of two years she'd lost grandmother, aunt and mother, a succession of blows that would give anyone pause— and perhaps as effective as being sold to a press gang at making one revaluate the world and one's place in it.

'Heartbreaking, certainly,' Greville summed up, once again unaccountably touched by the sadness in her magnificent eyes. He was trying to hit upon a way to redirect her thoughts when Miss Neville said,

'I was ill myself for some time, during which Mama carried the entire burden of running the household and tending me, my aunt and numerous members of the staff who'd also contracted the disease. Perhaps if I'd recovered more quickly and could have assisted her, she would have had the strength to survive once she herself succumbed to the sickness.'

'Surely you don't blame yourself,' Greville said. 'Likely nothing you could have done would have made any difference. Life brings tragedies to everyone; more frequently, it seems, to the blameless. During my first storm at sea, one of the foretop-men, the lads who work the sails at the very height of the mast, was swept overboard. He was a skilled sailor, well liked by all, while the man beside him, an ill-natured creature who caused no end of trouble, was spared. Why young Henry rather than the ne'er-do-well? The Devil protecting his own, perhaps.'

'You are likely right. Still, it's hard not to feel responsible, somehow.'

Miss Neville fell silent, obviously still grappling with her grief. Greville felt an upswelling of desire to comfort her that was as strong as his previous urge to kiss her.

Well, almost as strong. He yearned to pull her into his arms and promise her the moon, let the warmth of his body chase away the cold desolation in her eyes, tease her or even annoy her until he banished the lingering thoughts of loss.

Kissing her would certainly distract her, his body suggested hopefully. Why not satisfy both urgings?

Such a ploy would likely distract her right into planting him a facer, Greville answered himself. Still, he had to struggle to silence that tempting voice and quell the immediate effect the idea of kissing her produced in his all-too-needy member.

While he was thus preoccupied, Miss Neville said, 'Perhaps I should wait another year. But…there's nothing at Ashton for me save sad memories, and I did promise Mama.'

'Doing what your mama wanted is the important thing.'

'I know, you are right.' She uttered a strained laugh. 'It's ridiculous, but I am still so torn. Eager to embrace my future on the one hand, yet strangely resistant to leaving. It's as if, as long as I remain at Ashton, I haven't completely…lost Mama and Grandmama and Aunt Felicia. But once I go to London and embark upon my Season, the Season we spent so many evenings planning together, I can no longer escape the fact that they are truly gone…and I must live my life without them.'

'Tied to a past that cannot be recaptured, yet uncertain about moving forwards?' Greville said, thinking wryly he stood in almost the same position.

Her eyes widened. 'Yes, that's it exactly! How perceptive you are, Mr Anders.'

He waved a hand dismissively. 'I've had some…perspective-altering experiences myself this last year.' Like having his self-esteem and sense of position plunged into the maelstrom of the sea, to emerge eight months later, like a ship repaired after a storm, with a whole new rigging of attitudes about life and his place in it.

She nodded. 'Are you finding it difficult to move forwards?'

'My future plans are still…unsettled,' he conceded. 'About

yours, however, there can be no doubt: you shall become one of the Season's reigning Diamonds, intrigue a host of high-titled aspirants to your hand and choose one lucky man to be your husband.'

She chuckled. 'That was certainly Mama and Grandmama's plan. I was raised on tales about the dazzling Duchess of Devonshire, the premier light of society during Grandmama's years in London. Both she and Mama set their hearts on my making a brilliant match to a gentleman of high rank and political influence.'

With a smile, she continued, 'They made life in London sound so exciting! By the time I was sixteen, I was convinced I wanted to be just like Lady Georgiana—though not, of course, quite as much of a gamester. Or at least, not a losing one,' she amended with a laugh.

That small joyous sound dispelled the lingering sadness on her face and left him wondering whether her smile or her vulnerability was more appealing.

'You mustn't think I value myself too highly!' she added, her levity vanishing beneath a sudden seriousness. 'I realise I'm not a duke's daughter, nor one raised in political circles. I am, however, endowed with a very handsome dowry, which Grandmama said, for a gentleman with political or diplomatic ambitions, might well compensate for my lack of title and political connections. And the Bronning barony is a very old one. Both believed that, with my birth and dowry, achieving a grand match was quite possible. I hope you don't think me vain to express such aims,' she concluded, turning to him with an expression of concern.

'Not at all. From my experience in society, your family's expectations are quite reasonable.'

And they were. A young lady of Miss Neville's remarkable beauty, who also possessed birth and fortune, might look as high as she liked for a husband. That fact alone ought to extinguish his smouldering desire for her company.

Though he conceded that the political set to which she aspired performed important work, the London society of which she spoke so glowingly was a world he now considered shallow and barren of purpose. While it might be harmless enough to establish a teasing friendship with her, he'd best keep uppermost in his randy mind a clear understanding of just how divergent her future and his would be.

He wondered if she truly was prepared for the London she was so eager to reach. Despite her beauty and wealth—indeed, because of it—she was unlikely to find it the vibrant milieu teeming with charming, intelligent and superior individuals she seemed to expect. Instead, she was about to plunge into an often shallow, vicious world of exacting standards meant to trip up the unwary, peopled by idle, self-important social arbiters ready to seize upon any mistake to criticise and disparage a newcomer.

Heavens, he thought in some surprise, when had his view of society become so negative? Perhaps it was a distillation of his previous resentment over his lack of status, combined with the clarity of vision brought about by his life among those at the bottom of the social scale, who, despite their lowly status, spent their lives performing a mission of much greater urgency than the endless rounds of parties, gaming, and self-indulgence that made up the world of society. And used to make up his own.

He hoped whichever Grand Dame had agreed to act as Miss Neville's sponsor would be equal to the task of shielding her from the attacks of those who were jealous of her superior beauty, charm and fortune.

Deflecting the animosity she was likely to excite in London was not his problem, he reminded himself. Even if this curious protective instinct towards her persisted, unless cousin

Nicky performed his magic quickly indeed, he would still be in Devon, serving at the pleasure of the Coastal Brigade, while she went to London for her Season.

He was smiling at the image of Greville Anders, younger son with no prospects, protecting one as perfectly poised as Miss Neville for rising to the highest ranks of society when she asked, 'Are you familiar with London, Mr Anders?'

'Yes. I often visited the city while at Cambridge, and spent several Seasons there after leaving university.'

'Can you tell me about it, please? I've heard all of Grandmama's stories, of course, but she hadn't resided in the city for a decade. What is it like now? What sites and entertainments would you recommend I visit?'

When she looked at him like that, all innocence and persuasive appeal, he'd tell her whatever she wanted, Greville thought. Although, with her insidious presence beside him, it was very difficult to concentrate on any amusements other than the ones her potent physical appeal brought most strongly to mind.

Like kissing. With her cheeks flushed and her eyes shining with enthusiasm, her lips slightly parted and the hint of a pink tongue tempting him, all he wanted to do was bend his head down and sample her. Taste those plump lips and chase her tongue back into the sweet warm cave of her mouth, tangle his with hers and lave and mingle and caress...

London, he told himself, jerking that delectable line of imagining to a halt. The only delights she wanted to sample at the moment were the city's attractions.

Though he certainly did not mean to confess it, his sojourns in the city had usually been spent in diversions not normally mentioned in the company of ladies. Rapidly he scanned his memory for a list of activities suitable for a gently born female.

'There's the theatre—Covent Garden, which features the fabulous Mr Kean in Shakespearean roles, and the Theatre

Royal at Haymarket, where the social activity in the boxes and among the crowds on the floor is often as entertaining as the action upon the stage.'

'Yes, Grandmama particularly enjoyed the theatre! My sponsor keeps a box at Covent Garden, and I am most anxious to visit. What else?'

'There's Astley's Amphitheatre for equestrian displays. The Tower, where for a small tip the Guard will give you a tour and show you the places where the ghosts of Henry VIII's poor headless Queens, Catherine and Anne, are said to roam. Hatchard's bookstore, if you are of a literary mind. Gunter's for ices, and, of course, shops selling everything you could imagine.'

'Yes, Mama intended that we go to town early to begin acquiring a wardrobe, as she insisted nothing country-made would do. Oh, the evenings we spent, poring over fashion plates while Mama and Grandmama described the wonders of Bond Street and Piccadilly! Modistes, cloth-drapers, bonnet-makers, cobblers offering slippers soft as a glove, gloves in every colour of the rainbow.' Shaking her head, she said, 'Now you will be thinking me the most frivolous individual!'

'Fashion, frivolous?' he replied with a grin. 'Indeed not, Miss Neville. 'Tis practically the stuff of life in London. There's great artistry in the making of apparel that shows both the beauty of the material and the wearer to best advantage. It's said Beau Brummell went through an entire stack of neckcloths before getting his cravat tied to perfection and had a standing order for champagne, just to add to his valet's secret formula for blacking his boots.'

'I am so looking forward to it all. And to renewing my relationship with Lady Parnell, Mama's best friend, with whom we were to stay that first year and who will be my sponsor now.'

Surprise tinged with dismay banished Greville's amusement. Lady Parnell, one of the doyennes of society, was said to have more influence than all the patronesses of Almack's combined.

No need to fear that Miss Neville would fall victim to the petty cruelty of jealous schemers. No one who had any aspirations to society would be foolish enough to openly criticise the ward of so socially powerful a personage.

'If Lady Parnell is to introduce you, your success is assured.'

'Are you acquainted with her? She's my godmother, as well as Mama's best friend.'

'I've not had that honour.' Greville did not feel it necessary to add that this was hardly surprising, since the females whose company he'd normally sought while in the metropolis had been about as opposite as one could get from the virginal blossoms of society and the Grand Dames who sheltered them. 'I did know her nephew at Cambridge.'

Of all the matrons in the city, it would have to be Lady Parnell, he thought with rueful chagrin. If he were still clinging to any foolish thought of attempting a friendship, the identity of Miss Neville's sponsor ought to sound its death knell.

Not only was the lady wealthy, influential and needle-witted—and thus liable to allow only the wealthiest and most eligible gentleman to associate with her ward—she also had a keen awareness of everything that went on in London. He couldn't rule out the possibility she might even know about some of the questionable activities in which he'd participated with her nephew.

Time to stop indulging in—and tantalising himself with—Miss Neville's company before he grew too fond of it. What better way than to remind them both of his present position?

Halting with her in front of the French doors leading back into the house, Greville said, 'A most enjoyable stroll, Miss Neville, but now I must let you return to your duties. By the by, do you think I might find someone who could string a hammock in my bedchamber? I do miss some aspects of being at sea.'

There it was again, that flash of alarm, followed by irritation when she realised he was playing with her. 'I can certainly enquire,' she said frigidly, clearly not appreciating his teasing at her expense. 'Thank you for your escort, sir—and I will count upon your word as a *gentleman* in dealing with my cousin. Good day.'

She turned to stomp off, her posture as stiffly upright as a ship flying downwind under full sail. He chuckled, thinking it would only serve him right if he returned to his chamber this evening to find his bed removed and a hammock swinging gently from the overhead.

'My pleasure, Miss Neville,' he called after her.

How he wished she might be, he thought wistfully, watching the sway of her trim posterior as she walked through the doorway into the house. He could vividly imagine luring her to his chamber, burying his face in the scent of her golden hair while he pulled the strands free of their pins, loosing the ties of her bodice…

He could obliterate the pain of the past and uncertainty of the future with simple, all-consuming lust.

But that was the old Greville's favourite way of avoiding what he didn't wish to face. He was going to have to find a new way of handling difficulties.

Still, he thought with a sigh as he relinquished the tantalising image of Miss Neville in his bedchamber, despite knowing that he would doubtless end up a much better man for making the change, there were parts of being the old Greville he really, really hated to give up.

Becoming respectable, he acknowledged as he walked into the house and headed for the stairs, surreptitiously adjusting his suddenly restricting trouser flap, was turning out to be a deal more difficult than he could have imagined.

Chapter Five

Later that evening, Amanda left the kitchen and took the back stairs up to the first floor. Though she'd previously gone over the week's menus with Mrs Pepys, she'd felt driven to check one more time on tonight's dinner, pressed by an inexplicable compulsion to make doubly sure that their guest, if he in fact joined them this evening, would find nothing amiss.

It was ridiculous, the glow Mr Anders had ignited in her with his compliments about her management of Ashton Grove. Why should his approval matter? He was simply, as he seemed to take delight in reminding her, a lowly sailor.

She sighed. He was also, however, unmistakably a gentleman, by birth, speech and, teasing aside, usually behaviour. What was she to make of him…and the unprecedented, powerful attraction that had flooded her on the terrace this morning? For a moment, even knowing her destiny lay elsewhere, she'd nearly succumbed to a desire to kiss him!

And whatever had possessed her, burbling out all her thoughts, hopes and plans like a toddler visiting an indulgent grandmama? Her unusual loquaciousness merely underlined how starved she was for a sympathetic soul with whom to share all those details, from important to trivial, she used to confide to her mama.

Mr Anders certainly was not that...though he had been an attentive and sympathetic listener. A nearly instantaneous rapport seemed to spring up between them, so easy and natural that she'd not felt a moment's qualm about speaking to him like a close friend of long standing, rather than a near-stranger she'd just met. A rapport he'd felt, too, she was certain, as he'd certainly felt that flash of...something, heat and need and desire...that ignited between them once they were alone.

Before he'd put her back in her place. Strange, though *he* was the social inferior, *she* was the one who felt dismissed. The abrupt termination of their seductively intimate interlude had left her feeling...bereft.

Very well, she needed a friend and confidant. Soon she would have Lady Parnell. In the interim, since she wished neither to be the butt of his little jokes nor to subject herself to the disturbing allure of his company, best that she just avoid him.

With that conclusion, she turned down the hallway and walked towards the salon. On physician's orders, Papa took a glass of sherry there each evening before leading her in to dinner. Although if Mr Anders did join them, she suddenly realised, it would be her duty as hostess to go in on *his* arm.

So much for avoiding the man, she thought. At the image of his hand covering hers, another of those little shivers she seemed unable to either prevent or suppress trembled through her.

Trying to shake off the feeling, she turned her mind to the problem of Althea. After her too-intimate chat with Mr Anders on the terrace, she'd put him firmly out of mind, which perhaps hadn't been wise. Though she'd not seen him the rest of the day, she hadn't seen her cousin either. Had Althea managed to run their guest to ground after her ride?

Unsettled as their guest's teasing had made her, for some inexplicable reason she felt that Mr Anders would do Althea no harm. None the less, since he was a gentleman entirely unrelated to them and a stranger to the neighbours, she probably should have checked on them. To keep loose tongues from wagging, in the servants' hall if nowhere else, she must ensure that they were chaperoned during any walks and drives they took together.

Where the girl's reputation was concerned, it wouldn't do to trust any man, especially one as undeniably charming as Mr Anders.

She sighed. By the end of *their* walk, before he'd set her at a distance with that absurdity about hammocks, she'd been almost as won over by Mr Anders as her cousin. His sincere-sounding compliments, combined with the devilishly appealing trait he had of seeming to focus his entire attention on what one said, made him very hard to resist.

Adding to that, the handsomeness of his person—for a moment, she allowed the image of that tall, upright figure, the handsome face and arresting green eyes to play through her mind again—made him a vastly attractive gentleman.

Given how tempted she, who knew how indiscreet it might be, was to befriend the man, it was likely to be even more difficult than she'd initially anticipated to pry Althea away from him.

Perhaps, after dinner tonight, she'd have an opportunity to mention her concerns to Papa, much as she hated to burden him with any further cares. Althea had clearly found Amanda's presence during her excursion with Mr Anders an unnecessary interference. Papa was both the one ultimately responsible for Althea's well-being and the only one who might be able to point out the need for prudence without inciting a scathing response.

Even if Papa intervened to safeguard her cousin from falling into some impropriety, it was likely that Amanda would still have to continue supervising the two. This would mean abandoning, before she'd even begun to act upon it, her new-minted intention to avoid Mr Anders.

Unfortunately, the prospect didn't alarm her nearly as much as it ought to.

Which should've put her on her guard. Not only was she as vulnerable as Althea to having her reputation damaged by an over-close association with that gentleman, she'd had a potent lesson on the terrace in just how easy it was to fall under his spell. Tantalising as she—still, alas—found the notion of kissing him, it would be dangerously easy to be lured into improper behaviour.

Intriguing Anders might be, but after waiting so long to begin pursuing it, she had no intention of throwing away her lifelong dream of becoming a brilliant political hostess by compromising herself with a landless gentleman who possessed little more than a fine pedigree, a well-made body and a beguiling smile.

So she would just *have* to resist him. Upon that firm conclusion, she entered the parlour to find Papa finishing his sherry. Beside his chair, sipping a sherry of his own, stood Mr Anders.

Another of those annoying thrills rippled through her.

Willing it away, she noted he was properly attired in plain black evening dress, with a white-figured waistcoat beneath a modestly intricate cravat. With an inward smile, she recalled their discussion of Beau Brummell. Though his garb was simple, it was well cut and obviously of superior quality—and on him, elegant simplicity looked splendid.

She realised she was staring yet again and jerked her gaze

away. Just then, the door opened and, in a flurry of apologies for her lateness, Althea hurried in.

'As you see, our guest is finally able to join us this evening,' Lord Bronning informed them as she bent to kiss his cheek. 'Amanda, I trust you've instructed Cook to prepare something worthy of the occasion. Mr Anders, you've met my daughter, Miss Neville. Allow me to present my niece, Miss Holton, who always dines with us, although she is not officially out. As you see, we don't stand on formality among family.' His genial smile faded a bit. 'After the events of last summer, we treasure those still left to us.'

'It's I who am honoured, my lord, at being included,' Mr Anders replied.

Bows and curtsies exchanged, Amanda was about to take Anders's arm when, to her surprise, her brother George strolled in. She felt a pang of both resentment and concern to see how Papa's expression brightened upon realising that his son and heir had deigned to dine with them.

Fortunately, she was relieved to note, along with bestowing upon them that honour, George taken the trouble to remain sober, don fresh, crisply starched linen and wear proper evening dress, rather than show up still in riding breeches, as he had on several previous occasions.

It was Althea who offended propriety, dashing over to seize Mr Anders's arm and claim his escort into the dining room. Not wishing to reprimand or argue with her—though Mr Anders would know as well as she did that, as the highest-ranking lady present, it was *her* responsibility to escort in their guest—Amanda gritted her teeth and took her father's arm.

Her irritation over Althea's lapse was mollified by observing her brother's surprisingly good behaviour. Instead of remaining silent, staring moodily into his wineglass, as he had on the handful of other evenings he'd chosen to dine at home, George roused himself to enquire of his father how he had spent his day, then followed up by asking several quite intelligent questions about the state of the fields and cattle. Her heart twisted anew to observe how eagerly Papa responded to just the slightest indication of interest from his heir.

Poor Papa, who'd worked so tirelessly to exact a good return from a thin begrudging soil, deserved to turn over his acres to someone who loved them as he did, she thought, an angry tightness in her chest.

Still, the feeble interest George was now displaying was greater than she could remember his evincing upon any other recent occasion. Had her jobation of the other evening provoked some results after all?

Whatever the cause, George had definitely set himself to be pleasant. After speaking with Papa, he took a few minutes to tease Althea, who couldn't seem to decide whether to be flattered or annoyed by this unexpected interest, before turning to Mr Anders to politely enquire after his health and add a compliment about his recent naval service.

'You're to report to the Coastal Brigade station?' George was asking. 'Will you be working with the revenue cutters based there?'

'I'm not sure what my duties will be. I'm still not hale enough to man a tiller or haul a sail, but once I've recovered sufficiently to be of more use, I would expect to be assigned some duties. Although I understand Lord Englemere is working to obtain my release from the service, so I may not be here long enough to lend much assistance to the Navy in hampering the local trade.'

'I'm sure the Gentlemen will be happy to hear that,' George said. 'Though the men hereabouts know every rock and inlet of this coast so well, not many cargoes are hampered by the excisemen's presence.'

To Amanda's surprise, her normally genial father frowned at his son. 'And how would you know about the local trade?'

George shrugged. 'Everything about the Gentlemen is common knowledge hereabouts. The Devon coast has been a hotbed of smuggling since the days of the ban on wool trade with Flanders.'

'Though the wool is used locally, too,' Amanda pointed out, trying to steer the conversation away from a topic that seemed to distress her Papa. 'The Axminster Carpet works nearby recently began weaving floor coverings of exceptional beauty, some of the fibre in them from Ashton Grove sheep.'

Her father smiled at her. 'We've built up quite a good herd. Devon soil is often poor; corn planting alone cannot always earn the tenants a sufficient income, especially with the fall of agricultural prices since the war.'

'Although Papa encourages them to adopt the newest methods of enriching soil, rotating crops and planting new species,' Amanda continued, with a jerk of her chin at George, trying to silently key him to continue the conversation.

Though she failed to catch her brother's eye, Mr Anders joined in. 'I've not yet had a chance to see the fields and flocks, but I did walk a bit about the terrace today. The house and grounds are exceedingly lovely, Lord Bronning. I understand from Miss Neville that their pleasing arrangement was the work of renovations undertaken by your wife.'

Anders could scarcely have hit upon a better means of delighting her father than by praising the lady he'd loved so dearly. Even if he were not the most attractive man she'd yet to meet, Amanda could have kissed him.

She almost forgave him spending time as a common sailor.

'Thank you, Mr Anders,' her father was replying, a smile of genuine delight lighting his face. 'The renovation project was the consuming passion of my dear wife. The magnificent court and gardens you enjoyed today are her legacy to every succeeding generation of Nevilles. Only the children she bore me are dearer to me.'

''Tis a legacy every observer must cherish,' Mr Anders said—and focused on Amanda such an potent, heated gaze she felt scorched right to her stays.

Surely he wasn't saying he wanted to cherish…*her*, was he? Rattled by the intensity of his eyes, she tried to shake off that disconcerting, and surely erroneous, conclusion.

Indeed, she *must* be mistaken, for no one else seemed to find anything untowards about his statement. Oblivious to any undercurrents, her brother continued, 'What type of ship were you on, Mr Anders?'

'The *Illustrious* was a two-decker, 74-gun ship of the Common Class.'

'How well would she sail, compared to the Coastal Brigade's revenue cutters?'

'Since I've not seen the vessels yet, I couldn't say. The 74-gun is considered a good sailor for a line-of-battle vessel, well proportioned and weatherly. I understand the cutters, with fore and aft and square sails on a single mast, are quite swift. And very busy, if the county is as favoured by smugglers as I've heard.'

'The cutters might be busy,' George replied with a laugh, 'but they aren't usually successful, according to the sailors at the Sloop and Gull.'

Her father frowned. 'The Sloop and Gull isn't the best place to honour with your custom, George. It's known to be frequented by free-traders—dangerous men, many of them.'

'Really, Papa, I'm not a child. The sailors there are just drinking and lazing about. As for dangerous, "Rob Roy" and his men have never harmed anyone that I've heard of. Such wonderful stories of his exploits are told in the pubs in Beer. Besides, I wouldn't be too pious about disapproving of the trade. I'll wager there wasn't any duty paid on the brandy in our cellars.'

To Amanda's indignation, her father flushed. 'True, there's always been trade, and Rob Roy has been an honest dealer. But lately others, more ruthless than he, have been contesting his control of the coast. There've been some ugly skirmishes, I've heard.'

George shrugged. 'People love to talk, especially here, where Heaven knows, there's hardly much else to do. If someone wants to pay a penny for brandy or some China silk, what business should it be of the government to tax it, when enterprising men can sail to France and obtain the goods much more cheaply? The free-traders are doing us all a favour, I say.'

'Have you done much sailing, Mr Neville?' Mr Anders inserted. 'Before my sojourn in the Navy, I'd never been out of sight of the coast. What majesty there is in the sea! All the awesome power of the wind, harnessed by a fragile expanse of sail. The whine of a wind in the ship's rigging, the vibration of the hull as she hangs upon a crest, then plunges into the trough, a tiny toy at the mercy of the restless, roiling deep.'

'You make it sound wonderful!' Althea breathed. 'How do the sails harness the wind?'

Amanda listened appreciatively as Mr Anders went on to answer her cousin's question. More wonderful than his descriptions, she thought, was the skilful way he'd steered the conversation away from the shoals of discord between her father and brother over the matter of free-traders…just as, she suddenly realised, he'd intervened to turn the tide when she and Althea appeared to be at loggerheads this morning.

She didn't think his intervention in either case was merely coincidental.

No, he *was* perceptive, as he'd been when he'd sensed her reservations about his association with Althea. And straightforward, to immediately acknowledge her concern and discuss it with her.

He was a good storyteller, too, she noted as he spun out his tale of sailing the blue-water ocean, from the icy Irish sea to the turquoise warmth of the Mediterranean off the African coast.

His conduct when he wasn't recounting sea stories was also just as it should be. Unlike some of the *parvenu* lace merchants her father had hosted upon occasion, Anders gave the footmen serving the meal just the right amount of attention, neither ordering them about nor ignoring them. He might have spent time as a common sailor, but it hadn't led him to treat the servants with familiarity, as if he felt himself one of them.

All further evidence he was exactly the gentleman his breeding would lead one to expect. So how had he ended up on the deck of a man-of-war?

Resting her curious gaze on him, she watched his expressive face and the play of candlelight over his lips as he wove his tale. What would it feel like to have that mouth pressed against hers?

Heavens, now he had her thinking of kissing again! Jerking her thoughts from that vision, she sighed in exasperation. Given his disconcertingly strong pull over her senses, Mr Anders's presence was a complication she didn't need during her last few weeks at Ashton.

How much easier it would have been had he proven to be a boor! Slurped his soup, dripped gravy on his cravat, gulped wine by the glassful so that by the end of the meal, he was sitting red-faced and stupid.

Instead of looking as he did now, so regrettably handsome, with such a beguiling smile and knowing green eyes that sparkled, inviting her to share some amusement. He tempted her to share a friendship, to build upon the warm rapport that had sprung up between them…and the sizzling sensual tension just below the words.

But she must not give in to that inclination. Mr Anders was definitely not part of Mama and Grandmama's grand plan, a fact she would remind herself of hourly, if necessary. Tearing her gaze from his smiling face, she stood to lead the ladies out of the dining room.

As Amanda expected, her brother did not join them for tea. Mr Anders accompanied her father to the drawing room, but drank only one quick cup before excusing himself, citing the necessity to rest after his first full day out of his chamber.

From somewhere unbidden, the image flashed into her mind of him returning to his room, removing his garments, stretching out on the bed, all long strong limbs and bare skin… It was fortunate, she thought, flushing, that she'd soon be in London, all her efforts bent towards wedding and bedding, if a handsome face was going to keep turning her thoughts in that direction!

Before Anders left, Althea exacted his promise to go driving about the estate the next day—an invitation into which, to her cousin's obvious displeasure, Amanda had felt obliged to insinuate herself. Althea looked as if she wished to protest, but as Papa immediately agreed, telling Anders his daughter would be a prime guide, as she was intimately familiar with everything on the estate, from buildings to fields to manufactories, the younger girl could hardly object.

Had her father recognised the need to provide her cousin with a chaperon? She wasn't sure Papa even thought of his sister's little girl as a young lady with a reputation to protect. Alarming as the idea was, she'd have to remind him.

Once Anders left, Althea quickly deserted them too. Alone at last, Amanda smiled at her father. 'Another cup of tea, Papa? Or perhaps some of that smuggled brandy?'

'Perhaps a wee drop,' he agreed. 'For all that I enjoy the wine, I am concerned about the source.'

'The free-traders, you mean. There have been skirmishes, you said?'

'Distracted as I've been by our…troubles, I know what's about in Beer and Branscombe. The talk among the tenants is that since last spring, Rob Roy's control of the coast has been contested by a group out of Sennlach in Cornwall, sailing under a captain they call "Black John" Kessel, who's known for ruthlessness and making high profits. I suspect some of our tenants near the coast are being pressured not just to help land cargoes, but also to offer lofts and sheds to store his contraband goods. It's even said there was a barn burned last summer by one who refused Black John's request.'

Lord Bronning sighed. 'The increased activity worries me… especially with George home. The last thing an energetic young man wants is to rusticate here in the country.'

The sadness in his tone made Amanda want to throttle her brother on the spot. 'He does value Ashton Grove, you know,' she said, patting her father's shoulder. 'He's just…young.' And thoughtless. And careless. And unappreciative of all their father was doing for him.

Her father squeezed her hand. 'I know. Love for the land will develop—how could it not? It's bred into him! But with George bored and out of sorts, getting mixed up in the smugglers' operations is just the sort of mischief that might attract him. If it were only Rob Roy, I'd not worry…but this new man is an entirely different sort, much more dangerous than George can credit.'

Privately alarmed, Amanda sought a soothing tone. 'Mr Anders will be reporting to the Coastal Brigade soon. Why not ask him to check with the local officer? If there's anything dangerous afoot, they should know of it.'

Her father brightened. 'That's an excellent idea.' A moment

later, he put a hand to his chest, grimacing. 'I'm afraid I'm growing weary, my dear. Will you mind terribly if I abandon you?'

She'd just been about to broach the topic of Althea. But Papa did look tired and unwell, she thought with a pang of concern. Surely she could muddle along on her own a while longer. 'Of course not. I was about to go up myself.'

After her father kissed her goodnight and left for his chamber, Amanda lingered only long enough to put out the candles. She needed her rest, too, for tomorrow, in addition to her other tasks, she'd have to fit in a tour around the property with Althea—and Mr Anders.

A flurry of anticipation buoyed her to her room. She couldn't quite convince herself that the sense of heightened expectation was due only to the pride she'd feel in showing off Papa's estate.

'Mr Anders, you will truly enjoy this first site,' Miss Holton told him as he guided the gig down the Salters Bay Road. ''Tis the ruins of an iron-age fortification. The area has many of them, remnants of the ancient Dumnonii who inhabited this region before the Roman conquest. The hills are riddled with caves as well, one of the reason free-traders are eager to land goods here. If you would stop now, please?'

'At your command, Miss Holton,' Greville said, pulling up the horses.

For the third straight day, he was touring Ashton Grove land with Miss Neville and her cousin. The first time, when he'd not been sure how long he'd be able to tolerate the jolting of a carriage, they had confined their explorations to the immediate vicinity of Ashton Grove manor. Perhaps mindful of his condition, Miss Neville had maintained a dawdling pace, stopping frequently at a series of small farms. At each one, she greeted the tenants by name, enquired about their families and asked insightful questions about the condition of the fields and the current status of ploughing and planting.

Yesterday they'd travelled north, past velvety pasture land dotted with dairy cattle, up towards steeper, rockier ground where flocks of sheep grazed. Again, Miss Neville paused whenever they encountered men tending the animals, enquiring after them and their beasts. Farther north still, she'd told him, were tin mines in which her father had a controlling interest.

Today they were headed towards the coast at Salters Bay, where he meant to report for duty at the Coastal Brigade station.

After climbing out, Greville walked around the gig, buoyed with anticipation. One of the benefits of finally feeling well enough to take over the reins from Miss Neville, who had driven on each of their previous outings, was going to be the delight of lifting her down from the vehicle.

An instant later, she was in his arms. He revelled in this perfectly acceptable excuse to touch her…and if his fingers lingered a bit longer than absolutely necessary at her waist, allowing him to breathe in her light flowery scent and savour the sparking burn where his hands pressed against her—oh, that there were not so many layers of cloth and chamois between his skin and hers!—perhaps she'd attribute it to his not being recovered enough to complete the action swiftly.

Though her widened eyes and slight intake of breath as she looked up at him, standing motionless with his hands still upon her, hinted that perhaps she found the contact as stimulating as he did.

To his regret, she moved away, leaving his hands bereft. He turned to find Miss Holton staring at them curiously. 'What would you know about smugglers, Miss Holton?' he asked.

To his relief, the query deflected her attention, just as he'd intended. With a tell-tale blush that would doubtless have struck fear in the heart of Lord Bronning, who was already worried about his son's possible involvement in the trade, she said quickly, 'Oh, only what anyone hereabouts knows.'

Miss Neville gave her cousin a sharp look, leading Greville to suspect she'd just been struck by the same disagreeable suspicion. He sent her a sympathetic glance over Miss Holton's head, chuckling softly when she rolled her eyes heavenwards.

Thank the Lord he was not responsible for trying to supervise the Holton chit!

'The remnants of the hill-fort ramparts are this way.' Miss Holton turned back towards him, offering her hand. Obligingly he tucked it under his arm and let her lead him about the area, duly admiring the bits of stone and mounds of earth that excited her enthusiasm, Miss Neville trailing after them like a long-suffering chaperon.

Although the idea of the delectable Miss Neville as anyone's *chaperon* made his lips tremble with suppressed mirth.

Their inspection complete, they returned to the gig. 'What else shall we see on the way to Salters Bay?' he asked Miss Neville.

'First we'll pass the Trimmer, Smith and Mercer farms,' Miss Neville replied, 'all planted in grain. More pastures, and the cottages of Mrs Enders and the Hill family, lace-makers. Honiton is the centre of the trade, but the lace is actually made at home by a number of individual craftsmen. Papa assists those who occupy Ashton land, taking their products to Honiton in lieu of rent.'

'We're still on Ashton land, then?' he asked, surprised.

'Yes. We will be, almost all the way to Salters Bay.'

'I must say, the estate is vaster than I'd imagined,' Greville said.

'It's the largest landholding in this part of Devon,' Miss Holton said proudly. 'Nevilles have been here since the Conquest. The ruins of the original family dwelling, Neville Tour, sit on the cliffs just beyond where our road descends to Salters

Bay. With its commanding view from the sea to the mouth of the Exe, it was constructed by the first Baron Bronning, who'd been charged with keeping the King's peace from Exmouth to Exeter, from Honiton to Lyme Regis.'

'Vast acreage, grazing of cattle and sheep, fields of grain, tin mines to the north, lace-making to the south…Ashton Grove estate is a most impressive property!'

'It is indeed,' Miss Neville replied, giving him a warm glance. 'It's a vast amount to handle and make profitable, too, especially these last few years since the war, with the price of corn so depressed. Papa is a very skilled manager.'

'You are quite knowledgeable as well,' he said with sincere admiration.

Miss Neville blushed and Greville suppressed a smile. Apparently she really was unused to compliments, whether about her beauty or her talents. Once again, he found her unexpected humility endearing.

'I suppose, having ridden about with Papa since I was big enough to hold on to his saddle bow, I've learned a few things.'

'Far more than just a few!'

After his first two days of observation, Greville had concluded with chagrin that Lord Bronning's daughter knew far more about estate management than he had learned in nearly two years as titular manager of Blenhem Hill.

Even more surprising, he was finding himself actually interested in her observations about farming, flocks and fields.

Travelling about Lord Bronning's estate had opened his eyes to the truth he had somehow missed all the time he'd been Blenhem Hill's manager. Every interaction he observed between Miss Neville and the farmers demonstrated just how much a man of birth like Lord Bronning enhanced, rather than diminished, his stature and the respect in which he was held by intimately involving himself in the life of his land and tenants.

A fact the perceptiveness honed by his months aboard the *Illustrious* now made seem completely obvious.

What an opportunity he had wasted at Blenhem Hill! Not for the first time, he wished he might have the last three years back to live over again.

He wasn't sure when or how he would make amends to the tenants his ignorance had harmed or the cousin whose trust he'd abused. But some day, after he obtained his release from the Navy and built a new career, he intended to do so.

'Is your shoulder paining you, Mr Anders?'

Miss Holton's enquiry interrupted his reflections. Realising he must have been frowning, Greville replied, 'Not at all, Miss Holton. Just concentrating a bit too much on the road. Forgive me.'

'Around this next curve is the Trimmer farm, which has quite an extensive orchard,' Miss Neville said. 'We can rest the horses—and probably beg a mug of their excellent cider.'

'A mug of cider would be most welcome,' Greville said, dismissing the last of his lingering regrets and turning his attention back to his companions.

Chapter Six

Several hours later, after cider at the farmhouse drunk under the still-bare branches of the apple trees, stops at several other farms and a visit with the lace-maker Mrs Ender, they left Ashton Grove land and began the descent to Salters Bay. Conversation languished as the narrow, twisting lane and the steep grade forced him to focus all his concentration on driving.

Though Greville didn't mind the slow pace. He was in no hurry to get to their final destination and exchange the company of the glorious Miss Neville for that of a passel of crusty sailors. Though perhaps he ought to be.

In the camaraderie of admiring farms and fields, it had been all too easy to forget he had intended to keep his distance. Rather than tease and antagonise her, with each engaging conversation he moved closer to falling into an easy friendship with the beguiling Miss Neville, whose tantalising proximity made him yearn for the more intimate relationship that both honour and common sense forbade.

A good part of the effect she had on him, he reassured himself, doubtless arose from his being so long without attractive feminine company. The eager anticipation with which he'd awaited each of these day-long outings, the way it seemed as though the spring sun emerged after the chill clouds of winter when she smiled—all stemmed from a temporary fascination that would fade, as former fascinations had, once he could freely avail himself of the intimate contact he had lacked for so long.

Though he acknowledged, regretfully, such contact would probably not be possible until he was free of the naval service and residing in a metropolis large enough that one's neighbour didn't know about one's every indiscretion.

Suddenly a carriage careened around the corner, headed right for them. Returning to his duties with a start, Greville hauled back hard on the reins, pain searing his recovering shoulder as he struggled to control the rearing, plunging horses.

The other carriage was doing the same, and after a few moments of chaos, with the ladies crying out and hanging on to rails, the groom from the other vehicle ran to the horses' heads while two men jumped down and hurried over.

'Miss Neville, Miss Holton, are you both unharmed? I fear, while showing off my new curricle for my guest, I took that last corner far too swiftly.'

'Althea and I are quite safe, Mr Williams,' Miss Neville assured the newcomer.

'My thanks to the gentleman handling your reins for avoiding a collision! Had he not reacted so swiftly…' Mr Williams's voice trailed off and he shuddered.

'Fortunately, he did a magnificent job, for which we are all grateful,' Miss Neville said. 'May I introduce our guest? Mr Anders, late of the Royal Navy, recently wounded in action off the Algerine coast, is staying with us as he recovers. Mr Williams, our nearest neighbour, has property that marches with Papa's to the south-east.

After bows exchanged all around, Greville said, 'You were

just as responsible for averting disaster, Mr Williams. I'm only glad we were able to avoid injury to the horses and assembled company.'

'Amen to that, Mr Anders. Now, ladies,' Mr Williams continued, 'may I present my own guest, whom I was foolishly trying to impress with the speed of this vehicle! Lord Trowbridge, son of the Earl of Ravensfell. I have the honour of hosting him whilst he looks over the mills in Honiton as a possible investment for his papa. Lord Trowbridge, let me offer the pleasure of acquaintance with Miss Neville, the loveliest lady in Devon, daughter of my good friend and neighbour Lord Bronning! And Lord Bronning's niece, Miss Holton.'

All the hackles Greville had thought worn off by his sojourn at sea arose anew as he watched this sprig of nobility greet Miss Neville. Though he felt sympathy for Miss Holton's addendum of an introduction, most of his brain was occupied in fiercely resenting how Lord Trowbridge, while bowing and murmuring the appropriate courtesies, managed to sneak a quick, full-body inspection of Amanda Neville.

The swift appreciation registering in his eyes told Greville he found Miss Neville a sweetmeat he'd like to devour on the spot.

Greville struggled to rein in an unexpectedly fierce emotion that could only be jealousy. Why should he be so angry at Trowbridge? No man breathing could look at Amanda Neville without reacting in that manner. Knowing he looked at her like that himself, he should hardly resent another man doing so.

That didn't mitigate the fact that he minded it very much. Or perhaps it was the unconscious swagger that said Trowbridge, as an earl's son, thought he had an inherent right to her admiration in return.

In the meantime, Mr Williams was continuing, 'Miss Neville is to go London shortly for her come-out, are you not, ma'am?'

'I am indeed, Mr Williams. How kind of you to remember.'

'How could I forget, when your leaving will deprive the county of its greatest beauty?' he replied with ponderous gallantry. 'And one of our most tireless workers. Since the tragic death of her mother last summer, Miss Neville has taken over as chatelaine of her father's house and angel of mercy for the tenants. Ask Father Bricknell at the church or any farmer in the parish, they'll tell you no one in need fails to receive Miss Neville's gracious attentions.'

'You are too generous, Mr Williams,' Miss Neville protested, her cheeks colouring, which only enhanced her loveliness—unfortunately, Greville thought, his fingers curling into fists as he resisted the urge to plant a facer in the middle of Trowbridge's handsome aristocratic nose.

'Ashton's loss will be London's gain, then,' Trowbridge said. 'What a charming addition to society you will be, Miss Neville.'

'Will you be in town for the Season, Lord Trowbridge?' she asked.

'I'm in London whenever Parliament is in session, though assisting my father with his work in the Lords generally keeps me so occupied that I don't take part in many society entertainments. I see I shall need to change that.'

While Miss Neville blushed anew at his implication, Mr Williams said, 'Indeed, Miss Neville is quite interested in politics. Reads all the London papers and always asks for a report of what's going on when I return from town. Miss Neville, Lord Trowbridge's father has much influence with the current government, being often consulted by the Prince and Prime Minister. You will certainly wish to make the acquaintance of all his family while you are in town.'

The shy smile she gave Trowbridge had Greville clenching his jaw. 'I've read much in the journals of Lord Ravensfell, particularly in his capacity as advisor to Lord Wellington and

Lord Castlereagh at the Congress of Vienna,' she said. 'I should be honoured to meet your family, my lord.'

Trowbridge bowed again. 'I shall tell Mama to call upon you as soon as you get to town. Will Lord Bronning be taking a house there?'

'No, Papa dislikes the city. Besides which, having always some new project or planting that requires his supervision, he hates being long from home. I will be residing with Lady Parnell in Upper Brook Street.'

'Excellent!' Trowbridge said. 'Lady Parnell is one of Mama's dearest friends. We will certainly make a visit after your arrival…though I hope I may see you again sooner than that.' He gave her a significant look, to which Mr Williams added a wink.

To Greville's disgruntlement, she replied with the expected invitation. 'If time allows, you must dine at Ashton before you leave Devon. Papa would be delighted to meet you, Lord Trowbridge. He also has investments at Honiton and might be able to add some insight about the process. As for you, Mr Williams, we've not had the pleasure of an extended visit with you and Mrs Williams for far too long.'

Lord Trowbridge smiled, like a sleek, satisfied cat that has just polished off the mouse population of the barn. 'I should like that very much.'

'Mrs Williams will be charmed as well,' her neighbour said. 'A bit of merriment will do your poor papa good after the sadness of last summer, eh?'

She nodded. 'I'll send a note to the Grange.'

'We shall all look forward to it,' Lord Trowbridge said.

'Haven't we kept the horses standing long enough?' Miss Holton inserted, her tone acerbic. 'They must be getting chilled.'

Greville sympathised with her annoyance. Out or not, it

couldn't be very appealing to a girl to be totally ignored while men made much of her beautiful cousin.

Not that Miss Neville could help being beautiful. And irritated as Greville was by the invitation she'd extended, with her close neighbour hosting a distinguished guest, there was almost no polite way she could have avoided issuing one. Unfortunately, since Lord Bronning had insisted on treating him like a guest, he'd probably have to suffer being present at that dinner, even though Trowbridge appeared to be exactly the sort of complacent, self-satisfied aristocrat Greville found most annoying.

After an exchange of farewells, Williams and Trowbridge returned to their curricle and the two vehicles drove off in opposite directions.

'Well, that was certainly pleasant,' Miss Holton remarked. 'Being treated as if one were of no more importance than the carriage wheel.'

Glancing down at the girl's affronted expression, Greville had to grin. 'A carriage wheel is not nearly as noisy and troublesome as you can be, Miss Holton,' he teased, trying to amuse her out of her pique.

The ploy seemed to work, for her brow cleared and she threw him a saucy glance. 'I would have thought you felt so too! Since the conversation never allowed mentioning your relationship to a marquess, you might have been the other carriage wheel.'

'Then we could have rolled away, could we not?'

Miss Holton giggled. 'Oh, that we might have! Very pleased with himself, isn't he, that Lord Trowbridge? I wonder he dares ride out in an open curricle, lest his Brutus-cut locks or his elegant cravat be disordered by the wind.'

'You must not fault a town-bred lord from wishing to look his best, even in the country,' Greville said mildly, recalling the days of his own sartorial splendour. Some imp of jealousy forced him to add, 'A very handsome gentleman. Did you not think so, Miss Neville?'

'He's well looking,' she allowed.

'He's just the sort of man you are looking for, Amanda!' Miss Holton said. 'Titled, influential political family, government connections. Having made his acquaintance now, you'll be sure to see him again during your Season. You should be in alt!'

'I would hope to know more of a man's character before becoming overwhelmed with enthusiasm for his company,' Miss Neville replied a bit sharply.

Trowbridge might well be a prime contender for Miss Neville's hand, Greville realised; certainly he possessed all the right qualifications. Since Greville did not—and never would—he found the fact that she had not gone off into transports of delight over the earl's son more satisfying than he ought.

'It's never good to assume virtue—or lack of the same—based solely on someone's family name and connections,' he said. Hadn't he always been proof of that?

'Meaning many a wastrel bears a title?' Althea said. 'From what I heard the girls at school discussing, it seems most spend their days in idleness and dissipation.'

'London gentlemen, like any other group, consist of both good and bad individuals,' Greville said. 'Some of my Cambridge friends ended up being frugal, industrious guardians of their estates and family. Others…are less conscientious,' he concluded, his own conscience smiting him at the knowledge of which category, until recently, he'd fallen into.

Still, he had to acknowledge that sticking in his gut, indigestible as a biscuit after two months at sea, was the idea of Trowbridge cosying up to Miss Neville.

Never before having seriously vied for any woman's attention, he had little experience of jealousy. He found he didn't much like the feeling.

'You are quite right, Mr Anders,' Miss Neville was saying. 'One should refrain from judging upon first acquaintance. Character will out eventually, leading one to make a more informed decision later.'

Was that another subtle apology for her less-than-courteous initial treatment? With a swell of satisfaction that did much to dissipate his irritation, Greville hoped it was.

Around the next bend, they emerged from the stone walls sheltering the road to find spread out below them the small seaport of Salters Bay. An attractive collection of houses crowded together along several streets, their centre punctuated by the spire of a church, while in the far distance beyond a jetty unrolled the limitless vista of the sea.

'A lovely view, is it not?' Miss Holton asked.

'Lovely indeed,' he replied, feeling an instant connection to the tossing waves that had been the scene of his deepest desperation and the beginning of his transformation.

'The Coastal Brigade office is there,' Miss Neville pointed, 'at the end of the quay. I don't see any cutters anchored at present off the jetty, so perhaps you'll not have any duties to perform just yet.'

'I must report in any event. As I'm not sure how long that will take, could I have you ladies leave me at the office and rejoin you later? At a local inn, where I could offer you some refreshment, in thanks for driving with me today.'

As he made the offer, he sent another prayer blessing his sister for providing the coins that made that small gesture possible. The thought of the humiliation of not being able to do even that strengthened his resolve to swiftly find a new, income-generating occupation.

'The Knight and Dragon keeps a fine table. Papa and I often stop there when we have business in Salters Bay.'

'Oh, yes, do let us meet there!' Miss Holton said. 'Mrs Merriweather makes an excellent roast and apple tart!'

'The Knight and Dragon it is, then,' Greville agreed.

A few minutes later, they reached the quay and he stepped down, handing the reins over to Miss Neville. After the ladies drove off, he stood immobile, watching until the gig turned down the first street and disappeared from view.

Then, squaring his shoulders, he mounted the steps of the small seaside office where his chequered past and uncertain future were about to collide.

Chapter Seven

Greville entered the building to find a small, swarthy man in sailor's garb seated on a stool behind a desk in the anteroom. One side of the man's face was covered with a bandana, while his visible eye focused on the elaborate knot pattern he was creating with a length of twine. One of the hands plying the rope was missing two fingers, Greville noted.

As Greville walked over, the sailor jumped up and touched his forehead respectfully. 'Kin I help you, sir?'

Greville noted further that the old sailor balanced on one wooden leg affixed below his knee. No question, then, why this seaman was moored in port. 'Yes, Mr...?'

'Gunner's Mate Andrew Porter, sir, late of the *Indie*.'

'Ah, *Indefatigable*, a fine ship! I'm Greville Anders, late of the *Illustrious*.'

Porter's one eye brightened with interest. 'Was you on board for her action against the Algerines a month or so back?'

'Yes, I was.'

'Ah, what a fine fight it were, or so I've been told! Had a dust-up with that ship and her captain back when we was battling the slave trade off the Africa coast. Fierce fighters. Carrying quite a cache of gold this time, I hear, instead of the poor Europeans they used to sell off to them harems and such.'

'So it was rumoured. I took the sharp side of a cutlass before we breached the hold. Though I fared better than you, the wounds were bad enough that they shipped me back.'

'Aye, luckier by half,' the man acknowledged with a nod. 'I couldn't tell you'd been wounded, whereas there'll be no more deep-water sailing for old Andrew, more's the pity. But why are you not in uniform, sir?'

With him wearing gentleman's dress, the sailor took him for an officer, Greville realised. 'I was transferred off in the rags of the clothing in which I fought the action. I had no seaman's trunk to follow me, nor spare uniforms; I was impressed as a landsman.'

The sailor's eyes widened as he took in that information. 'Thought we weren't impressing no more, now that the war against Boney's over. And it weren't never legal to impress gentlemen.'

'The circumstances of my entering the Navy were rather… unusual. In any event, proceedings are underway to have me honourably released from the service. In the meantime, I am to report to the commanding officer here.'

'That would be Lieutenant Belcher,' the sailor said. 'I'll tell him you're here.

Greville was duly escorted into an inner office with a window overlooking the harbour. Behind the desk sat an older man in a naval lieutenant's uniform. Since he was wearing civilian dress—and if cousin Nicky prevailed with the Navy Board, he would remain garbed that way—Greville did not salute.

After the gunner introduced them, Belcher said, 'Mr Anders, what can I do for you?'

'Technically, Lieutenant, I'm still a landsman attached to the *Illustrious*, although I expect soon to have word from the Admiralty Board directing that I be released from service.'

Belcher frowned. 'You, sir, are obviously a gentleman. How did you come to do service as a common sailor?'

'Apparently the ship was vastly undermanned due to an attack of virulent fever among the crew. Eager to set off immediately for the Algerine coast, the captain instructed the press gang to take every able-bodied man they could find. Once underway, he had neither the inclination nor the opportunity to send me back.'

'If you were confined with the crew, 'tis little wonder you seek a discharge! Most are scurvy knaves, working only for their rum ration and out of fear of the lash.'

Greville's initially favourable impression of the lieutenant abruptly declined. How could an officer expect to inspire the respect and allegiance of his crew, if he held *them* in so little respect? There had been one or two such officers among the wardroom of the *Illustrious*—all uniformly despised by the men.

'True, there were slackers and malcontents, but the majority were good solid men,' he replied. 'The ship ran with an admirable efficiency that would not have been possible without a skilled crew performing their respective jobs as a unit.'

Belcher sniffed. 'If the ship ran with "admirable efficiency", it was because the captain knew how to get work out of scum. I'm astounded that you, who claim to be a gentleman, could have served for any time aboard ship and remain ignorant of so obvious a truth. Unless your common sense was tainted by the common associations you formed below decks?' he proposed, chuckling a little at his own joke.

Greville was not amused. Association with hard-working common sailors had made him a better man than he'd been a year ago. His entire view of life had radically altered after spending months as one of the powerless at the mercy of those who exercised power—for good or ill.

Without the compassion and assistance of several of those 'scurvy knaves', he wouldn't have survived the experience.

'That wasn't my impression of the men aboard the *Illustrious*, but I allow you your opinion.'

'Oh, will you now?' Belcher cried, drawing himself up stiffly, as if to move away from the contamination of Greville's views. 'That's not the manner in which a sailor addresses a superior officer, a fact I advise you to remember for such time as you remain attached to the Navy. In fact, I'd be of a mind to discipline you for it, but as I haven't yet received word from Admiralty apprising me of your exact position, for now, I will exercise leniency.'

He leaned towards Greville, a banty rooster ruffling his feathers. 'Don't count on it happening again, sirrah. In any event, given your scant experience, you can't be entrusted with any naval duties. You shall remain in Salters Bay until Admiralty sends me word of their decision.'

'Am I dismissed, then, Lieutenant?'

Ignoring Greville's question, Belcher said, half to himself, 'I've got Black John Kessel moving in, intimidating villagers, even attacking my revenue officers. I need more veteran sailors to man my cutters, and they send me a useless landsman with peculiar opinions.' He shook his head in disgust. 'Very well, Anders, you may go.'

By now as angry as Belcher, Greville inclined his head. 'Lieutenant,' he said by way of farewell, determined not to accord the man a 'sir.'

As he turned to the door, the lieutenant said, 'I suppose I should enquire if you need billeting? I can have Porter find you something in town since you are, apparently, still the Navy's responsibility.'

'No need to trouble yourself,' Greville said. 'I've been offered hospitality for the duration by Lord Bronning.'

The lieutenant was nodding absently, but at that name, his eyes snapped wide. 'Lord Bronning?' he echoed. 'Can you mean...*Miss Neville*'s father?'

Greville suppressed a smile. Apparently the glorious Amanda had made a conquest here. 'The same. You are acquainted with his lordship and Miss Neville?'

'We've been introduced, though I've never been invited to Ashton Gr—' Belcher halted abruptly, his ruddy colour deepening with indignation as he realised this man whom he disdained was on familiar terms with the most important family in the locality—and he was not.

'A most handsome property,' Greville said. It might be ignoble of him, but he was enjoying Belcher's chagrin. 'You must visit it, should you ever have the opportunity.' Leaving the lieutenant with his open mouth gaping like a beached halibut, Greville walked to the door.

Gunner Porter sprang up as he reached the threshold. 'Should I add Mr Anders to the duty roster, Lieutenant?'

'No!' Belcher barked. 'I'm not sure what to do with such a person,' he added, his aggrieved voice still vibrant with anger. Turning to Greville, he said, 'I shall dispatch a letter to the Admiralty, enquiring about your case. Report back here in a week, Anders.'

'Mr Anders,' Greville corrected softly, holding the man's gaze. He might pay for it later if Englemere's intervention didn't succeed and he ended up under this man's authority, but he had ultimate confidence in cousin Nicky's influence. And he did not intend to bend to this petty tyrant.

The lieutenant looked away first. 'You are dismissed.'

Greville closed the office door after him and turned to see the gunner grinning. 'Mustn't mind ol' Belcher, sir. Likes to act important, as if he was still aboard a man-of-war, standing the quarterdeck watch. Hard on him, being passed over for promotion. With the cutbacks in the Navy and the war ended, he knows he'll probably never get a command—unless he finds a rich wife to buy him one, like that Miss Neville you was speaking of.'

'Gunny, were you listening at the door?'

'Can't help if yer voices was a bit loud,' the sailor replied.

Recalling Belcher's contempt for sailors, Greville said, 'Though I imagine you'd welcome his transfer, I have to say I'm glad the lieutenant will never get a command.'

'The devil of it is, I understand he's a damn good sailor. But he's got the making of a flogging captain if anyone does, and there's nothing worse in the fleet. So you lived on the deck plates, you a gentleman 'n all?' Porter shook his grizzled head. 'Seems near impossible.'

Greville remembered his shock and despair when the truth had finally sunk in that he was not going to be able to talk his way off the ship. 'It nearly was.'

With neither the training nor experience as a sailor, suffering from the unaccustomed labour and poor food, for a time he feared he might never leave the fleet save with his feet weighted down, slipped over the side under the cover of a Union Jack.

'Had it not been for the doctor who tended me and one old salt who'd been at sea since he was a five-year-old powder monkey, I might not have survived. He kept the bullies from tormenting me, went out of his way to teach me how to perform my duties.'

'Had a friend meself among *Illustrious*'s crew. Everyone called him Old Tom, been in the service since sails was first made, he used to say. You woulda known him, I expect.'

'Indeed, I did! It was Old Tom who helped me. An excellent sailor, and I've never met a finer man,' Greville said warmly.

'We sailed the China coast together, and there weren't never a better Jack Tar in a gale or a fight. Sure wouldn't mind having more of his ilk here, what with what's going on now.'

Greville recalled Lord Bronning warning his son about smugglers and the concern the lieutenant had just expressed. 'What is going on?'

'Always been smugglers here—how could there not be, close as we be to the French coast and duty on brandy and fripperies being so high? Things been run for years by John Rattenbury out of Beer, a right kindly gentleman the folks hereabouts call Rob Roy. But lately, a gang from Sennlach near Land's End been trying to take over his territory, led by an out-and-out cutthroat more fit to captain a pirate crew.'

Porter shook his head. 'Black John fired at the last revenue cutter that got close to his ship, wounding three and killing one sailor outright afore he slipped away into the mist. I hear he gets local people to move goods for him—whether they be willing or not.'

'Is that why there are no cutters at anchor now?'

'Aye, they're all out looking for him, though I'm not so sure the next dust-up won't come on land. There were a fight between Black John's men and Rob Roy's last month over how they was forcing some folk to store his cargo. Then, just last week, Farmer Johnson was found murdered. It's said he refused to hide contraband for Black John. My friends in the village tell me some in Salters Bay been saying they better stand up to Black John afore he takes out them what resist him, one by one.'

'Sounds like a man who needs killing. I don't think I'm able yet to wield a cutlass with any force, but I'd be glad to help out if I can.'

'You get yourself healed first afore you think of joining a fight,' Porter advised. 'Well, I reckon the lieutenant will send word when the Admiralty makes up its mind.' He patted Greville on the arm. 'It's the Navy, though. Don't expect it will be quick.'

Greville thought of the enticing Miss Neville. 'Slow is fine with me.'

The old seaman chuckled. 'Wouldn't expect nothing else from a man who's hanging his hammock in the house of a beauty like Miss Neville!'

Who was by now probably waiting for him at the inn. Cheered by that thought—and by recalling the arrogant Lieutenant Belcher's teeth-gnashing indignation at finding his subordinate on familiar terms with so rich and beautiful a lady—Greville bid the sailor goodbye and headed off to find the Knight and Dragon.

Chapter Eight

After an enjoyable lunch at the inn, during which Mr Anders kept them amused with naval anecdotes, Amanda let him hand her into the gig for the drive home.

For a few moments, the pleasant tingling sensation created by the touch of his hands at her waist halted all other thoughts. Then it faded and her present worries rushed back.

Their excursion was almost over, and she'd still not worked out how to have a private word with Mr Anders about whatever he might have learned of the smuggling threat. She didn't think it wise to broach the matter in front of Althea; she had enough to worry about without having her Navy-mad cousin decide to go haring off investigating on her own. Or worse, take it into her head to help the free-traders bring in cargo, as Amanda suspected her bored brother George might be doing.

She hadn't wanted to voice the fear to Papa, but after what he'd said about the local smugglers, the many nights her brother had absented himself and the mornings she'd caught him creeping in had taken on an ominous new meaning. If something as exciting as a battle between rival smuggling groups was going on, George would very likely want to be right in the thick of it.

She'd tried to send Althea off on an errand before they left the inn. But since the girl was perfectly indifferent to visiting the haberdasher or the local modiste and there was, alas, no bookseller in town, Amanda hadn't been able to shake herself free of her cousin's company after Mr Anders rejoined them.

There'd be no opportunity for a private chat now, with Althea seated right beside them in the gig. Tuning out her cousin's chatter, Amanda tried to figure out how she might create a chance to talk with Mr Anders once they reached Ashton Grove.

'…open air so energising, I believe I shall ride once we get home.' Althea's words penetrated her abstraction. Amanda looked up sharply to see her cousin direct a hopeful glance at Mr Anders. 'Would you like to accompany me?'

To Amanda's relief, Mr Anders said, 'Perhaps another time, Miss Holton. Poor spirited as that makes me appear, I must confess to being somewhat wearied by our excursion today.'

Amanda didn't doubt it. She'd seen how he'd grimaced, one hand going instinctively to cushion his wounded side after he'd hauled back on the reins to halt and then control their frightened team during the near-collision earlier.

He'd steadied them masterfully. That incident and the way he drove today demonstrated a skill at handling the ribbons any Society Corinthian might envy.

Had he been a Corinthian? He'd not yet explained how he came to enter the Navy as a mere common sailor. Amanda wished for once she was as heedless of proper behaviour as Althea and could just boldly enquire about this and several other very personal matters.

She knew he'd attended Cambridge. What else had he done for what looked to be thirty-odd years? Amanda had to admit to a very ill-bred curiosity.

She came back from her reverie to hear Mr Anders encouraging Miss Holton to proceed without him and chose a favourite path on which he might ride with her later.

Excellent, she thought. When Althea stepped down at the entryway to go change into her habit, she'd invent some excuse to remain in the gig while Anders returned it to the stables. That would gain her a snippet of time on their way back to the manor for her to speak with him.

It would be only a short walk across a flat bit of Ashton Grove land, but an unexpected thrill of anticipation ran through her. Would he think she was asking for something other than advice if she were bold enough to solicit his company?

She recalled that moment on the terrace at Ashton when, startled, her eyes had locked on his. Heat had blazed across her skin, her bosom, her lips. Every nerve awakened, she'd sensed the descent of his lips towards hers, anticipated the brush of his hands at her sides. Urgency flooded her to feel the warmth of his hard chest against her body, the press of his mouth upon hers.

Her face and ears flaming at the memories, surreptitiously she fanned herself, blessing the fact that Althea continued to chatter on, holding Mr Anders's attention. Though her experience was limited, she did have some notion of what had transpired between them on the terrace. Now she felt acutely aware of him seated beside her, radiating a strength, warmth and boldness that urged her to draw closer.

Lust was the blunt name for the force pulling them together, a force, she was nearly certain, he felt as strongly as she. A year ago in the autumn, before her second aborted Season, Mama had taken her to the local assemblies in Exeter, to acquire a bit of town bronze before she had to appear under the far more exacting eyes of the London *ton*.

Several attractive young gentlemen had pursued her. She'd felt a flurry of excitement in the pit of her stomach when one particular man, a rogue with knowing eyes and a wicked smile, let his fingers linger just a bit longer than was proper on her waist and wrist when he helped her in or out of her carriage.

Mama would have been horrified had she ever learned, but she'd even let Lord J. of the dancing smile and roving hands walk her into her cousin's garden and steal a kiss behind the rose arbour.

Like the scent of the autumn blooms that masked their intrigue, the kiss had begun as a sweet, light sensation. Then came the shock of a wet tongue brushing her lips, a firm hard hand stroking her breast.

Aghast, she'd broken away immediately and run from the garden...not sure whether it was the audacious Lord J. or her own response to him that had frightened her the most. She'd returned to Ashton Grove the next day, never able to decide whether she was glad or happy she wouldn't see her rogue again.

She was honest enough to admit she'd be delighted to repeat the experience—with Mr Anders's hand at her breast and Mr Anders's tongue tasting her lips.

In fact, the thought of him doing so sent a veritable blast of sensation through her, making her nipples tingle and sending a rush of liquid heat between her thighs, far dwarfing in intensity the response she'd had to Lord J. that long-ago afternoon.

She drew in a shaky breath, not sure what had just happened. She only knew it was fortunate the rose garden at Ashton was now nothing but sad brown sticks stripped of foliage, awaiting spring.

As she and her desires must do. If she wanted to fulfil Mama's dream of making an advantageous match, she couldn't racket about Ashton Grove, kissing available men when the fancy struck her.

Even though the urging to do so had been stealing over her with increasing frequency ever since that interlude on the terrace, she thought—and realised she'd instinctively slid closer to him.

This would never do, she told herself, moving towards the outer rail of the gig and firmly yanking her thoughts away from his too-attractive torso.

Ah, yes, it was time to get herself wedded and bedded indeed!

Since Mr Anders was not a member of the political elite into which she aspired to wed—assuming wedlock was of any interest to him, which he'd given her no reason whatever to believe—she'd do better to turn her thoughts to someone who was...like Lord Trowbridge.

If what their neighbour said was true, here was a gentleman who seemed a perfect choice to make all her plans a reality.

Not that she doubted Mr William's word, but he, like Papa, preferred to tend his acres and remain in country. He'd have no way of knowing whether Trowbridge's attractive exterior was matched by an excellence of character worthy of his family's position among the *ton* and his father's prominence in government.

Lady Parnell would know. Amanda would just have to wait until London, where she could rely upon that lady to guide her choice. But in the interim, it wouldn't hurt to get to know Trowbridge better. After finding a way to speak privately with Mr Anders, she would speak with Papa about arranging a dinner.

She squelched a *frisson* of unease at the little voice pointing out that, despite her appreciation for his many assets of family, title and position, she felt for him nothing like the strong, instinctive attraction that pulled her towards Mr Anders.

Stealing a few moments with her guest turned out to be easier to arrange than she'd hoped. By the time the gig turned into the entry gates at Ashton Grove, cloud banks had blown up, accompanied by a sharp wind that promised rain. Anxious to get in a ride before the weather turned, as soon as Mr Anders pulled the gig up before the entry Althea scrambled out and flew into the house. While Anders waited for the footman to assist Amanda down, in a voice she hoped sounded quite natural, she informed him she'd like to continue on to the stables, as she needed to speak with the head groom, and would like to claim his escort to the house afterwards.

He made no comment, only setting the horses back in motion, though she dared not sneak a glance at his expression.

It took only a few moments' thought to come up with a topic to discuss with Jenkins. Though the head groom gave her an odd look when she enquired about the ordering of tack, a matter that was certainly not of sufficient urgency that she needed to seek him out this particular afternoon, thankfully he asked no awkward questions while Mr Anders stood by, waiting politely.

Then, finally the moment arrived. Heart hammering in nervous anticipation, she turned to Mr Anders, who offered her his arm. The jolt of sensation as she laid her hand upon it, for a moment, blew every other thought out of her head.

Obviously not as affected by the contact as she, Mr Anders was able to chat politely about their pleasant day's outing, giving her time to recover.

Gathering up her scattered wits, she said, 'I must offer my apologies for kidnapping you, but I needed to speak to you without Althea being present.'

'You flatter me,' he replied. Then, a naughty light gleaming in his eyes, he added, 'Do with me what you will.'

Back into her head flew the image of kissing him behind the arbour, his mouth on hers, his tongue seeking…

Jerking her thoughts away, she said, 'You may recall my father mentioning his concern about a rather ruthless group of smugglers who've moved in to challenge the local men. My brother George, after being sent down from Cambridge, asked and was refused Papa's permission to await the beginning of his next term in London. I fear that, bored and resentful of being forced to remain far from his friends and amusements, he may have become involved. Confounding the revenuers and maybe earning himself a cut of the profits is just the sort of thing that would appeal to him.'

By the time she'd finished, the teasing light had gone out of his eyes. 'What makes you think he might be involved?'

Quickly she described the many nights her brother had been absent and the mornings she'd caught him sneaking in, not always in his cups. To her dismay, rather than passing off her concern with a joke about hovering womenfolk and a recommendation that she loosen the young man's leading strings, Mr Anders's expression turned more serious.

'He's certainly been absenting himself during the hours that smugglers would be moving their cargoes. And both Lieutenant Belcher and Petty Officer Porter at the Coastal Brigade station mentioned there'd been a marked increase in tension lately between the local men and a group of newcomers for control of this stretch of coast. The Cornish group seems not at all averse to violence.'

His words confirmed her worst fears. 'Did you learn anything more about the situation?'

'Nothing specific. But Porter did say he thinks some sort of altercation might be imminent.' Anders shook his head. 'I wish I'd known of your concern before I reported in. Though I'm not due to return for more than a week, perhaps I will drive in sooner, see what else I can discover.'

'I would be most grateful! And if you would, please don't mention this to my cousin. She might be moved to try to investigate on her own, and she is as heedless of danger as my lackwit of a brother.'

'Poor Miss Neville!' he said with a sympathetic smile. 'Yet

more concerns to occupy you. No wonder you wish to escape to London.'

She flushed, feeling both ashamed and resentful. Was it so wrong that she wished to escape dealing with such a tangle of problems? 'That makes me sound self-centred and frivolous.'

'I meant nothing of sort!' he protested. 'Excuse me, but you seem far too young to have been saddled with the many responsibilities you must shoulder. And shoulder with excellence, I should add.'

Her resentment dissolved in a glow of pleasure at his compliment. 'But here I am, selfishly chattering on about my own concerns. What of you? Did Lieutenant Belcher have any information about your situation?'

He grimaced. 'Precious little. He wasn't even aware that I'd be reporting. He's going to send a note to the Admiralty, requesting their guidance.' He grinned. 'I'm afraid he didn't think much of this former gentleman-turned-landsman. He made it quite clear he doesn't want me involved in any of his patrol work.'

'If there's a confrontation in the offing, I should think he would want to muster every able-bodied hand.'

Too late, she caught the connection and could have bitten her tongue. He must have as well, for as he watched her face flame, a slow, teasing smile curved his lips.

'I'm glad you think I'm…able-bodied,' he said softly, his velvet voice rich with sensual undertones.

Oh, she did indeed! With his head tilted towards her, those arresting green eyes fixed on her face, his lips curved in a wicked smile, he was temptation incarnate. Her fingers itched to explore, from the broad shoulders down his chest to the trim waist…and lower. Lean up just a bit, rest her hand on his shoulder, and she might brush his mouth with her own…

Her pulse hammered and she jerked her gaze away. With a shuddering breath, she forced her feet back in motion. If this was how well she was going to resist the pesky attraction that kept pulling her to him, she'd better get back to the house, and quickly.

When he caught up to her, it seemed he'd accepted her silent rebuff. In a normal tone, he said, 'Belcher was probably right. I'm feeling infinitely better these last days, but if I had to shoulder a weapon or wield a sword, I'm afraid I still wouldn't be of much use.'

Perhaps his nearness had rattled her normal sense of propriety, for she found herself asking, 'Did you wield a sword when the pirate ship was taken?'

'I did.' His mouth thinned and his gaze went to the far horizon. 'I served in the Quartermaster's Corps during the Waterloo campaign, which mostly involved coordinating the movement of provisions in and around Brussels. We never saw any actual fighting. I hope I acquitted myself well when we took the pirate's vessel, but battling for one's life in a skirmish is nothing like fencing at Angelo's.'

Amanda wondered if he'd killed a man. He must have at least injured some, if only to protect himself and his shipmates. With the grim look on his face, she didn't dare ask.

In any event, they'd reached the manor. Amanda was about to walk up the steps when the entry door flew open and Althea, the train of her habit caught up over one arm, dashed out.

She stopped short, staring at Amanda with her hand on Mr Anders's arm, her eyes widening.

A flash of guilt wafted through Amanda—as if she'd been caught kissing him.

Trying to damp it down and prevent a flush from mounting her cheeks, she said, 'Thank you, Mr Anders, for a most illuminating discussion. I expect I'll see you at dinner.' Nodding to Althea, whose expression had gone from shocked to betrayed to accusing, she continued up the steps and into the house.

Chapter Nine

Two days later, Greville entered the breakfast room to find it deserted. In answer to his unspoken question, Sands said, 'Miss Amanda rode out early to visit some tenants, but Miss Althea should be down soon.'

Conscious of a disappointment he shouldn't be feeling, Greville nodded and went to fill his plate. He'd not seen the glorious Amanda yesterday. After awakening with his left side on fire and the cutlass wound weeping, he'd cursed himself for his foolhardiness in insisting on driving and spent the day resting.

He really shouldn't seek her out anyway. For the second time, he'd almost committed the impropriety of kissing her, the urge to do so stronger than the occasion before, on the terrace. This time, she'd nearly initiated the caress herself, before sanity returned and she prudently broke away from him.

He should respect that prudence and keep his distance.

Except…he just didn't want to. What was the harm in a little dalliance? an insidious voice asked. He wasn't a green youth, to be catapulted beyond the limits of control by a simple kiss, and she had her cap firmly fixed on catching a husband much grander than him. A few stolen caresses would titillate her and gratify them both, after which she'd be off to London and he could concentrate on settling his own future.

While he wrestled with temptation, Miss Holton entered. 'Are you feeling more the thing today?' she asked as she accepted a cup of coffee from Sands.

'Much better, thank you.'

'I'm so glad. We hoped you'd not re-injured your shoulder avoiding the collision with Mr Williams.'

'A temporary setback, no more.'

'Excellent. The day looks to be fair. Would you like to ride out? I could show you the ruins of Neville Tour.'

After the irritation of his aching shoulder and a day of forced inactivity, the idea of being out in the fresh air was so appealing that he replied at once, 'I should like that very much.'

'Wonderful!' Miss Holton gulped the rest of her coffee and set down the cup. 'Just let me change into my habit and I'll meet you at the stables.'

Not until she'd dashed off did Greville recall that, with Miss Neville off somewhere and unable to act as chaperon, he probably shouldn't have accepted Miss Holton's invitation.

By now, he'd had several occasions to observe the strain between the two girls. He suspected that, after seeing him with Amanda on his arm two days ago, Miss Holton had leapt at this opportunity to circumvent her cousin's attempts to prevent her from spending time alone with him.

But the day was truly too fine to waste, so by the time he arrived at the stables, he'd decided he could ride while still respecting propriety by getting one of the grooms to accompany them.

Miss Holton arrived a few minutes later. She looked askance when, after the servant gave her a leg up, he threw himself up on his own mount.

'You needn't come with us, Billy,' she said, a touch defiantly.

The flush that accompanied her words told him he'd been wise to be cautious. 'I asked him to do so, Miss Holton. The consequences of our excursion two days ago reminded me that I'm not yet fully healed. If I should tire and need to return early, I wouldn't wish to spoil your ride. Billy could accompany you home.'

'I've ridden these hills and valleys since I was a child,' she protested. 'I don't need help getting home.'

'Perhaps, but you are a young lady now. A gentleman never leaves a lady without an escort.'

He bit back a smile, watching the play of emotions on her face as gratification at being considered a lady warred with her desire to refuse a chaperon. 'I suppose I must bow to the preferences of a guest,' she said at last.

For a time after they set out, Greville tried the horse through its different paces, seeing how his body responded to the jolt of being astride. Requesting the services of the groom hadn't been entirely a matter of maintaining propriety; on this, his first ride since his wounding, he wasn't at all sure how much stamina he'd have, especially after the strain of fighting the team to a standstill two days ago.

But after a mile at an easy trot, he felt surprisingly well, the familiar rhythmic motion paining neither his arm nor his side. Joy suffused him; for the first time in almost a year he was on horseback, surveying the countryside like a hale, whole, independent man again.

Soon, he'd have an occupation that ensured he stayed that way.

Worries about his endurance dispelled, he turned his attention to determining whether his speculation about Miss Holton's intentions had been correct.

'Will Miss Neville be joining us?' he asked casually, pulling up his mount beside her.

Her chin rising defiantly, she halted her horse as well. 'Do you not wish to ride with only me for company? If that is the case, just say so—'

'Of course I wish to ride with you,' he interrupted, a bit annoyed by her prickly temper. Still, after the way he'd watched her being virtually ignored by her neighbour, he could understand her sensitivity on that point. 'You promised me a tour, did you not? Besides, I find you a most interesting and unusual girl,' he added with perfect truth.

That modest compliment earned him a smile. 'I don't see why we can't ride without her,' she replied. 'She was strolling with you the other day without a chaperon. If being alone with you won't sully her reputation, why should it harm mine? I think she just likes telling me what to do. Ever since Aunt Lydia fell sick, she's taken over at Ashton and ordered everyone about.'

Her tone was belligerent, but the vulnerability he read in her eyes touched him. She was an orphan, after all, and very much in her beautiful cousin's shadow. He knew all too well what it was like to stand in the shade of a more famous and compelling relation.

'She probably didn't have much choice about taking over from her mother,' he pointed out mildly, recalling what Miss Neville had confided to him. 'With all in chaos and distressed by the illness and then loss of those most dear to her, perhaps she did not exercise that authority as lightly as you might have wished. I expect it was a difficult time for everyone.'

'You can't imagine!' the girl burst out. To Greville's alarm, tears sheened her eyes. 'Do you know, they didn't even send me word that Mama was so ill? And then, when I finally did get to Ashton Grove, she was—' Miss Holton's voice broke.

Swallowing hard, she continued, 'She was so delirious, they wouldn't let me see her.'

'She had contracted a virulent fever, I was told. Probably the family wished you to avoid the infection.'

'Amanda sat with her.'

'Had Miss Neville not already recovered from the fever? Perhaps it was thought no longer dangerous for her.' By now, Greville was wishing he'd tried to turn the subject rather than enquiring further. What did he know about consoling a distraught young female?

Still, something about her—her bravado, her desire to escape being held to the rigid standards required of young ladies—reminded him of himself at her age, rebelling against a world in which the possession of wealth and property was everything, yet at the same time, priding himself on belonging to that ruling class, by birth if not status. He'd battled his relegation to an inferior position ever since leaving university—until a turn of fate reduced his existence to the most elemental level. His months at sea had taught him character was a much more important measure of a man than title and position.

'Perhaps,' Miss Holton said, sounding unconvinced. 'In any event...' she looked away, her voice dropping to a gruff murmur '...I expect Mama never asked for me. She always liked Amanda better. The whole time I was growing up, all I ever heard was how pretty my cousin was, how well she played the pianoforte and how beautifully she painted. Her behaviour was always the standard Mama held up for me to copy.'

Unsure how or whether he ought to halt the stream of words, Greville remained silent as she rushed on, 'It wasn't so bad while Papa was still alive. He took me riding, let me jump all the fences, even promised to teach me to shoot, until Mama found out and forbade it. I was already too "unnatural" a female without him encouraging me, she said.

'They didn't let me see Mama until the night she died, and

then only for a moment,' she continued, abruptly shifting back to her first narrative. 'She was already beyond recognising anyone. They rushed me out before I could try to make p-peace with her, though Amanda and Aunt Lydia stayed until the end,' the girl concluded bitterly.

Even the old Greville, before his experiences had given him a keener appreciation for the suffering of his fellows, couldn't have failed to be moved by her grief and regret. 'I'm so sorry,' he murmured, curling his fingers to resist the urge to pat her on the back or gather her in his arms.

With the speed of a jack rabbit darting away from a pursuing hound, her face cleared and she put on a determined smile. 'But heavens, why am I nattering on to you, who can have no interest in those events? It's all in past, anyway. With Amanda leaving soon, I intend to stay here with Uncle James. He'll not make me return to school or try to turn me into someone I'm not. Now, the castle ruins are just around the next turn.'

He had to admire her quick recovery, accomplished, praise Heaven, without any clumsily offered assistance from him. During the misery of days he'd spent aboard the prison hulk, confined with the other impressed men while they awaited transport to the *Illustrious*, he'd experienced the awful sense of being powerless and absolutely alone in world. Miss Holton's situation was by no means as dire, but losing the support of those nearest to you and being forced into a position you did not want was something he understood only too well. If her behaviour sometimes bordered on the churlish, perhaps she had cause.

Leaving Billy with the horses by the remains of the old curtain wall, Miss Holton led him inside. 'This was the bailey,' she said, indicating a large, oval open space. 'You can see the remnants of what were stables and storehouses, and over there, the keep.' She gestured towards the square stone tower at the cliffside end of the expanse. 'Being as useful as a lookout point during the centuries as it was at its construction, it has remained in remarkably good repair. Shall we look within?'

Nodding, he followed her across the open space towards the arched entryway. 'Duke William gave the first Lord de Bronnaut all the land along the coast, with orders to build a fortification and hold it against attacks by wild Cornishmen or resurgent groups of Angles and Saxons,' she said, pacing through the doorway. 'Supplies were kept below, so the defenders could hold out for quite some time, even if the bailey wall was—'

She stopped abruptly, frowning. Looking over her shoulder, Greville saw the remnants of a stamped-out fire on the stone floor.

'The tower has never been secured, but Uncle James wouldn't like someone trespassing,' Miss Holton said. 'Do you think a poacher was here?'

'Probably not—the heights are barren, with no cover to entice game. Probably some farm lads or shepherds took refuge from a storm.' Greville didn't believe that, but he had no intention of voicing to Miss Holton the suspicion that had sprung immediately to mind as soon as he saw the remains of the fire.

Neville Tour, with its unimpeded view down the coast and convenient storage areas below, would make as perfect a spot for signalling a vessel to land its cargo as it was a secure, dry place to stash it.

Indeed, something about the whole area, from the bailey into the tower, set the hair on the back of his neck prickling. Might someone be watching them?

All his protective instincts at high alert, Greville said, 'I believe I'm a bit weary, Miss Holton. Shall we head back?'

'You don't wish to see the cellars?'

'Another time, perhaps.' If smugglers were making use of the place, he had no intention of descending to the storage areas and letting Miss Holton discover contraband—or be knocked over the head by a free-trader anxious to protect his cargo. Not when he had not even a knife on him with which to defend her.

The ploy worked; instantly solicitous, Miss Holton took his arm and walked with him back across the bailey. The itch between his shoulder blades didn't abate until they left the castle enclosure to meet the groom with their horses.

Billy helped Miss Holton mount and they set off. After their return, Greville thought as they trotted back towards Ashton Grove, he'd report his findings to Lord Bronning and suggest he send a party—a large, armed party—back to investigate.

The sunshine and mild breeze had made the ride back as delightful as the journey out. After they'd reached the stables and turned their horses back over to the staff, Greville walked Althea back to the manor.

'Thank you, Miss Holton. The ride was quite refreshing, and Neville Tour is a fascinating place.'

'Isn't it? When you've fully recovered, we must go there again. The view from the paths along the cliff edge is breathtaking. And please call me Althea. We are friends now, aren't we?'

'Friends,' he agreed. 'You can call me Greville—though probably not when your uncle or cousin can overhear.'

She sniffed. 'No, Amanda would chide me about the impropriety for sure.'

Though it was certainly no business of his to become involved, it did seem to him that the cousins were working at cross-purposes. 'Have you ever spoken with Miss Neville about what happened at the time of your mother's death? I suspect she may not be aware of how shut out and ignored you felt.'

Althea shrugged. 'She'd just fob me off with some excuse, or give me a lecture about not knowing my place.'

'She might. But she might also apologise and say it had never been her intention to slight you. Family is important—a truth I've only recently come to fully appreciate. One shouldn't remain estranged without making a push to heal the breach. Consider it, anyway.'

At least she didn't cut him off this time. After a moment, she nodded. 'Perhaps I will.'

Encouraged, Greville nodded back. And then had to bite his lips to keep from smiling as it suddenly hit him what an enormous transformation had taken place.

The old Greville's hosts would have taken care to keep him far away from any fourteen-year-old daughter of the house lest he attempt to debauch her. Somehow the new Greville had gone from dangerous rake to confidant and confessor.

He wasn't sure whether the change was a tribute to his evolving improvement or a great joke being perpetrated by the Almighty to whom he'd made that heartfelt promise to reform his character. But if any of his former companions in wenching and gaming could see him now, they'd laugh themselves silly.

They had just reached the steps leading to the entryway when, in a reverse of the previous afternoon, Miss Neville walked out and stopped short. Irritation registered in her eyes as she took in Althea in her habit, both of them carrying whip and gloves.

'I didn't know you were riding out,' Miss Neville said.

'Why shouldn't I?' Althea shot back, immediately defensive.

'I don't mean to criticise,' Miss Neville replied, 'but I didn't know where you were. It took me some time to piece together that you'd set off on horseback—with Mr Anders as your escort.' She sent him an accusing look over Miss Holton's averted face.

'Why should he not accompany me? You don't need Mr

Anders to flirt with now, not since that *ever*-so-elegant Lord Trowbridge has arrived. Why don't you practise for your début by charming him? Though he seems impressed enough with his own company, he probably doesn't need anyone else's flattery.'

Miss Neville's face flushed, as if she were controlling her reply with an effort. Finally she said, 'It's hardly fair to disparage a gentleman we hardly know after one short meeting.'

Althea tossed her head. 'I know from listening to him once that *I'm* not interested in his company. Or is that what annoys you—that Mr Anders enjoys my company, when you clearly do not?'

Not wishing to be in the middle of the storm that looked to be breaking between the two and hoping somewhat guiltily that it hadn't been his speaking about her cousin that had set Althea on the defensive, Greville was trying to find a way to excuse himself when Miss Neville responded, 'That's not true! I'm sure Mr Anders appreciates your energy and enthusiasm, as we used to appreciate each other, once upon a time. But our guest isn't yet fully recovered. You shouldn't tease him to go on excursions that will tire him—as, forgive me for saying so, Mr Anders—he appears to be now.'

'Who else is there to accompany me?' Althea retorted hotly. 'If I mix with the servants, you criticise my speech and conduct. All I have is Uncle James, and he scarcely listens to me, only stares off into the distance. I know you don't want me here, but it's not fair that you try to keep me from making any friends!'

Her flush deepening, Miss Neville said, 'That's not what I'm trying—' Halting in mid-sentence, she took a deep breath and made a valiant attempt at a smile. 'I hardly think Mr Anders wishes to hear us brangle. Could we not cry pax? I don't mean to tease you. I know I probably say the wrong thing sometimes, but I'm only trying to guide you as Aunt Felicia would have done.'

'Well, you're not my mama. And if you truly want to get on better, leave me alone.' With that parting shot, Althea flounced up the stairs and stomped through the door.

For a moment, Miss Neville stared after her. Turning to Greville, her cheeks scarlet with mortification, she said, 'I am so sorry you had to witness that.'

'I have noticed a certain...tension between you.'

She gave a shaky laugh. 'Indeed. She's still very young... and for some reason I can't puzzle out, resents me very deeply.' An expression of sorrow washed over her face, mingled with hurt.

His strong inclination was to make some light remark and put the uncomfortable interlude behind them. But as it had before, her sadness pierced his heart.

After struggling a moment, failing to convince himself to let the matter drop, he said, 'I spoke with Miss Althea at some length during our ride—for which, by the way, I did manage to take along a groom, so you may be easy about the matter of a chaperon.'

'Thank you for looking out for her, Mr Anders.' She gave a rueful chuckle. 'I certainly could never have persuaded her to employ such a precaution.'

'It's not my place to intervene, but Miss Althea did share some reflections with me that I think you might wish to know.'

The concern on Miss Neville's face sharpened. 'Please, do continue.'

'Oh, nothing that would threaten her safety or reputation,' he added hastily. 'Rather, they shed light on her attitude towards you.' Briefly he related how Althea had described what transpired during the time of her mother's illness and death.

At his revelations, Miss Neville looked appalled. 'But we never intended…how could she have thought that?'

He shrugged. 'Why do people perceive what they do? When one is labouring under extreme emotion, I imagine it's easier to misconstrue. You might want to talk with her about it, although I'd appreciate your not mentioning why you came to do so. She did not expressly forbid me to repeat her remarks, but I'm sure she would feel betrayed if she learned I'd spoken to you about them.'

She nodded. 'I'll consider how I might broach the matter. I would like to end the antagonism between us. Not that I think she ever could—or should—be again the little girl who trailed after me adoringly, but this past year has reduced what was already a small family. We've always been close, and I miss that.'

She reached over to press his hand, sending little eddies of delight up his arm. 'How can I thank you enough? You've been a true friend—to both of us.'

'My pleasure, Miss Neville. I wish you luck in your chat with her.'

She nodded and he followed her in, the imprint of her touch still tingling. There was a pleasant warmth deep in his chest as well.

He was glad now that he'd ignored his natural disinclination to discuss emotional matters and related what her cousin had revealed. Over this last year, he'd come to fully appreciate how important it was to have a caring family; but for his sister, he might at this moment still be languishing on board the *Illustrious*, or stranded penniless in some foreign port, left to heal under the care of indifferent strangers.

Had Miss Neville so overcome her prejudice about his status that she now truly considered him a 'friend'? That attitude would be a decided improvement over her initial disdain.

Having a *friendship* with a woman would be a new experience for him. However much his randy body might prefer something more physical, since that wasn't a possibility anyway, he decided he rather liked the feeling. There still wasn't any future in the connection, of course, but perhaps while they both remained under one roof, he could cautiously explore the waters of this uncharted territory.

Chapter Ten

Two nights later, Amanda returned to her chamber from the kitchen after ensuring all was in train for the impromptu dinner she'd arranged for her neighbours and their guest Lord Trowbridge. As she pulled the bell to summon her maid, she thought again about Althea, who'd been scrupulously polite since her outburst. Though she'd also avoided all of Amanda's gentle attempts to engage her in conversation, at least she seemed to have abandoned her efforts to sneak off with Mr Anders, either riding alone now or accepting the escort of a groom if he accompanied her.

One worry set to rest, it seemed. As for the other…she'd observed George arriving home two of the last three early mornings, looking sober and dressed in plain, dusty clothing. Moving with a furtive air, he too had avoided speaking with her.

Now virtually certain he must be somehow involved with the smugglers, she'd debated speaking with Papa. But he'd looked even more grey-faced and weary of late; she hated to add to his worries by voicing her suspicions.

What she needed was for Mr Anders to express a desire to drive back into town, so she might ask him to enquire further about the matter with his contacts in the naval service.

Struggling to loosen the ties of her afternoon gown, Amanda wondered where in heaven her maid had got to. She was about to ring again when Betsy came running in, red-cheeked.

'So sorry, miss,' she panted, going at once to the gown ties.

'You've been out in the cold?' Amanda guessed. 'It's a chill day for a walk.'

To her surprise, the maid burst into tears. All Amanda could glean from her tangled speech was 'sorry' and 'shouldn't have gone' and 'so worried'.

'There, there, now,' she said, trying to soothe the distraught girl. 'What happened to so distress you?'

'Oh, miss, it's such a tangle. My da, like most folks hereabouts—' that said with defensive look '—he's helped the Gentlemen upon occasion, and been happy for the coins and sometimes the jug of brandy that come with it. Never had no problem when Rob Roy was running things, but this last six months, a new man's come in. Da heard he wouldn't book no opposition, but as men like to talk, he never paid much mind. Then this morning, Jenkins come up to tell me my brother Billy, what's a groom down at the stables, weren't back after a…visit home last night. I'm sorry, Miss Amanda, I know it weren't my half-day off, but I just had to go and check on him.'

Dread a growing knot in her belly, Amanda replied, 'Of course you did! What did you discover?'

The girl shook her head, tears dripping down her cheeks. 'Billy were home, all right—but he'd been beat within an inch of his life. He told Pa Black John got him, said Billy would help him—or nobody—and that if he caught him running goods for Rob Roy again, Billy wouldn't live to tell the tale. Now Pa's talking about calling up other farmers in the valley and some of the townspeople, saying it's time to stop Black John once and for all.'

She twisted her hands. 'But, miss, how can they? Black John's men got rifles and pistols, good ones. Pa and his friends will likely get themselves killed, and then who will take care of Ma and the little ones? They can't go to the preventatives for help, not when they've all of them been involved in free-trading. I left Ma weeping and Pa cleaning his old army musket and Billy abed, still half out of his senses.'

Heavens, it appeared matters were even worse than Amanda had feared! 'Yes, something must be done,' she said sooth-ingly. 'But surely your father knows a confrontation will lead to certain bloodshed.'

'Already been bloodshed, Da says. Billy and some others been beaten, and Farmer Johnson was shot dead, not long ago.'

'Someone needs to persuade them to avoid a pitched battle they would surely lose. Perhaps my father—'

'Oh, please, don't tell Lord Bronning, miss! He's such an honourable gentleman, he'd probably feel he had to call out the riding officers. Billy and Da and all the rest could be arrested for moving smuggled goods, or transported, or worse!'

'You know my father would never involve the authorities in a way that would bring harm to people he's known all his life,' Amanda objected.

'He might not want to, but it could turn out that way. Please, mistress, promise you won't tell your papa.'

'Very well, I won't…yet, anyway, while I try to think of something else.' Damping down the fear curdling in her stom-ach, she tried to ask casually, 'Is Master George involved?'

Betsy's eyes widened. 'Oh, miss, I hope not! It's best not to ask questions nor look too close, Pa always told me. I don't know for sure, nor do I want to.'

The maid took a shuddering breath. 'Thank you for listening, ma'am. I'm feeling better now. Da's a smart man; he'll not be off doing something foolish. Let me get you into your dinner gown; the gong will be sounding any minute.'

Betsy might feel better, but Amanda did not. While she let the maid help her into her gown and arrange her coiffure, her mind raced furiously.

Some sort of altercation was obviously brewing between the rival smuggling groups, and she was almost certain George was involved with one or the other. How would Papa react if his son and heir were taken up by riding officers? If the confrontation turned violent, George could even be injured. Or shot dead, like Farmer Johnson.

Amanda could throttle him for worrying her so! She felt the strongest urge to proceed directly to George's room and demand he tell her everything.

Gratifying as that might be, George was unlikely to admit he was involved, even if he was. Like Althea, he would probably resent what he would see as her unwarranted interference in his private affairs.

Perhaps she was doing him a great disservice. He might be entirely innocent, but his clandestine behaviour and her instincts said he was not.

The anxiety in her gut spiralled tighter. If only they were not hosting this blasted dinner tonight! She debated going immediately to consult Papa. Though she hated to alarm him, wouldn't he feel he had a right to know if she suspected George was caught up in some dangerous enterprise?

No, she decided, best not to talk with him yet. Rather than alarm him making what might be baseless accusations against George, she must discover more about the struggle between the rival bands and her brother's possible connection to it.

'There, miss,' Betsy said with satisfaction as she settled a shawl of spangled gauze about Amanda's shoulders. 'You look like a fairy princess. I hear there be a prince dining with you tonight, too,' she added with a wink.

Amanda stifled a groan. Trust the unfailing accuracy of servants' gossip to have ferreted out that an eligible young man had been invited to Ashton Grove.

Never had she felt less like entertaining. Girding herself for the task, she dismissed Betsy and walked towards the parlour.

In spite of the guests, some time tonight she'd find a way to exchange a few private words with Mr Anders, implore him to go into Salters Bay tomorrow and consult his Navy contacts.

The idea of confiding in Mr Anders brought a surprising measure of calm. He'd already shown himself to be intelligent, perceptive and discreet in his dealings with Althea. Her initial impression of him as a man of subtly leashed power, someone who could—indeed, had—held his own in a fight, had only strengthened as she'd come to know him better. She felt instinctively she could count on him to assist her.

Despite the worry gnawing at her, the idea of stealing a few moments alone with him sent the now-familiar flare of excitement through her. Though she told herself she intended only a brief chat, still her mind embraced the image of other things a man and a maid might do in a midnight-dark chamber. Kissing. Caressing.

Impatiently she shook her wayward thoughts free. She needed to concentrate on extricating George from potential disaster and finding a way to prevent what might be a dangerous, destructive confrontation.

As she paused on the threshold of the parlour and pasted a polite smile on her face, she couldn't help a sigh. Just when she thought she might begin concentrating on her preparations for London, everything at Ashton had grown much more complicated.

* * *

After putting his bit about Althea into Miss Neville's ear, Greville had tried to avoid them both these last two days: Althea, so he didn't become a further bone of contention between the two cousins; Miss Neville because he was so powerfully drawn to seek her out. He wasn't sure this hazy new concept of maintaining a friendship would triumph over the old, well-worn habits of seduction, and temptation was much easier to resist if he remained out of her enticing presence.

He lingered in his chamber, wishing he could avoid the dinner tonight as well. He had no desire to be present to observe Trowbridge practically salivating over Miss Neville while he paraded his perfectly bred, perfectly connected, perfectly handsome body before her.

He would have asked for a tray in his room, except that Althea had tracked him down in the library to tell him, in tones of dismay, that her uncle had said she would be included in the dinner tonight, as a special favour. Uncle James seemed to be so delighted at offering her the treat, she hadn't had the heart to refuse him. She begged Greville to make sure he was seated near her so she'd have someone with whom to converse, since the Handsome Lord and her neighbour and his wife would surely concentrate all their attention on her uncle and her cousin.

His host and hostess would be distressed as well, should he fail to appear. Besides, he knew he couldn't pass up a chance to admire Miss Neville in a dinner gown.

He could hardly blame Trowbridge for salivating. Her delectable form embraced by a thin veiling of silk, a tiny puff of sleeve displaying her slender arms and graceful shoulders, while a sliver of bodice offered the arousing sight of her breasts emerging from a deep décolletage…. Ah, he was ready to salivate himself.

Still, he considered it a torture not much easier to endure

than five lashes from the ship's cat to remain in her presence when he would be forced to watch the blandishments sure to be cast in her direction by Trowbridge.

Who was, Althea had said, 'just the sort of man' Amanda was looking for, he recalled with gritted teeth.

Well, tortured or not, he had to attend, so he might as well get himself to the parlour before he compounded his social failings by being late.

When he arrived in the salon a few minutes later, Lord Trowbridge and the Williamses had already come in. The young nobleman looked every bit as polished as Greville had expected: his masterfully cut black evening coat and cravat tied in a perfect Waterfall would have excited Greville's admiration back in the days when such fripperies consumed his attention. Greville forced himself to keep straight fingers that wanted to curl themselves into fists.

Greville would bet the hands encased in his lordship's gloves, unlike his own tanned, callused, hardened ones, were white and soft. The man might be the high-born son of an earl, but Greville knew if he were about to storm the deck of an enemy ship, he'd rather have the low-born Gunny Porter or Old Tom or seaman's son Captain Harrington at his side.

The before-dinner chat was mercifully brief. Miss Neville led in their highest-ranking guest, while Lord Bronning escorted Mrs Williams, a garrulous woman who spared him scarcely a glance. Althea went in on his arm, murmuring a 'thank you'.

Galling as it was to watch Trowbridge monopolise Miss Neville, during most of the meal he was left out of the conversation, which suited him quite well. Mr Williams engaged their host; Mrs Williams, after enquiring if Althea was yet out and being informed that she wasn't, but had been included by her uncle, as he considered this nearly a family party, said 'oh' in a disapproving tone and then ignored her. Greville supposed she must have already learned through the infallible local grapevine that he was not a person of importance, for she had paid him no heed either.

The only break in the tedium was the mischievous Althea, who rolled her eyes and mimicked their neighbours when they were not watching. Greville almost spat out his soup when she put her napkin to her lips in an exaggerated fashion that parodied Lord Trowbridge.

He was chuckling at another of her antics when, to his surprise, Trowbridge addressed him. 'Mr...Anders, is it not? I understand you are related to the Stanhopes.'

'Yes, the current marquess is my cousin.'

'And you've lately served in Navy?'

'I had that honour,' Greville replied warily. Trowbridge's expression was guileless; perhaps he simply wished to include the Nevilles' guest in the general conversation.

Still, something about him—the tone of his voice, the odd speculative light in his eye—warned Greville of an impending ambush as surely as if the foretop lookout had called out the sighting of an enemy sail.

If Trowbridge had an interest in Miss Neville, he might see Greville as a potential rival. And if he were seeking ways to diminish that rival, given the attitudes certain to be shared by most of the company, exposing Greville's recent occupation would be a simple means to do so.

'Should I address you as "Lieutenant"?'

'No,' Greville replied, his suspicions hardening. Though he was not ashamed of his service—rather the contrary—neither did he mean to let Trowbridge use that information as a weapon to try to embarrass him, distressing his kindly host in the bargain. 'I'm currently on furlough.'

'Mr Anders was injured in a skirmish with pirates,' Lord

Bronning inserted, already looking uneasy. 'As I understand is customary, he's been temporarily assigned to the Coastal Brigade while he recovers. When Lord Englemere learned that Ashton Grove is situated not far from the station at Salters Bay, the marquess asked if his cousin might reside with us during his time there. It's been our pleasure to have him as our guest,' he added, with a nod to Greville.

'Ah, that's why you are not wearing a uniform,' Trowbridge said. 'You look fit enough now.'

'Fit enough to halt stampeding horses two days ago,' Miss Neville inserted, giving him a smile.

Warmed by her compliment, he said, 'I am much recovered.'

'Will you be resuming your naval duties shortly?' Trowbridge persisted.

His suspicions of Trowbridge's intent revived, he said shortly, 'Once I am *fully* recovered.'

'Indeed. I heard the most shocking rumour in town yesterday,' Trowbridge said, his tone studiedly casual. 'That Mr Anders had served aboard ship as a *common seaman*! Of course, I informed the man that he must be mistaken. Stanhope's cousin, a mere member of the ship's company?' Trowbridge laughed. 'I cannot imagine how such a story got out.'

Was Trowbridge truly ignorant, assuming from his lineage that the informant must be mistaken? Somehow Greville didn't think so. Best to meet attack with immediate counter-attack.

Greville fixed Trowbridge with a stern look. 'Surely you know that, without the selfless service of those *common seamen*, who suffered years of deprivation whilst manning the blockade, Bonaparte might have succeeded in invading England? But with your esteemed father such a knowledgeable member of the Lords, as his *assistant*, of course you understand that truth.'

As swiftly as a chain following its anchor into the deep,

Althea took up the cause. 'Forgive me for disputing with a guest, Uncle James,' she cried, 'but I find it shocking of Lord Trowbridge to disparage our loyal seaman. Oh, the stories Mr Anders has related of their bravery and endurance under the harshest of circumstances!'

Trowbridge couldn't have looked more surprised if the table leg had leaned over and bit him. With a glance at Lord Bronning that said girls not yet out would be better confined to the schoolroom, he replied, 'I didn't mean to diminish our seamen's efforts, Miss Holton. The fact that, though most are very rough individuals, they none the less perform well in battle just demonstrates that even the most unpromising of material can be moulded into an effective fighting force, led by superior officers.'

Spoken like a seasoned naval veteran, Greville thought with disgust. It sounded like Trowbridge had been gossiping with Lieutenant Belcher. 'Have you much personal acquaintance with seamen, my lord?' he asked drily.

Trowbridge looked uncomfortable. 'Well, no, but everyone knows—'

'I thought not. Forgive me, but I fear you have been gravely misinformed. It's true that many sailors are illiterate and come from humble backgrounds, and certainly the Navy has its share of rogues and reprobates, like every rank of society.' *Including yours, you privileged, self-satisfied, pampered bastard.* 'But in the main, the hard life roots out the undesirables, leaving only those with the skill and grit to survive long months at sea on short rations, performing difficult jobs under nearly impossible conditions. As Miss Holton mentioned, after my short time among them, I came away having personally witnessed more than a dozen instances of most *uncommon* bravery and self-sacrifice.'

'I didn't mean to imply that most are not valiant men,' Trowbridge protested, retreating rapidly.

'I'm sure you did not,' Greville said. 'But all this naval talk cannot be of much interest to the ladies. Mrs Williams, I believe you were about to describe the clever comedy you lately attended in Exeter?'

Nothing more was required to launch that lady off into a long recitation of the play, the theatre and all the notables in attendance. Satisfied, Greville sat back, while a disgruntled Trowbridge pasted a smile on his face and gave the appearance of listening with great interest to Mrs Williams. And for the first time since dinner began, Greville noted with delight, the earl's son did not try to engage the attention of Miss Neville.

She gave Greville a speculative look. He bit back a grin. Trust that clever lady to have noticed that his impassioned speech masked the fact that he'd never directly answered Trowbridge's question about his naval service. However, though he might owe the host and hostess who had opened their home to him some explanation of how and why he came to be at Ashton Grove, he certainly didn't owe one to Trowbridge.

His high-and-mighty *lordship*, Greville felt sure, would think twice before trying again to ambush plain *Mr Anders*.

Althea's muffled giggle interrupted his thoughts. When he turned towards her, one eyebrow raised quizzically, she mouthed a 'well done', then swirled her hand in a circular motion before dropping it into her lap.

In recognition of his sinking of the conversational fireship Trowbridge had launched to destroy him? Amused, he grinned back.

Not until after Mrs Williams finally finished her lengthy account did the earl's unusually subdued son once again address a remark to Miss Neville.

After returning him a brief reply, she rose and said, 'I believe it's time for the ladies to leave you gentlemen to your spirits. Mrs Williams, Althea, if you would accompany me?'

The men stood politely as the females left, Greville watching Miss Neville disappear with a mingled sense of triumph and sadness. She'd refrained from comment during his short skirmish with Trowbridge. Had his verbal vanquishing of her guest, whom she had to consider a prime potential suitor, angered her?

The possibility ought to remind him how fragile and temporary their 'friendship' was likely to be. Though in the battle of public opinion Althea was firmly among his crew, Miss Neville would almost certainly sail with Trowbridge in lamenting the low nature of his naval service. His cordial association with her was based merely on politeness and proximity, a connection that would never survive the parting when she left for London and he went on to pursue a new career.

The sense of loss that settled in his chest at acknowledging that fact was dismayingly sharper than it should have been.

Since Trowbridge now carefully refrained from even glancing in his direction, Greville was left in peace to sip his brandy. He considered making his excuses and departing at once—but then he'd not be able to see Miss Neville at tea and assess the damage.

His logical mind tried to convince the rest of him that forfeiting her friendship, however painful now, would prove wiser in the end, since ending it was inevitable anyway. The rest of him simply didn't want to listen. Every illogical impulse impelled him to see her, mollify her and worm his way back into her favour, if he had indeed forfeited it by engaging Trowbridge.

Why this imperative to return to her good graces? Watching the brandy as he swirled it in the glass, he admitted that, for the short time she remained at Ashton Grove, he just didn't want to deny himself the pleasure of her company, even though being with her was neither safe nor wise.

Not when desire suffused him whenever he gazed at her, emptying his mind of everything but the almost tangible need to taste and touch her. Even more dangerous was the hold she was coming to have over his thoughts and emotions.

The day was simply brighter when he walked with her. Like it or not, the music of her laughter lightened his heart. He felt an absurd sense of satisfaction when he managed a remark that pulled her from preoccupation with the many burdens she carried and provoked her into a laugh or a smile. A wave of exuberant delight washed through him each time he teased her into an exchange of wit, energising as the flash of cutlass blades.

He didn't want to give that up. Surely the earth wouldn't shift off its axis if he indulged himself in her company for the short time she had left at Ashton Grove.

Enough arguing, he thought. He didn't mean to probe any further into the significance of his reluctance to abstain from her company. For a while at least, he'd be the 'old Greville', enjoying the moment without a worry for the future.

Perhaps because, without her presence in it, that future was beginning to seem a bit bleak.

Waiting for the bustle around the tea table to subside, Greville contented himself with simply observing Miss Neville— her lovely profile, the effortless grace with which she poured tea while maintaining a flow of conversation with her guests. When at last the crowd thinned and he approached, ready to man the scuppers and salvage the leaky vessel of their relationship, to his surprise, she leaned close. 'Could I have a word with you later?' she whispered. 'It's very important.'

'Of course,' he murmured back. 'When and where?'

'In the library. After our guests leave, and Papa and Althea go up to bed.'

He nodded. 'I'll meet you there.'

'Thank you,' she whispered, then turned away. 'More tea, Mrs Williams?'

Could he really have just made an assignation with his host's daughter? Greville wondered, still not sure he'd heard her properly. After running her words through his mind again and finding no other possible meaning, a thrill of anticipation sent his spirits soaring.

She might be seeking a private audience to dress him down for embarrassing a guest…but he didn't think so. Could that invitation imply what he hoped it did? Though logic said there couldn't possibly be an illicit meaning beneath the words, deep within, a fierce sensual expectation uncoiled.

He should put a halt to any wild imaginings before they began. This was no time to indulge in lustful hopes. Amanda looked troubled, not seductive. Almost certainly she needed his help, not his kisses.

Even though, try to restrain it as he might, kisses were all he could think of.

Tea dragged on what seemed an interminable time. He had to endure watching Trowbridge with his gaze fastened on Miss Neville like a starving beggar anticipating a feast. Listen to him making her pretty compliments, promising to have his mama call on her as soon as she arrived in town, to all of which she replied with courtesy but not, he thought, anything warmer.

Greville knew he shouldn't resent the man so much—but with his wealth, title, status and good looks, Trowbridge was just too perfectly placed to carry off the prize Greville was coming to admire much too much for his own good.

Finally the party broke up, Trowbridge and the Williamses setting off in their carriage. At an arched eyebrow and a nod from Miss Neville, Greville left the drawing room and headed for the library.

Chapter Eleven

Greville's accelerating heartbeat already thudding in his chest, he entered the darkened room, wondering what was so urgent Miss Neville felt compelled to sneak out and discuss it this very night. He tried, he really did try, not to think wicked thoughts… but he just couldn't help it.

Images of fevered kisses and stolen caresses seemed to shimmer in the dimly lit air around him. Desire rose in a fierce wave, swamping him.

Not at all sure he could control it, he was halfway to the point of leaving when the door opened softly and, bearing a single candle, Miss Neville crept in.

She jumped when his figure materialised out of gloom. 'Whisper the secret code,' he joked, trying to set her at ease and rein in the desire that pounded in his ears and pulsed through his body with every rapid heartbeat.

He yearned to draw closer, but he couldn't risk that now, not with the strong sensual connection sizzling between them. Not when the shadows and the teasing scent of her perfume and her lovely face, gazing up at him, would make leaning down to claim her lips so very easy.

He took a step back from temptation, his hands shaking with the effort to resist touching her. Forcing himself to focus on the reason for this meeting, he said, 'What has transpired that is so dire you must sneak about in the dark to discuss it?'

Without preamble, she related the troubling news her maid had confided. 'I fear some altercation is imminent, for George did not appear tonight, though he knew we had guests and that Papa would surely be distressed by his absence. Even my brother is generally not that heedless. Could you ride to the Coastal Brigade station tomorrow and see what you can discover? I know I should confide in Papa, but…he's been looking so ill these last few days. I hope my fears are only wild imaginings, and don't wish to add to his anxiety without good cause.'

He wished he could reassure her—or, better still, kiss the worried frown from her brow, but the circumstances she'd just described were so troubling and potentially dangerous, they managed to check even his passion, at least for the moment.

'I will ride into Salters Bay first thing tomorrow.'

She exhaled a sigh. 'Thank you! I'm sorry to involve you in troubles that do not concern you, but I had no one else to confide in. And I knew I could count on you.'

His rational mind tried to rein in the ecstatic leap of his heart at that avowal. She counted on her maid to dress her and her cook to prepare a good meal. He was making a great deal too much of out of nothing.

Or was he?

Overriding that speculation was the imperative, now that she was here, to make the most of this rare opportunity. With every atom within him, he ached to kiss her, but since that was nearly certain to send her scurrying to the safety of her room, he'd settle for luring her to remain here so he might savour her presence.

Ease off, he cautioned himself. A direct reference to the incident at dinner should cool his ardour and remind them both of his place. 'I thought you might want to berate me. If so, prime your weapon.'

He succeeded in part of his mission; the frown smoothed from her brow and she gave him a reproving look. 'You were rather hard on poor Lord Trowbridge.'

'Poor' Lord Trowbridge. Now that was a hopeful sign. Ladies generally did not favour men they referred to as 'poor'. Though the eventual possession of a powerful title must have a wonderfully strengthening effect, even on a weakling.

'Surely you see he deliberately provoked my response.'

'Yes, his attempt to ferret out information was surprisingly ill bred.'

The words trembled on his tongue to ask if she realised Trowbridge's purpose had been to injure someone he saw as a possible rival. Before he could decide whether such a question was wise, she said, 'May *I* ask a terribly ill-bred question?'

A sinking sensation spiralled in his belly. Though he feared he knew where this was headed, he replied, 'Of course.'

'How did you come to join the Navy?'

After the look she'd given him in the dining room, he wasn't surprised by her enquiry. He was her guest, imposing upon the hospitality of her family. She must be as curious as Trowbridge had been...and though revealing the arrogance and folly that had led him on to the deck of the *Illustrious* might well lower him in her estimation, she deserved the truth.

'It's rather a long story.'

'I should like to hear it, if you don't mind the telling,' she replied, motioning him to the sofa.

He followed, thinking ruefully that once his tale was done, he'd not have to worry about tempting her with kisses. She'd probably bolt from the room and take care to stay far away until she could put the distance from Ashton Grove to London between them.

'As I expect you know, my family is a junior branch of

the Stanhope tree, without land of our own. When I returned home from the army after Waterloo, I approached my cousin Lord Englemere, who offered me a position managing an estate near Nottingham. Knowing little about running a property, I intended to turn it down, but Sergeant Barksdale, my assistant in the Quartermaster's Corps who'd returned to England with me, persuaded me to accept. He'd grown up in the country, he said; hire him as my foreman and he would show me how to manage the estate.

'I trusted him, unwisely as it turned out. Instead of taking me in hand, he urged me to leave the details of running the estate to him…and I did.'

With a bitter curl of his lip, Greville recalled how completely Barksdale had gulled him. And he'd been perfectly content to be so gulled, he thought with brutal self-appraisal, as long as he could fancy himself 'lord of the manor' on his occasional rides around the property, his vanity stoked by his assistant's assurances that supervising the work of manual labourers and common clerks was beneath the dignity of a gentleman's son. It had been all too easy for Barksdale to lull him with wine and loose women into ignoring what was happening under his very nose on the estate given into his charge.

'It shames me to confess that even after my time in the army, I was still indolent, arrogant and far too sure of my own worth. Not until I'd been more than a year at Blenhem Hill did I discover how badly wrong things had gone. One of the farmers came to me demanding justice, claiming Barksdale was overcharging for rents, delivering less than promised of seed, tools and equipment, and refusing to make repairs, even the most essential. At his insistence, instead of a cursory ride about the estate, I made a more thorough inspection of the farms.'

Greville shook his head, the shock and dismay of what he'd uncovered that day still painful to recall. 'Even to one of my inexperience, conditions looked grim. I returned to the estate office and inspected the books, discovering entries that showed far less rent recorded than had actually been paid. That same day, a message arrived from my cousin. The former estate agent, now retired, had written him about the state of affairs at Blenhem Hill. Englemere's letter informed me I'd been relieved of my position.'

Greville felt the burn of humiliation that had scorched him that day, reading Englemere's dismissal. 'My cousin was right; I'd let him down; I'd failed the people who'd depended on me. However, though Barksdale's guilt in no way relieved *me* of responsibility for the situation, before I informed Lord Englemere of his crime, I wanted to give my confederate the chance to make retribution.'

Greville laughed bitterly. 'Even then, I didn't have his true measure. Once he saw I could be misled no longer, he begged for some time to consider how he might repay what he'd stolen. The last thing I remember before waking up with a pounding headache on some low back street in Portsmouth was turning away to pour him a glass of wine.'

'He attacked you?' Miss Neville asked with gasp.

'With the fireplace poker, I suspect. Since I have almost no memory of what would have been several days' journey, he must have drugged me as well, then turned me over to some disreputable associate. With the threat of prosecution hanging over him, I expect Barksdale paid his confederate well to make sure I was sent off to sea, hopefully never to return. Delivered to the press gang stripped of my clothing and everything else of value, I didn't much resemble a gentleman, and despite my seemingly drunken state, they judged me otherwise in good health. Anxious to return the ship as quickly as possible, they hauled me into a wagon and set off. By time I was fully conscious, I found myself aboard a prison hulk off Portsmouth, under guard and awaiting transport to the *Illustrious*.'

'Surely you protested this injustice!'

'Of course. But apparently pressed men often try to talk their way out of service, and I had nothing but the quality of my speech to support my claim of being a gentleman. The lieutenant in charge, doubtless not wishing to make another foray ashore to find someone to replace me, told me I could present my case to the captain once we were on board.'

'But by then, you were at sea and nothing could be done,' she surmised.

Greville grimaced, remembering those first wretched days. 'Since the first lieutenant was no more impressed with my protestations than the shore guard, I wasn't permitted to see the captain until long after the ship left British waters. So, yes, by then, nothing could be done.

'Although I came to believe my service aboard ship was divine intervention, sent to help me correct my life's course, there's no avoiding the truth that I was beaten, drugged and sold to a press gang.' He looked away, not wishing yet to see the condemnation and disgust that should by now have replaced any tentative approval he'd earned in her eyes. 'It probably *was* outrageous for Lord Englemere to prevail upon your father to offer me hospitality. I'm still amazed he didn't send me packing that first day.'

'It's you who have been outrageous, Mr Anders, right from the start,' she replied.

So much for their budding friendship. Ah, well, 'twas doomed anyway. He was about to agree and bow himself off when the tenor of her voice sank in.

Surely that couldn't have been…*amusement* he heard in her tone? Certain he must be mistaken, he whipped his gaze back to her face.

Rather than looking repulsed or offended, though, she merely seemed…thoughtful. 'Not that I do not recognise you made grave errors. But in the end, you recognised the wrongs that had been done and took steps to correct them.'

'True, but by then, many had already been forced into desperate need. And even then,' he said, still disgusted by his arrogant *naïveté*, 'Barksdale was able to take me unawares, like a drunken country boy rolled for his purse on his first trip to London.'

'How could an honest man predict the depths of evil to which a villain would descend?' she countered. 'Certainly you conducted yourself well aboard *Illustrious*.'

Greville nodded. 'Once I accepted that there was no escaping my fate, I believe I did, at such limited tasks as a landsman can perform.'

He laughed ruefully. 'The unexpected sojourn at sea gave me plenty of opportunity to reflect upon my life, to promise myself and the Almighty that I would do better, if granted a future. And while confined aboard, I had much time to observe sailors, from deckhands to senior officers. Most of the men, though rough and unlearned, were honest and hard-working, the sort one would want at one's back in a fight and be proud to call friend.' With a touch of defiance that reminded him of Althea, he concluded, 'I admired them.'

She nodded. 'As I admire the farmers here. Many have so little, yet they make much out of it. It's…humbling.'

Greville sucked in a breath, feeling as if the ground had been cut away from beneath his feet. There could be no mistaking her words: she actually…*understood*.

Awe and amazement filled him that a girl of her beauty, class and privilege seemed to share his unconventional views. He'd been right when he'd seen her that first moment in the hallway: she *was* an angel.

It took a moment for his scattered wits to summon a reply. 'It is humbling indeed,' he agreed, adding wryly, 'and over the last nine months, humility is a subject in which I've received a thorough grounding. Not without good cause. Save the service I rendered aboard ship, I've done little else of worth in my life.'

'A little more humility would benefit us all. But I should not too much disparage a gentleman who endured what many of his class would not have survived and emerged from the ordeal a better and wiser man.'

Once again, she'd surprised him, pronouncing a judgement far kinder than the one he'd levied upon himself. 'A most charitable assessment, Miss Neville, that I fear I do not deserve. I'm not nearly as good a man as I'd like to be.'

Because when she looked at him like that, with sympathy and understanding and, yes, *respect*, all he wanted to do was tip up that lovely face and kiss her. Pull her into his arms, absorb the warmth of her beauty and goodness deep within him. Hold her so tightly, her lush curves moulded into the hardness of his body while he went on kissing her, mindless and senseless with wonder and need, until she was as gasping and as needy as he.

Then lead her to his room, gentle her with caresses and more drugging kisses until she urged him to ease her out of her garments. Savour her sweet eager innocence as he taught her how to use her mouth and breasts and body to give and receive joy, to experience the fulfilment only the union of a man and a woman could bring.

His mind was so carried away with sensual imagining, he was shocked to discover, moments later, that her face was indeed closer, her lips only a breath away from his. Had he moved towards her, or had she leaned up of her own accord?

Whatever brought her mouth so near, he bent that last small distance, compelled to brush his lips against the ones she seemed to be offering.

Just a taste, his body urged. Just a taste, it promised.

And then he was kissing her, light and long and slow—had

he ever kissed a virgin? He didn't think so—long and light and slow while his body hummed and buzzed and pulsed and sparked.

Stilling the hands that burned to explore her, he went on kissing her, letting her decide when to pull away. When, finally, she did so, the effort required to force himself to let her go made his whole body shake.

'I'd…better leave,' she said, trembling as well.

'You most certainly should,' he agreed when he could speak.

'You'll tell me what you learn tomorrow?'

'Yes. But better not to do so in a dark library at midnight. I am *trying* to become a better man, but flesh and blood can only resist so much.'

She gave him the wicked smile of a temptress. 'Good,' she said. And walked out.

Greville sat down abruptly, then sprang up, sitting in his tight breeches having become suddenly uncomfortable.

What was he to make of that interlude—and her parting remark? He shook his head, wishing he had more—any—experience with virtuous young maids.

She certainly hadn't seemed affronted. No, his body confirmed, she'd been an enthusiastic participant in the caresses they'd exchanged, melting compliantly against him, her little murmurs of pleasure urging him on.

Had it been a tease? A desire to experience a forbidden thrill?

A mistake?

Or something natural and inevitable for them both, a confirmation that she was drawn to him as powerfully as he was to her, despite everything that should keep them apart.

And would. He mustn't forget that. She was destined to become the wife of a wealthy, powerful peer. He would go into government service or land management, tending important affairs…but as secretary or agent for a man like the one she would marry, who could offer her more status and wealth than he would ever amass.

Impatiently he brushed that brutal fact from his mind. For now, he would embrace whatever joy life offered, an old Greville principle the new Greville intended to practise.

He'd start by fulfilling her request that he find out all he could at the coastal station. He hoped the information might relieve her anxiety, though he doubted it. In any event, he intended to search out one George Neville and have a pointed chat with him, and discover if Bronning's heir was dabbling in illegal activities that could get him killed, injured or transported.

Where could they safely meet for him to report back to her? If he couldn't keep his hands off her, they had no future even as friends.

Tenderness and awe flooded him again as he recalled the amazing fact that, rather than consider her tenants simply as menials who worked the estate, mere implements like farm tools and draught horses, she saw them as *people*, valuable and worthy of respect. It seemed he'd been teasing her from the first about a sense of superiority she did not possess.

But how was he to have guessed she shared his values, she who had enjoyed from birth every advantage meant to make a lady of her class feel superior and indifferent to those beneath her?

Though he should have seen it; indeed, he was sure, on some level, he had already realised the truth after watching her converse with field hands and shepherds, lace-weavers and farmer's wives. The genuine concern and mutual respect were evident in her interactions with these people who knew her well, whom she had no need to impress. How could he not have tender feelings for such a beautiful, accomplished, compassionate lady?

Now that was a dangerous conclusion, he thought, tossing out a mental sea anchor to bring this suddenly perilous line of reflections to a halt. Resolving to focus instead on what he needed to discover tomorrow in Salter's Bay, Greville headed for his chamber.

Chapter Twelve

By late morning of the next day, Amanda had to force herself to continue with her daily routine. Tense and distracted, she went about consulting the housekeeper and the estate agent, supervising maids, footmen and laundresses, though she was too anxious to give these domestic matters her full attention.

She'd not seen George since early yesterday; unable to prevent herself, she'd checked his bed and confirmed it had not been slept in. She'd not seen Mr Anders at breakfast, either, but Sands told her he'd already ridden into town. Oh, that he might discover what was going on and end this painful uncertainty, let her know just what sort of danger was afoot!

As she hurried down the hallway to meet Mrs Pepys in the kitchen, she passed the library door, and her feet stopped of their own accord. An unconscious smile curved her mouth as, in her mind's eye, she pictured Mr Anders within, his handsome profile and tempting lips outlined by candlelight.

A much more complex man than she'd thought upon first meeting, she reflected. He'd begun by teasing—and tempting—her, while he disconcerted her with his unexpected perception.

She'd come to rely on his logical, level-headed approach and his discretion. She thought she'd come to know him well—until last night, when he'd confessed to lapses in judgement and responsibility that should have shocked and disappointed her.

The way he'd gazed directly into her eyes as he revealed his disgraceful past said he *expected* her to be shocked and disappointed. That he expected his revelations would likely cause him to forfeit her good opinion.

He had acted badly. She probably should be more appalled and disapproving. But the very fact that he *did* confess, fully aware of what his honesty could cost him, swayed her in his favour. He had offered no excuses, nor did he try to equivocate about bearing full responsibility for his mistakes.

True, he had failed in his duty, but who among us has not? she thought, recalling her clumsy handling of George and her ignorance of Althea's despair during her mother's final days.

However slow to respond, Mr Anders had eventually recognised his lapses and tried to rectify them. When thrust into truly dire circumstances, he had responded with courage and fortitude. She could think of no reason he would own up to faults that he himself expected would diminish him in her eyes, unless he possessed a character worthy of her respect.

That he trusted her, and valued her enough to offer the truth, impressed and touched her.

His experiences were far different from those of any gentlemen she'd met or was likely to meet in London. Might that be why he fascinated her in a way the much more eligible Lord Trowbridge—whom he'd routed handily at dinner—did not? A unique and different man, moulded by living in a clash between two radically different worlds, one of privilege and one of poverty.

The fact that he was handsome and she was attracted to him probably also factored into her judgement of his worthiness, she admitted. The powerful physical force that had pulled her to him from the beginning was fully present last night, despite her anxiety. She probably shouldn't have ignored the little voice of caution warning, even as she whispered the invitation, that meeting him alone at midnight wasn't wise. All the while she told herself the situation with George and the free-traders was urgent enough that she would be able to ignore Mr Anders's annoyingly persistent magnetism, she'd known in her heart that wasn't true.

She had thought the initial pull to her intriguing guest would diminish, once she grew accustomed to the novelty of having a handsome, amusing young man about the house. Instead, the fascination seemed only to intensify the longer she knew him and the more she learned about him.

Pulsing just beneath her worry and concern last night had been a wicked thrill at the idea of meeting him alone, an insistent, insidious desire to test him and discover if her effect on him was as powerful as his effect on her. A hunger to taste his mouth she didn't have the will to resist, once opportunity, need and clandestine desire collided.

She'd been driven to discover if one taste would satisfy the urgent need to touch him. Though deep down, she'd known even before she let him—nay, nearly begged him—to kiss her, that the first taste would only make her want more and more and more. The moment his lips touched hers, a sensual haze enveloped her, blocking out every warning of risk and all notion of prudent behaviour.

Thank Heavens, he had the presence of mind *not* to go on kissing her, since it seemed she'd left sense and restraint at the library door. After he moved away from her, she'd quit the library with reluctance, drifting to her chamber still in state of heightened arousal that made her body tingle and her nipples spark as the material of her nightrail slid over her naked flesh.

She'd pictured not soft flannel, but his strong, tanned hands and his warm persuasive mouth moving over her skin.

When she at last drifted into sleep, her dreams were filled with confused images of kissing and touching and more. Sensations so strong she felt a surge of heat and a throbbing between her legs, a tingle in her breasts, recalling them now.

Good sense and restraint had not re-emerged until the cold light of morning. Which should warn her, that with her thoughts, senses and emotions all inclining her towards him, she'd better be as vigilant on her own behalf as she was trying to be on Althea's, lest she end up doing something stupid that would ruin careful plans that had been years in the making.

First and most important, she must resolve not to be alone with him again.

Ignoring the little voice within protesting that decision, Amanda resumed her walk towards the kitchen. Suddenly, Betsy appeared at the far end of the hall.

Stopping short when she spied her mistress, Betsy gave her an agitated wave, obviously entreating Amanda to wait as she rushed towards her. A stab of alarm scattering all other thoughts, Amanda hurried to meet her.

'What is it? What have you learned?'

'I slipped away to check on my brother—and found none of the menfolk home. Ma says they left at dawn. There'll be a cargo to land come nightfall, and she fears they plan to settle with Black John once and for good. Billy wouldn't tell me nothing, but the way he looked startled when I asked about Master George, I'm afraid he may be with them, though with Rob Roy or Black John, I don't know. But you might try to keep him here tonight, miss, for I'm guessing whatever happens will come about once the sun goes down.'

'Thank you, Betsy. I'll do my best to keep my brother at Ashton Grove tonight.'

'Aye, that would be safest. I just hope all turns out aright!' Wringing her hands, the maid hurried off.

Amanda stood motionless, anger, worry and fear roiling in her gut. Before she could keep George home, she'd have to find him. Surely he would return before the run, to rest and change clothes, if nothing else.

Except…a new worry intervened, dashing her relief. If this cargo were truly that important, George might *not* return, fearing his prolonged absence could cause Papa to raise uncomfortable questions that would make it difficult for him to get away again.

There seemed little doubt now that he was somehow involved in the smuggling. Oh, how could he be so rash and thoughtless as to get tangled up in something potentially disastrous?

Unable at the moment to dispel any of her pressing worries, Amanda forced herself to the kitchen, where she listened in distracted fashion to Mrs Pepys, then continued with her endless list of domestic duties.

But as the hours ticked by, she grew ever more restless and anxious. Though she made several detours through the breakfast and billiard rooms, the library, the gun room, his own chamber, she saw no sign of her brother, nor had Mr Anders yet returned from his trip to Salters Bay.

By mid-afternoon, she could stand the waiting no longer. She'd still have enough daylight to ride to town, enquire about her brother at the Sloop and Gull, and return before dark. Once—she refused to let herself think 'if'—she located him, she'd lure him back to Ashton on some pretext, then use cajolery or outright threats about Papa's delicate health to talk him or shame him out of participating in whatever mischief was brewing on the Saltern Hills.

Anxiety beating a pulse within her, hastily she changed into her riding habit and set out for the stables.

Chapter Thirteen

Both she and her frisky mare feeling better for a hard gallop, Amanda slowed Vixen to a walk as they mounted the rise where the road to the village curved past the track leading to the ruins of Neville Tour. A feeling uncomfortably like jealousy struck her at the thought that Althea had already taken Mr Anders to what had always been one of her favourite places, the still-impressive ramble of walls around the stone tower where her long-ago ancestor, the Conqueror's lieutenant, had kept watch over the sea and the river far below.

Reaching the heights, she pulled the mare to a halt, waiting for the trailing groom, who'd not been so intent on a gallop, to catch up. As she recalled picnics on the ruins shared with her cousin in summers past, when they giggled together as they spun tales about the valiant knights and ladies fair who had once inhabited this site, a melancholy pang went through her.

Could she break through Althea's resentment over the inadvertent slights of last summer and bring them back into harmony again?

Jenkins having almost reached the crest, she let Vixen proceed around the next bend, then down where the sharply descending road cut deep between the surrounding fields. Suddenly, a small party of men emerged through the thicket from the adjoining field into the roadway. Quickly she jerked Vixen to a halt.

Surprise turned to unease as she surveyed the men facing her. Their leader—tall, black-haired with flashing dark eyes, and dressed in sailor's attire—had two pistols tucked into his belt. Her alarm grew when she realised she recognised neither that man nor his handful of similarly garbed and armed compatriots—several of whom had neckerchiefs pulled up to conceal their faces.

They must be smugglers—few farmers could afford such expensive matched weapons and none would need to hide their identity. But what were they doing here, far above the beach where goods were normally landed, in full daylight?

'Well, what have we found?' the leader said, interrupting her racing thoughts. 'What a winsome prize to collect on a chill winter day!'

Wondering uneasily how far behind her Jenkins was, Amanda tried to instil her voice with a calm she didn't feel. 'Please let me pass, sir. My man and I have important business in town.'

The black-haired bandit made a show of looking from side to side. 'Man? Don't see no man. But I reckon a pretty lady like you be needing one, eh, boys?' he said, earning a laugh from his followers.

Trying to quell the fear rising queasily in her belly, she replied, 'My groom is riding just behind; he'll arrive at any minute.'

Grinning, the black-haired man leapt from the saddle and came over to seize Vixen's bridle. 'I can help you out right now. I've an itch I wouldn't mind scratching.'

One of his men gestured impatiently. 'Now, Black John? We got business to accomplish.'

'When I need advice, I'll ask, Kip,' the leader threw over his shoulder. Turning to her, a smile on his crudely handsome face, he said, 'This lady and I will do some business first.'

At that moment, the leader's name penetrated her fog of alarm and she had to swallow a gasp of horror. This must be the man her maid had spoken of, the one who'd been terrorising the local citizens and had beaten Betsy's brother senseless.

Her pulse hammering with fear, she was frantically considered what to do when a man in farmer's dress, his face also masked, walked over to the smuggling chief. 'There'll be willing dames at the inn later. Kip's right, we ought to check the goods and be gone.' Leaning closer, he said in an urgent undertone, 'She's Lord Bronning's daughter.

Her momentary flare of hope was dashed as the smuggler replied, 'Is she? Even better. I imagine old Lord B. would pay a few golden guineas to get his daughter back…only a little used.'

At that moment, Amanda finally heard the longed-for sound of hooves approaching. It must be Jenkins!

The leader heard it, too, angling his head to look behind her. Taking advantage of his momentary inattention, Amanda slashed her riding crop down on the hand holding her bridle and urged Vixen into motion.

Black John cursed, but rather than releasing his grip, in an unnerving display of strength, he held on. He yanked down sharply to halt the mare before she could move.

After inspecting the blood welling up in the welt on his hand, he looked back up at Amanda, something ugly glittering in his eyes. With a chilling smile, he said, 'Might have to give you more than a bit of use for that.' Then, as Jenkins appeared over the rise and trotted towards them, he said, 'Pull him down, men.'

Jenkins put up a strong resistance, but against so many, the result was a foregone conclusion. Pulled, struggling and fighting from the saddle, he ended up with his arms bound behind him, his cries of outrage silenced by a kerchief gag. With her last hope of help subdued, Amanda could only stare back in silence at the ruthless commander.

He gave her another of those emotionless smiles. 'Come along, little lady. Time to taste your sweetness and determine your worth.'

Meanwhile, down in the village of Salters Bay, Greville was hoisting a mug at the Knight and Dragon with gunner's mate Porter. He'd found the old sailor manning the Coastal Brigade office alone, the lieutenant having departed aboard one of the cutters the previous night.

There'd been a rumour of troubles ahead this day, Porter told him. Revenue officers had seen lights flashed from the cliffs across the Exe to Dawlish Warren, where the ferry boatman confirmed more than the usual number of patrons had gathered at the Mount Pleasant Inn, one of the most notorious of smugglers' taverns. Belcher had ordered all available cutters to sea to patrol the coast in anticipation of an attempt to land illicit cargo.

After inviting the old seaman to meet him at the inn, Greville paid a visit to the Sloop and Gull, looking for George Neville. He found that establishment mostly deserted; to his enquiries about any topic remotely related to smuggling, the taciturn proprietor returned replies either guarded or evasive.

On the one hand, he had to smile at the notion that the innkeeper clearly thought he was some sort of covert agent for the crown, intent on sniffing out free-traders. But on the other, the man's suspicious demeanour and reluctance to speak aroused every instinct warning of imminent danger—instincts well honed after months aboard a man-of-war.

After his unproductive meeting with the innkeeper, he'd made for the Knight and Dragon to join Porter for a brew and one of the cook's justly famed meat pasties.

'Aye, something's amiss,' the gunner confirmed, pulling him out of his thoughts. 'Hardly any patrons here, at a time when most labourers should be coming in from the fields. And where's the barmaid? Come to think on it, I've not seen the baker's wife, nor butcher's neither, when I bought my meat pie for supper. Seems strange, but not being from these parts, the shopkeepers don't tell me nothing.'

Greville smiled ruefully. 'I spoke with the innkeeper of the Sloop and Gull, but couldn't get any useful information either.'

Porter nodded. 'Some of the seamen tell me after the last landing, 'twas a dust-up between the men working for Rob Roy and Black John's crew. Old Jeb, master of the *Lively Lass*, says both villagers and farmers have had their fill of Black John, and that there'll be a full-out battle with him soon.'

Hardly had Porter spoken the words when they heard the noise of a musket discharging. As they jumped up, the innkeeper ran out of the kitchen, tossing down his apron. 'Must leave you fellows!' he cried as he passed them. 'It's begun!'

'What's begun?' Greville asked, the two men following as the proprietor raced to the bar and rummaged between the kegs.

'Black John said before the landing tonight, he'd be sending his men to town for horses and wagons to transport it,' the innkeeper told him, drawing an old pistol from its hiding place. 'Said them with hollow walls and storage buildings better be ready to receive his goods, or get a belly full of lead. After Farmer Johnson was shot for refusing to co-operate and Wilson's boy Billy was roughed up, the men hereabouts decided to send all the womenfolk away and fight Black John's men when they came before the raid.' Catching up a powder horn, flint and a leather pouch of balls, the innkeeper hurried out.

Porter looked at Greville. 'Won't be like boarding a ship at sea, but it there's a fight brewing, we'd best assist. Have ye any weapons?'

Greville thought of the fine matched pistols and Baker rifle he'd brought home after Waterloo, left at his London lodgings. 'Not with me.'

'Come along, then,' Porter urged. 'Got some stored at the station. Sounds like firing's coming from the churchyard. We'll pick them up the way.'

Porter loped ahead of him, surprisingly quick on his peg leg. Scrambling through a cabinet inside the door as they arrived, he tossed two pistols at Greville and helped himself to two others before leading him towards the churchyard, from which sounds of firing had intensified.

They found the farmers and townsmen sheltered behind the stone wall that encircled the graveyard, armed with an assortment of weapons ranging from muskets and pistols to shovels and scythes. The group of smugglers, approaching from the north, had taken cover behind the few trees that bordered the lane.

'Got them on the run,' the Sloop and Gull's owner shouted as they joined his position. 'If ye've weapons to fire, take aim. Some here are already out of balls and powder.'

'Best get some shots in before the fun's over,' Porter told him.

Fun? With a shudder at his memories of the boarding of the pirate vessel, Greville knelt to level his pistol on the rock edge and fired towards a smuggler in red headscarf. His opponent was forced to pull back his own weapon and duck out of range as Greville's shot went home. Quickly changing pistols, he followed up with a second shot, equally accurate.

As he turned to pick up the first pistol, it was thrust back at him, already loaded and primed. 'Got better aim than me, mate,' a man said. 'I'll keep the sparkers loaded if you'll keep 'em firing.'

So Greville fired on, picking a new target when the first man bolted behind the line of trees. His second quarry soon abandoned the contest as well, taking to his heels down the lane. He was looking for a third when a cheer went up from the churchyard defenders.

'They be on the run, the cowards,' one man shouted.

'Aye, they be not so bold when met by men armed to resist them,' another cried.

'Quick, gather round, men!' the innkeeper of the Sloop and Gull called out. As the scattered group converged from around the churchyard—Miss Neville's brother George among them—the innkeeper said, 'Jake, take a group to the *Black Prince* moored at the cove, board it and retrieve any goods you find. The rest of you, grab your weapons and come with me. The cargo still ashore is most likely hidden up at Neville Tour. Let's go take back our own!'

While the innkeeper gave orders, Greville went over to grab Neville by the arm. 'What's this nonsense? Surely you haven't involved yourself in this.'

'Not with Black John,' the boy said. 'But what's the harm in helping out Rob Roy? Half the men in the county are here.'

'Half the men in the county take the risk because they need the income. You've no such excuse—and your father a magistrate! When Lieutenant Belcher sees the noise and smoke coming from the churchyard, he'll send a naval vessel back to investigate. You don't need to be here when they come ashore.'

'Aye, imagine they're beating to land as we speak,' Porter said. 'Sound of firing carries a long way across the water.'

'Hasn't your sister enough to handle with your father ill and the whole household to manage, without worrying about you getting yourself hung at the crossroads?' Greville demanded. 'How would Lord Bronning feel if he learned his son had been arrested by preventatives, or shot dead by one of Black John's men? Do you want to have to flee England, ruin your whole future, for a lark?'

'I'm not stupid,' Neville retorted, an angry flush on his face. 'I care about my father and sister. I wouldn't have risked staying here, but I couldn't run from the fight like a coward.'

'You acquitted yourself well, lad,' the Sloop and Gull's proprietor put in. 'But this gentleman is right; Lord Bronning's son best not be present if we have to tangle with the King's officers. You'll be lord here one day, though, and the men of the Devon coast won't forget how you stood with us against Black John.'

Neville's face flushed again. 'Thank you, sir.'

With a nod, the innkeeper slung a Baker rifle over his shoulder and stuffed his pockets with powder and balls. 'We must make all speed, if we are to catch those slimy villains before they can warn their leader and make good their escape.'

Greville turned to George. 'Tell me you'll see reason and head home now.'

The young man nodded reluctantly. 'I hate not to finish the fight…but, yes, I'll go back to Ashton Grove.'

'Good,' Greville said, clapping the lad on the shoulder. 'There are better ways to occupy your time than worrying your relations. Take it from one who learned that bitter lesson well.'

'Will you go with the men to Neville Tour?' Porter asked.

Greville remembered the prickly feeling at the back of his neck the day Miss Holton had taken him to the Tour. Had there been smugglers there, hidden and watching them?

Althea also told him it had always been one of the girls' favourite places. A sick feeling gathered in his stomach at the thought that either of the Ashton Grove ladies might stop at their old haunt and encounter the likes of Black John.

'Yes, I'll ride with them. Are you coming?'

'Nay, I'll head to the cove. Been a long time since I've boarded a vessel, cutlass in hand,' Porter said, his face glowing with enthusiasm for the task.

Giving Greville a cheerful salute, he stumped off. Foreboding in his gut, Greville snatched up his own weapons and followed after the innkeeper.

In the shadows of Neville Tour, Amanda stood within the walls of a now-roofless building that might have once been a kitchen. Her jailor, one of the local farmers, his identity concealed by a mask, stood guard at the entrance.

Keeping his gaze fixed on Black John and the men assembled on the open ground of the bailey beyond, the masked farmer murmured, 'So sorry you be caught up in this, miss. Weren't no call for Black John to take you like that. You just hold fast. I'll make sure no harm comes to ye, if I've got to take a bullet to stop him.'

'Thank you. I sincerely hope it doesn't come to that.'

'As do I, miss,' he replied, a touch of amusement in his voice, despite the grim circumstances. 'Once they finish the parlay, I'll see if I can distract them and give you a chance to slip across the bailey. Your mare's tethered just outside the entrance.'

'Thank you,' she murmured, grateful and fully cognisant of the danger in which the man placed himself by helping her. 'I won't forget your kindness.'

The farmer touched his fingers to his cap. 'Don't hold with harming women, surely not one of Lord Bronning's own kin. He and his lady, your mama, been good to me and mine. Ah, they're breaking council now. I'll see what I can do, miss.'

As her sympathetic captor paced away, Amanda gave her

small prison another assessing glance. She knew from her many explorations as a child there was no other way out but through the gate to the bailey, in which Black John and his compatriots now sat, drinking from a breached barrel of brandy.

What if the farmer couldn't find some pretext to lure the ruffians away long enough for her to cross the open ground? A rising despair checked when she recalled that it wouldn't be unusual for smugglers to have fashioned another entry into their stronghold, excavating out a portion of the curtain wall or even digging a tunnel beneath it, like one of the many that dotted the cliffs along the coast. Might Black John's men have made some new breach in the walls of this structure?

While her heart thumped anxiously in her chest, she began a cautious circuit of the small chamber. Packed into the space, completely masking the walls, were a number of brandy tubs, with parcels stacked atop them that might contain anything from tobacco to French lace to China silk.

She tugged at a barrel, but couldn't budge it an inch. Undaunted, she'd renewed her efforts, tugging and clawing at the heavy tub, when she heard the sound she'd been dreading.

'Need a drink, sweetheart?'

She turned to find Black John standing at the doorway, a feral look in eyes. Trying to peer around him to locate her sympathetic guard, she said, 'I'm waiting for you to come to your senses and release me. Abduction is a capital offence.'

He merely laughed. 'And smuggling is not? If the prospect of the gibbet swayed me, I'd still be tending bar at Pa's inn in Sennlach. Nay, I like a challenge. I think you'll be one.'

Where was the farmer? she wondered while Black John spoke. Had he already made his move and been overcome?

Regardless, it didn't appear he was in a position to help her now. She could either cower before her captor…or stand her ground.

The outcome would likely be the same in either event, but

Amanda vowed she'd not submit meekly. 'If you mean to lay hands on me, I'll certainly resist.'

'I like a lass with some spirit,' he said, grinning. 'So, girl, let's see how much you have.'

He advanced on her. As soon as he was in range, Amanda swung hard, landing a blow that knocked him a bit off-balance. Panic giving wings to her feet, she used that instant to dart past him and race into the bailey.

Hampered by her skirts, she got only a few paces before a strong arm grabbed her shoulder and wrenched her around to face him.

'Never ken a lady'd be handy with her fives,' he said, a grudging respect in his tone. But any hope that respect would translate into his releasing her died as he dragged her close. 'I think that bravery deserves a reward.'

Desperate with a fear that fuelled her strength, she pummelled at his chest with her fists. Growling, he crushed her against him, trapping her hands, and brought his mouth down on hers, his tongue jabbing at her firmly closed lips. The sharp smell of brandy and heated male filled her nostrils as he moved a hand down, tugging up the skirt of her habit.

Oblivious to the sudden shouts of the men around them, Black John didn't release her until one of them pounded his shoulder. As he turned, snarling, his confederate cried, 'Our men were attacked in Salters Bay. The whole damn village and half the men of the countryside were there, armed with pistols, shotguns and rifles. They're on their way here now!'

Another cluster of men, one clutching a bleeding arm, ran up to them. 'Leave the wench, damn it! We gotta grab what we can and go now, John. They've sent a separate party to try to seize the *Black Prince*.'

'If we don't get there quick, they may burn her to the water-line,' another added. 'With all that brandy aboard, she'd go up like a devil's torch.'

To her immense relief, the brigand nodded. 'All right, we secure the ship first, then come back here for any cargo we can't carry. Jack, Harry, get those parcels of lace; Tilden, you take the tobacco. Spring it, boys!'

As his crew rushed off, he looked down at Amanda, whom he still held in an iron grip. 'Don't fret, sweetheart. I'll be back for you later.' Hauling him against her, he kissed her again, hard, before pushing her away and striding towards the road to the sea.

The scurrying men ignored her as they loaded up as much cargo as could carry from the stone chamber and hurried after their leader. Pressing herself against the curtain wall, heart hammering, Amanda waited until the sounds of the departing men and horses faded.

She raced towards the gate of the bailey, then stopped short, gasping. Her sympathetic guard lay face down on the ground near the entrance; Jenkins, struggling to free himself from his bonds, sat nearby.

She ran first to the groom, pulling off the gag and wrestling to untangle the knots that bound him.

'Are you all right, Miss Amanda?' he asked. 'Your father will discharge me, and rightly, for letting that blackguard take you!'

'I'm unharmed. Of course Papa shall not discharge you! How could you have known there would be brigands on the road in full daylight, any more than I did? Nor could you resist such superior numbers. But the guard!' she cried. 'Did they…?'

'Knocked him out,' Jenkins replied. 'The group from town arrived before they could finish him off.'

Leaving Jenkins to free the last knots, she turned and put her fingers to the temple of the downed man. Mercifully, a pulse still beat strongly.

'Could you carry him on your horse back to village?' she

asked Jenkins. 'And look for Master George. I'm afraid he may be involved in this.'

'Nay, miss, I can't leave you! I didn't bring no weapon, more's the pity, but if we hole up inside Neville Tour, won't nobody be able to take you.'

She shook her head. 'There's no need; you heard Black John's men. They're heading back to secure their vessel. If I set off for Ashton straight away, taking the path over the fields that only the local men know, I'll be safe enough. Please, you know how precarious my father's health has been since losing my aunt and mother. I fear for his life itself, should his son be killed or injured. You must go for George at once!'

The downed farmer began stirring. Helping him to sit, Amanda said, 'Let my groom help you into town. I haven't anything here to treat your hurts.'

'I'll just make my way home, miss.' He touched his bloody head gingerly and grimaced. 'Never thought it would happen, but the innkeeper at the Sloop and Gull were right. The folks rose against Black John at last.'

Amanda argued with him for a few minutes, but the farmer was adamant. Amanda suspected he wanted to be home and gone before any revenue officers made an appearance.

'Will you at least give me your name, so my father can thank you?'

The injured man managed a grin. 'Now, miss, you know with the Gentlemen it's best to ask no questions, in case the authorities was to question you later.'

He was probably right, Amanda thought. She wasn't very good at dissembling. After sending off the farmer with an admonition to take care, she turned to the groom.

'You'll find my brother now, please?'

'Aye, miss. You get yourself home, too, afore whoever be coming here arrives. You hear anything while you're going through the fields, you spring that mare. Ain't a horse in the country can catch Vixen.'

Moments later, the groom was on his way and the farmer had limped out of sight. Time to collect her mount and ride home, before the townsmen arrived or any hint of the disturbance reached Papa.

As she recalled the shocking events since her departure from home, her legs suddenly went too weak to support her. Shocked, horrified, at what had happened, what had almost happened, she sagged back against the curtain wall.

Never in her life had she given a thought to travelling the countryside with more than a groom to accompany her. There had always been smugglers about, but they'd never operated in daylight and never, ever, accosted women.

She remembered Black John's mouth on hers, his rough hand snaking under her skirts. Nausea welled up, her head swam; for a moment, she thought she might be ill.

Sitting down on the ruined wall, she forced herself to take deep, steadying breaths. Nothing had happened, really. She'd lost her hat somewhere in the struggle and the brigand had threatened and manhandled her, but she was not truly hurt.

She'd not think of what he might have done. She must calm herself before she arrived home, lest her father sense her distress.

But as she rose to fetch her mare, she heard the pounding of hooves that announced a rider approaching at a gallop. Panic slashing through her again, she glanced about wildly for some crevice in the ruins where she might hide herself, for a stone or even a stick she might use as a weapon. Oh, why, believing a skirmish was imminent, had she not brought even a small pistol with her?

Finally she settled on a large round stone, pitiful as protection, but better than nothing. She'd just secreted herself behind the crumbling walls of one of the outbuildings when she heard a shout. 'Miss Neville! Amanda! Are you there?'

Surprise and joy welled up as she recognised Greville Anders's voice. She had no idea why he would be riding up, calling for her, but never in her life had she been happier to hear her name on anyone's lips.

Relief making her weak, she sank back against the rock wall. 'Here,' she called, her voice despicably weak and trembling. 'I'm in here.'

Chapter Fourteen

Thank heavens, Miss Neville was still at the fortress! Greville thought as he pulled up his horse. Putting from his mind any thought of what the brigand might have done to her, the mere idea of which would make him crazy, he tossed down the reins, took his weapon in hand and sprinted in the direction from which her reply had come.

His poor mount was blown, after he'd urged him uphill at a steady gallop ever since he encountered Jenkins on the road from Salters Bay and learned Miss Neville had been held captive by Black John and his men. Despite Jenkins's assurance that she was quite unharmed, Greville vowed that if that brigand had laid a finger on her, he'd search him out and tear him limb from limb. Terrified for her safety and furious, he'd let the innkeeper and the other townsmen head back to the coast to intercept the smugglers while he proceeded on alone, driven by the need to make sure she was safe.

He'd never seen a lovelier sight than her slender form, seated on rock beside one of the ruins in the bailey. Picking up his pace, he rushed to her side, forcing the nightmarish visions of brutal violation back into the dark cave from which they'd sprung.

'Thank God you're all right!' he told her. 'I met Jenkins on way, told him I'd come for you while he went back to Ashton to let everyone know you are safe. You…are unharmed?'

She nodded, trying to control her trembling lips. 'I am now. But what of my brother? I sent Jenkins to find George and send him back to Ashton Grove.'

'I already did. I think today's violence finally impressed him that dabbling in smuggling is not a game, but a risk that carries serious consequences. Are you truly all right? That villain did not touch you?'

She shook her head, but one hand went unconsciously to her lips.

'That blackguard!' Greville exploded. 'He did hurt you? By St George, I'll strike him down where he stands!'

'He didn't have a chance to steal more than a kiss before news of the ambush in Salters Bay reached here. He and his men left with all speed for their ship, desperate to reach it before the townspeople got there. Anyway, I would have fought with everything I possessed to prevent him taking m-more.'

To his dismay, her voice broke and her calm demeanour splintered. Lips trembling, she gasped out a 'sorry', hugged her arms about herself and dropped her gaze, tears tracking down her dusty cheeks.

The need to offer comfort was too strong to resist. 'Poor sweetheart,' he murmured and pulled her into his arms.

Once she was safely cradled against his chest, her tears came in earnest, great gasping sobs that clawed at his heart while her fingers clung to his shoulders. He hugged her close, as he'd wanted to do for so long, savouring her scent and her softness.

Before his body got other ideas, he warned himself sternly

that comfort was all he would offer, no matter how tempting her lips or how deliciously soft the breasts pressed against him.

At last the storm of weeping subsided and she pushed away. Reluctantly he released her.

'Mr Anders, I am indeed sorry. First I stumble into danger, then I weep all over your coat. You've no reason to believe me, but I'm not usually such a poor honey.'

Smoothing back a stray wisp of golden hair, he wiped a tear from under her eye. 'It's my privilege to offer comfort. I'm only glad nothing else happened. I would have had to put to sea in pursuit of Black John and I'm still not quite healed enough to handle a tiller.'

That earned him a wobbly smile. 'You'd have pursued him, for me?'

'To the gates of hell. Him, or anyone who tried to harm you,' he replied, with implacable steel in his tone that could leave her in no doubt of his sincerity.

She took his hand and kissed it, then laid it against her cheek. 'Thank you,' she murmured.

The sheen of tears as she looked up at him made the already bright blue of her eyes even deeper. Helpless to resist, he ran one gentle finger over her reddened lips. 'It's an outrage that brigand touched these,' he murmured.

She stilled as he caressed her, mesmerised, then with an articulate murmur, leaned towards him. They both froze, held motionless a mere breath apart by the power of the attraction arcing between them.

The new Greville said to ignore it, to help her up, to send her home.

The old Greville whispered it was just a kiss, one she wanted as much as he did, and he'd been wanting to kiss her with every breath he took since their interlude in the library. Just one more sweet brush of the lips, then he'd put her firmly at arm's length and escort her home.

The long lashes shadowing her cheeks fluttered closed and she angled her face up, her lips offered in invitation. Even as his brain issued one last warning 'no', he felt himself lean down and kiss them.

He half-expected, after the fright she'd just had, that she'd push him away and slap his face. He even had a quip of an apology for his effrontery half-formed in his brain.

Instead, she did something much more dangerous. Murmuring a breathy little sigh, she put her arms around his neck and kissed him back.

Sweetness and lust and pleasure and anticipation flooded him. It had been so long, so very long since he'd felt the exquisite joy of a woman's embrace. But this was more than just a woman, any woman.

This was Amanda, a lady for whom he not only lusted, but whose kindness and generosity touched him, whose intelligence and competence he found admirable, whose independent, egalitarian views sparked in him a fascination as strong as his desire.

Then he felt the tentative, exploring touch of her tongue and all his good intentions of ending the kiss scorched into ash and crumbled. On a wave of remembered delight, the old Greville took command, his one driving impulse to take and give pleasure.

He opened his mouth to her, teased and encouraged her tongue to enter, exulted when she accepted that invitation, her lack of experience evident in its uncertain slide. Meeting it with his own, he licked playfully, lured her deeper, revelling in her gasp of pleasure as he stroked her tongue with his own and sucked gently.

His hands went under her cape, insinuating themselves upwards, his thumbs seeking her breasts. To his absolute delight, still she did not repulse him, instead gasping anew when his questing hands found the nipples as tight and hard-peaked as he knew they'd be, palpable despite the barrier of her stays.

Oh, if only he could dispense with that garment, feel the silk of her skin beneath his fingertips, trace the pebbled tips, draw their budded beauty into his mouth and show her what delight he could give her with lips and teeth and tongue!

Ah, delight she would find indeed, for already she was gasping, her tongue now actively seeking his while she thrust her breasts into his hands.

He plumbed her mouth for maximum delight, using all his years of expertise, tucking his tongue into the crevice beneath hers, sucking the tip, drawing it into his mouth, then withdrawing to trace her swollen lips, to bite and tease and nibble. All the while, his fingers kept circling, pinching, caressing the taut nipples.

She gave a murmur of protest when his lips abandoned hers, only to arch her neck back with a gasp as he moved his mouth down her throat, tasting the hollow where the pulse beat wildly, nibbling and sucking at the tender skin at her jaw, nipping his way to her ear, dipping his tongue into its fragile shell.

His hands craved bare flesh. Enflamed by her ardent response, he wanted her pleasure to be complete, wanted to feel her shuddering with release in his arms. Leaning her back against the rock wall, he lowered one hand from her breast and dipped it beneath her skirts.

For an instant she stilled, but only for an instant. Then she was urging his hand up her leg as he revelled in the velvet softness. He toyed with her calf, the back of her knee, until her legs fell apart limply, allowing his hand to continue its upward quest.

He felt his own member, painfully hard in the confines of his breeches, leap when at last his seeking fingers reached the object of their desire, the tickle of moist curls at her centre. Her body tensed, then trembled as he gently parted her and found the plump little nub rigid and already wet with the urgency of her desire.

Clutching him with desperate fingers, her head writhing against the wall, she widened her stance, offering him full access. Taking her mouth again tenderly, he licked her lips in rhythm to the slow stroke of his finger across that supremely sensitive spot.

Then, when the sobbing of her breath and pounding of her heart told him she had nearly reached her peak, he slid a finger into her tight wet passage as he continued to stroke the nub above. Seconds later, with a sharp cry, she came apart in his arms, thrusting her torso into his caressing hand as her pleasure crested.

For long sweet moments, rejoicing, exultant, he held her while she gasped as fulfilment rippled through her.

She was as beautifully passionate as he'd imagined. Only burying himself deep within her could have made the moment more exhilarating, and even the old Greville had retained sanity enough to refrain from attempting that.

Finally the shuddering ceased and she collapsed limply in his arms. As he cradled her on his chest, her eyes fluttered closed.

Though his needy member pulsed with regret that he'd not followed her on the path to ecstasy, he knew as sense returned to her, he'd likely pay a heavy enough penance for the liberties he'd just taken. But with old Greville insouciance, he refused to worry about the consequences.

Instead, a heady sense of exultant euphoria filled him. He wanted to wrap her in his arms, ride back with her to Ashton, shouting his joy to the countryside all the way. Take her to her chamber when they arrived and show her the even more remarkable ways he could make her body respond. Sleep with her in his arms, see how many times he could wake her to even greater heights of joy. Teach her to pleasure him along the same path.

Take her to church.

Shock rolled through him at the implications of that thought. But though it surprised him, he didn't retreat in panic. Cradling her closer, grimly Greville admitted what he'd been avoiding this last week and more.

He, Greville Anders, former rake and gadabout, had tumbled mast-over-keel, complete and for all, into love with a women whose lifelong dream was to occupy a world which no longer had any appeal for him. Who aspired to a status and a role he could never provide for her, even if he wanted to. A woman with whom he would never share any more joy than he'd tasted in this stolen interlude.

The truth of that stark prediction settled in his bones and made them ache. For a long moment he went perfectly still, savouring her nearness and soft slumberous breaths, until he could bear to face the truth.

If this were all he'd ever have of her, he'd best make it memorable. Gently he traced her lovely face with a fingertip as, eyes closed, she murmured and nestled into his caressing touch. Settling her against his chest, he buried his face in her scented golden hair, every pad of his fingers memorising the contour of her ribs and back as he held her tight, tight enough to sear into him the feel of her body against his. Using hands and arms and body to express all the cherishing he wished he could voice, and wouldn't.

He refused to tempt her with the power of their attraction, an attraction she obviously felt as strongly as he did. To lure her to stay with him, persuade her to cast aside her dreams because she was what *he* wanted, would be to act against every tenant of honour bred into him, an honour that was perhaps even stronger for having been only lately discovered.

He could hardly expect her to suddenly decide she wished to

throw away her brilliant prospects and cast her lot with a man she'd known barely half a month. Nor, greatly as it would pain him to let her go, would he *want* her to choose him, unless and until she'd had the opportunity to experience all that London offered and decide if the reality of the dream she'd cherished so long was what she truly desired.

He recalled how she'd tried to smooth the tension between himself and Trowbridge at that dinner. How she soothed and cajoled her angry cousin. With her entrée among those of high estate and her empathy for the powerless, she was uniquely suited to claim the political role for which she longed.

If he must give her up, he hoped the leaders whose decisions would be discussed around her dining table and in her salon would be grateful; that the important legislation she helped move forwards by promoting compromise between opposing parties with a witty word or insightful remark would properly appreciate her intervention.

While careening along his previous indolent, sometimes angry, self-destructive course, he'd never sought or desired to find love. How ironic to unexpectedly encounter it now, when he'd matured enough to appreciate its worth, and to have to let it go.

He'd allow himself a final few minutes to indulge in bitterness over the fact that he'd been born a mere 'mister' instead of a marquess, who might with untarnished honour offer his hand to the woman in his arms. The old Greville would have decried the unfairness of it, cloaked himself in anger and determined to debauch his way through the pain.

But he'd spent too many months among those who'd faced even taller odds and meaner futures. They toiled on, meagrely provisioned with hardtack and grog, daily facing dangers and privations. His position now was far more privileged and comfortable.

So the new Greville steeled himself to a hurt that stabbed

bone-deep. Fiercely glad, even if he could not hold her for ever, to have had this one afternoon stolen from time and fate and circumstance when she had been his alone.

He wasn't sure how long he cradled her there as the shadows lengthened and the stark outline of Neville Tour began showing black against the western sky. Finally, inevitably, her eyes fluttered open.

Stretching with sleepy satisfaction, she murmured, 'That was…remarkable.' Then her eyes blinked fully open, and he saw the exact moment she recalled what they'd just done. 'And incredibly ill advised.'

'I suppose I should say I regret it, but if ever lightning bolts would be dispatched to strike down one uttering an untruth, that would have to be the time.'

His speech had the desired effect; some of the alarm in her eyes abated. 'I'd speak carefully, lest a lightning bolt be dispatched for your calling down the Almighty in so inappropriate a situation.'

'The giving of pleasure is a pure gift, devised by God himself,' he said, his heart in every word.

She looked away, her cheeks pinking. 'I don't really know what to say.'

He tipped her chin back up so she had to meet his gaze. 'You don't need to say anything.'

He knew he would pay for the episode, but he was struck with grief as he saw recognition of the gravity of what she'd just permitted begin to register. A frown of alarm and regret creased her brow, while the panicked urge to flee widened her eyes.

All these years, he'd avoided compromising a virgin so as not to be forced into wedlock; now the girl he'd just thoroughly compromised wanted to escape this place—because she didn't want to be compelled to marry *him*.

The bitter irony of it twisted his lips in a grim smile. But what strong emotion, repressed passion and a reprieve from danger had led them into sharing, threatened the dream she'd nourished since she was a girl. He'd better reassure her she had nothing to fear from him before dismay led her to renounce even a vestige of friendship.

Cursing the old Greville for letting things spin out of control, he said, 'It was unwise, certainly, but with no lasting consequences. Except, I hope, a memory of the joy pleasure can bring.'

She bobbed her head quickly as, avoiding his eyes, with more force than necessary, she pushed away from him. 'I must go. Papa will be worried.'

'Yes,' he agreed, sorting through all the words he wished he could say to find something that might prevent her from chastising herself for a weakness she already regretted. 'We mustn't have you go from one abduction to another. But you needn't worry; I'm wonderfully inventive. By the time we arrive, I will have concocted a story to explain any lost time. To make it creditable, however, we must tidy you.'

To his relief, she let him adjust her bodice and smooth down her skirts. With aching fingers, he helped her pin up her hair, keeping himself from placing another kiss on her head as a sorrow keener than that cutlass slash seared his heart.

She took a step towards her horse, then hesitated. 'Whatever story you concoct, make sure there's nothing in it to alarm Papa.'

'There won't be,' he assured her. 'Nothing to alarm you, either. You mustn't feel uneasy; no one but the two of us will ever know what happened here.'

The lessening of the anxiety on her face both relieved and pained him. So she did dread discovery—and the threat of being trapped into wedding him.

'I know you would never hurt me.'

Meaning, she trusted him never to reveal their indiscretion. He supposed that was something.

'Of course I wouldn't. I only hope my rashness hasn't destroyed our friendship.'

She blushed a bit. 'I believe we've rather shockingly bypassed the bounds of "friendship".'

'My fault. You are irresistible, you know.'

'I, at least, am supposed to be able to resist.'

'You mustn't feel ashamed! In another time, another place, your passion will be blessed and sanctified. Remember this afternoon, if you do at all, as a preview of the delight to come with the one to whom you eventually pledge your hand.'

'Oh, I'm not ashamed!' she replied. 'Or…not much. Oh, how awful that sounds. I enjoyed it immensely, as you have good reason to know. I'm just…disappointed in myself, I suppose, for my weakness in going far beyond what I should have allowed.' She shook her head wonderingly. 'I had no idea I possessed so…unruly a nature. Thank you for trying to make me feel better about my lapse.'

'I assure you, your eventual bridegroom will treasure that "unruly nature".' *A man that will never be me.*

With a short nod, she turned away, although she allowed him to give her a leg up on to her mare. 'I shall not bother you chatting on the way home, but let you put that "wonderfully inventive" mind to perfecting your explanation of our long absence.'

At that, they set off for Ashton Grove.

Greville had no heart for light banter in any event. They'd escaped the consequences of indiscretion this once, but in her averted eyes and wary stance, Greville read that Amanda would not place herself into temptation again. There'd be no more walks or rides, no more intimate chats at midnight.

No more stolen kisses and secret caresses.

This journey together would be their last. In riding home, she'd be riding out of his life.

But that outcome had been ordained from the beginning. If he'd foolishly allowed his heart to become too involved, that was his own fault. He would just have to batten down his emotional hatches and ride out this gale. Doubtless there'd be days of rough sailing ahead, in which he paid in anguish for the folly of falling in love with her, but he'd survive them and move on.

After all, he'd survived hard times before. Could sending her off to London make him feel any worse than the despair of that filthy hold of a prison hulk, waiting to be forced into a role for which he had neither inclination nor training?

He resisted the woeful voice saying it could.

Chapter Fifteen

Amanda rode home in silence, a churning mass of thoughts crowding her brain as the pleasant sensual haze finally burned off. As she considered her behaviour, she grew more and more aghast. She hardly dared glance at Mr Anders.

Mr Anders…Greville. It was rather silly to avoid thinking of him by his first name, after all the liberties she'd just allowed him. Liberties, a painful honesty corrected, she'd not just 'allowed', but enthusiastically encouraged.

She could still scarcely believe her recklessness. Bewitched beyond prudence, she'd risked her reputation, her whole future, Papa's good regard and the respect of her neighbours and friends. A paroxysm of distress twisted within her at the knowledge of how much embarrassment and shame she might have brought upon a dear man who'd already suffered so much, if her lewd behaviour were ever discovered.

Of course, she'd not been herself, her equilibrium rocked by having her safe world and almost her very person violated.

She had good excuse for her relief that the newcomer to Neville Tour had been a man she knew and trusted. There'd been some excuse for throwing herself into his arms and weeping out her fear. Some excuse, even, for the boiling over of the desire that had simmered between them since that first morning in the breakfast room.

But there was no excuse for becoming so swept away that she allowed him intimacies only a husband ought to share.

It should be a sobering lesson in how little restraint character, upbringing and morality exercised over the powerful passion he evoked in her. A warning not to trifle again with so uncontrollable a force.

Thanks heavens Greville, at least, had kept his head, for, possessed by mindless craving, she'd certainly not have stopped him, had he pushed for the consummation the hardness pressed against her said he'd wanted. Her chagrin and remorse increasing, she acknowledged that he—and he alone—had saved her from total ruin.

Despite her current embarrassment, she should have the courage to make herself face Greville now, before they reached Ashton and private talk became impossible, and acknowledge how much she owed him. Not only had he not taken what could have so easily been his, she suddenly realised, but afterwards he'd done what he could to reassure her. Rather than treating her like the lightskirt she'd shown herself, he had gentled her with a caressing touch and spoken eloquently of the purity of passion between a man and wife.

Perhaps she hadn't lowered herself in his opinion after all. An immense sense of relief warmed her at the thought. She'd grown to value his approval as she valued his companionship and delighted in his company.

Just how deep did her feelings run for Greville Anders?

Sudden panic pulled her back from even examining the question. It didn't matter how much she esteemed him; a man in his position had no part in her future. She couldn't allow herself even to contemplate disappointing Papa, breaking her solemn vow to Mama and horrifying society by following the reckless path of desire and throwing herself away on a man in what everyone in her world would consider a shocking *mésalliance*.

Assuming he even wished to wed her. He was, after all, very experienced with the ladies, a self-proclaimed former rake and rogue not yet fully redeemed. Though she knew he cared about her, she had no assurance he was interested in anything more permanent than dalliance.

Something about him drew her like iron filings to a magnet. She'd been deceiving herself all along, thinking she could befriend him and keep leashed the strong attraction that flared whenever they were together. The episode at the Neville Tour today showed just how dangerous that assumption was.

Since she'd just demonstrated she couldn't trust herself to resist him, for the time remaining before she left for London, she would have to avoid his company. No more walks and chats, shared laughter...or burning kisses.

A wave of desolation swept through her.

It must be the lingering effects of the upsetting events at Neville Tour, she told herself, trying to suppress it. Before they reached Ashton, she would allow herself one more opportunity to speak with Greville before she turned him back into 'Mr Anders' and kept him there.

And then get herself to London with all speed, before her resolve wavered, and her newly discovered weakness dragged them both into a dishonour from which there was no escape.

By the time she'd got all the sorry details sorted out in her mind, they'd reached the stable drive. By the copse of trees before the final turn, she pulled up her mare, signalling at Greville—Mr Anders—to stop as well.

'Before we go in, I need to thank you.'

He shook his head. 'There's no need.'

'No, you must let me say it. Bad as our indiscretion was, it could have been much worse. The fact that it wasn't, I owe solely to your prudence. You exercised restraint while I exhibited none. Not that I will be hypocrite enough to deny how much I enjoyed it. But…' she felt her face flaming '…as I hope you know, that episode cannot be repeated.'

'I know,' he replied quietly, with a smile that looked somehow…melancholy. 'I shall try hard to remember not to tempt you.'

'And I will try not to place us in a position where you can tempt me.'

He nodded. 'Best we get back, then.'

As her stomach dropped to the vicinity of her kneecaps, he kicked his horse into motion. After a shocked moment of immobility, she urged the mare after him.

What did she expect from him? she asked herself angrily. To beg her to continue their friendship? To say he'd be desolated if they spent the next few weeks meeting as polite strangers, before she left for London and walked out of his life for good?

He'd been more realistic than she all along, never more so than today, after that episode at Neville Tour. He apparently recognised well before she had that their indiscretion meant the end of their friendship.

Would she find anything in London to replace it?

That dismaying thought made her want to weep again.

As they drew within sight of the stables, Jenkins ran out to meet them. 'Hurry straight to the house, Miss Amanda. Your papa's taken ill again.'

Instantly every other concern fell away. 'Another attack? How bad is it?'

'Don't know, miss. But Miss Althea sent for the physician, who arrived about half an hour ago, and told us we was to send you in the second you got home.'

An awful thought occurred to Amanda. 'Lord Bronning didn't hear anything about Black John and—'

'No, Miss,' the groom assured her. 'He'd already taken to his bed by the time I got back. Master George was back, too, and neither he nor I saw the need to tell anyone what happened in town or at the Tour.'

Urging the mare forwards, Amanda felt a guilty wave of relief that nothing in her behaviour had contributed to her father's condition. The relief was swiftly followed by a renewed alarm.

The attack could be serious. Papa had been ill, too, during that awful summer. He'd never fully recovered his strength and vigour after Mama's passing.

A few minutes later, they reached the front entrance. Greville dismounted and stood ready to help her down. After a moment's hesitation, she let him.

'You go on in,' he said, his touch at her waist light and impersonal. 'I'll see that the horses get back to the stable.'

'Thank you…for everything.'

He gave her the shadow of a smile. 'I can say with perfect honesty, it was a pleasure.' The smile faded; an intense look came over his face, as if he wanted to say something else. Shaking his head instead, he said, 'Go on in, now. Your cousin will be waiting.'

Despite her anxiety to reach her father's side, with him standing there close beside her, a treacherous longing rose in her. She knew she dare not see him alone again; this had to be the last time. Oh, how she ached to kiss him, to show by that tender salute that she esteemed him and would always treasure the friendship they'd shared.

But then he moved away, leading the horses towards the stable, and the moment was lost. A bittersweet ache rose in her throat. 'Goodbye, my dear friend,' she whispered to his retreating back before turning to hurry up the steps.

'Lord Bronning is in his chamber, Miss Amanda,' Sands told her as he held open the door. Tossing her cape in his direction, she headed for stairs, moving as rapidly as her skirts would allow. She rushed down the hallway to her father's room, and, after a soft tap, walked in.

The physician looked up, put a finger to his lips and inclined his head, indicating her sleeping sire. Motioning Papa's valet to remain, he escorted her back into the hall.

'How is he? What happened?' she demanded urgently.

'It appears he's had another of the attacks he suffered last summer. I won't dissemble; this one was serious, with sharp pains in his chest and a great difficulty in breathing. I've given him a few drops of digitalis and some laudanum. He's weak, and still in pain, but resting now.'

'What should we do for him?' she asked, fear consuming her. She simply couldn't bear to lose one more person dear to her.

'Keep him calm and quiet, let him rest. I recommend that he remain abed for at least a week. Light food, no spirits. Let his body recover.'

'Is there nothing else?' she asked, dismayed by how little it appeared she could do.

'I'm afraid not. His constitution must recover in its own time. But…'

'What?'

'I understand you are shortly to leave for London. On no account should Lord Bronning accompany you. The jarring in the coach, the dust and damp of an inn, the noise, smoke and commotion of London would be most injurious. In order to properly recover, he must remain quietly here at Ashton Grove.'

'Of course. Thank you, Doctor.'

The physician nodded. 'If it will not trouble you, I'll remain the night, in case I should be needed.'

'I'll have Mrs Pepys prepare you a room at once.'

'I believe Miss Althea has already done so. I must say, she showed uncommon presence of mind. Evidently she was the first to discover Lord Bronning after his attack. Gave him some of the tincture I'd left, then summoned Sands and his valet to convey him to his chamber. If, instead of taking such prompt and effective action, she'd had gone off in useless hysterics, your father might not still be with us.'

'I'll give her my heartfelt thanks. Will you dine with us?'

With a smile, he shook his head. 'I very much doubt you will wish to entertain tonight. Don't worry about me; I'll take a tray in my room, as I suspect you'll wish to take a tray here, where you can watch over your papa.'

'Thank you, Dr Wendell. I'll go back to him now.'

She slipped back into the room, to find her father still sleeping. After whispering to his valet to go to supper, she took his place by her father's bed.

Covering his hand with hers, she watched him, tears tracking down her cheeks. Poor, dear Papa. How she wished she could take all his cares upon her and will him back to health!

As she settled in beside him, a sudden realisation broke through her anxiety. She wouldn't be going to London after all. Although Papa had never intended to accompany her into the noise and confusion of the city he disliked, there was no possibility she could leave here with him so ill.

She'd have to stay at Ashton Grove…and put off her Season yet again. In the midst of the wave of frustrated disappointment, a sneaky little thrill sparked through her. She'd have to stay at Ashton Grove…where Greville was.

How long could she resist his appeal with them both here, residing under the same roof? The turbulent emotions of their ride back resurfaced: her attraction to him, her longing for his company pulling against a well-founded fear of his effect on her and a new appreciation for the strength of her passionate nature.

Her mind flew back to those delicious moments at the Neville Tour.

Oh, the sensations he'd sparked in her, his mouth exploring hers in a tangle of tongues! His lips against her throat, her ear; his hands smoothing and fondling her breasts until the nipples peaked under his stroking thumbs. And then, the wonderful, wicked blaze of pleasure as he caressed her knee, her thigh, and up into that hot, sweet secret place. Desire accelerating in a rush until she was breathless, mindless, racing towards a peak more exquisite than she could ever have dreamed.

Exhilarated by her first taste of fulfilment, a deep hunger consumed her to experience it all, to feel within her the hardness that had pressed against her belly, probing the passage his fingers had pleasured…

Her father stirred and she came back to the present with a jolt. Heavens, if she couldn't keep herself from lustful thoughts of Greville while seated beside her gravely ill father, how could she hope to hang on to prudence and discretion during the long slow weeks necessary for Papa to recover?

Even with the best of intentions, avoiding Greville's company would be difficult if she remained here for any length of time. How was she to resist the desire that pulled her to him, the urge to deepen a friendship that should rather be curtailed, lest passion propel them into folly?

Before she could begin to sort out the tangle of anticipation, dread, confusion and uncertainty this new situation evoked, her father stirred again. As she clutched his hand tighter, he opened his eyes.

He focused on her, his face relaxing in a smile. 'Hello, puss. I expect I gave you quite a scare.'

'You did indeed,' she replied, willing the tears away. 'It was most unhandsome of you.'

Patting her hand, he chuckled softly. 'I'm heartily sorry.'

The door opened softly and Althea peeped in. 'Come in, my dear,' Papa said. 'I expect Dr Wendell told you how resourceful our girl was today. Before I'd barely realised what was happening, she knew just what to do.'

'For which I will be eternally grateful,' Amanda said emphatically.

Althea looked over quickly, as if doubting her sincerity. When she realised Amanda had meant every word, her cousin coloured a little. 'I'm only glad I was nearby.'

'So are we both,' Amanda replied.

'I told Mrs Pepys to ready a room for the doctor,' Althea said. 'Perhaps I should have waited for you to do it, but I didn't know when you'd return. I hope you don't mind.'

'Not at all! It's one less thing I need attend to. Though my time shall be much less hectic now. Once I write Lady Parnell to tell her I shan't be coming, we can settle in and—'

'What's that?' her father interrupted. 'Not going to London? Why ever not?'

Amanda looked at him blankly. 'Of course I shall remain at Ashton until you are fully recovered. I mean to pamper you and make sure you follow every one of Dr Wendell's directives. Since your return to health is not a process that can be hurried, and I don't wish to leave Lady Parnell in uncertainty, it will be best just to cancel the journey outright.'

Her father shook his head. 'No, you will not cancel it,' he said firmly. 'You will go to London as planned. There have been delays enough; I'll not have you miss another Season.'

'Well, I am getting rather on the shelf,' she teased, trying to make him smile, 'though it's unkind of you to remind me. Since I've already passed the age of most hopeful young misses, waiting another year will not make much difference.'

'It will to me,' Lord Bronning replied. 'The last thing I promised your dear mama was to let nothing else postpone the

Season she'd wanted for you. If she didn't wish even mourning her loss to delay it, I shall certainly not permit my infirmity to do so.'

'But, Papa—'

'No, my child,' he interrupted again. 'I insist that you go. And if you dig in your heels and say you won't leave me, then you shall just have to pack me up and take me with you. Since leaving my beloved Ashton Grove would certainly send me into a decline, unless you want to have my death on your head—'

'Papa!' she cried. 'Don't even joke of such a thing!'

'Very well, puss. But you must continue your preparations. I want you to have everything you desire, everything you and your mama always dreamed of. Nothing is more important to me...even if it means sending you away.'

'I'll be here,' Althea inserted. 'I can take care of Uncle James.' She looked earnestly at Amanda. 'I know you don't think much of my abilities—'

'That's not true!' Amanda protested.

'But Uncle James is as dear to me as my own papa. I promise, I will care for him better than the best nurse. I'll follow to the letter everything Dr Wendell recommends. You deserve to have your Season,' she added gruffly. 'You'll be brilliant.'

It was as close to an apology as Althea was likely to come, Amanda thought, touched. 'I do trust you to care for Papa. I know you'll do whatever you can to help him regain his health.'

'You see,' Papa said, squeezing her hand and taking Althea's. 'She'll watch my every step, scold me if I sit in draughts, bring me warmed soup and in general coddle me so much I shall have to improve just to get out of the house. By the way, while I am confined, I intend to ask Mr Anders to ride about Ashton Grove for me, since it doesn't appear the Navy plans to make use of him. He has several times expressed an interest in learning more about managing an estate. Who better to teach him than a master like myself?'

'I'm sure Mr Anders will be happy to assist, Uncle James,' Althea said. 'How could he not be an apt pupil with so excellent a professor? I'll help him as well. And Mrs Pepys will aid me in managing the household, so you may be sure of it continuing to run smoothly.'

Looking at the two faces gazing at her earnestly, Amanda said, 'I suppose I am going to London after all.'

Chapter Sixteen

The next two weeks flew by in a flurry of activity: letters to Lady Parnell to advise of her arrival, setting the schedule for Papa's nursing, preparing gifts for staff and some to take to London, and final instructions for the household. For her last visit to the tenants, she took Althea along, presenting her as the mistress who would carry on in her stead.

When they returned to the carriage after their final stop, Althea said, 'So you really do consider me a useful member of the family now.'

Impulsively, Amanda gave her a hug. 'I always have! Do…do you think you could let go of that time last summer, so painful to us both, and let us move forwards?'

After a moment, Althea nodded. 'I can try.'

'Good,' Amanda replied, squeezing her cousin's hand, her heart lightening.

In all the bustle, one thing was missing. Seeming more determined than she to maintain the distance they'd both agreed was necessary, Greville Anders had made himself conspicuously absent.

Though she was rising early, he rose earlier still, and had already breakfasted and gone by the time she reached the morning room. He never returned to the hall for nuncheon and didn't join them at night in the dining room, which seemed so empty and echoing with just she and Althea that by mutual consent, they gave up eating there and took their meals in the small back parlour, or with Papa in his chamber.

The one time she had met him by chance in the hall, he begged pardon for his frequent absences, telling her there was so much to learn, and he needed to do it all immediately. Though he kept his gaze averted, to the delight of her starved senses, he rested his hand for a moment on her arm, until he apparently realised what he was doing and jerked it away.

By the evening before her departure, as she helped Betsy pack the few gowns she'd need for the trip—very few, as she'd be acquiring a whole new wardrobe in London—she still hadn't had a private word with Greville since returning from the Neville Tour. Was he really going to let her leave without any more than the few sentences they'd exchanged in the hallway? she wondered, restlessly pacing her chamber after sending Betsy off to bed.

Unless…being so often away from the house, perhaps he didn't realise she'd be leaving on the morrow?

As an excuse, it was feeble. She stopped by the window, gazing out at the moonlit park, wrestling with the decision. This unconquerable compulsion to see him again defied logic; she didn't even know what she wished to say.

But proper to seek him out or not, she simply couldn't leave Ashton without speaking with him one more time.

Knowing he'd be in the estate office, where he went every evening, she walked there and paused outside the door, gathering her courage. Even now, she wasn't sure what she was going to tell him. A small, nervous smile flitted to her lips: if she had observed Althea or of the housemaids behaving in so addle-pated a manner, she'd have laughed herself silly.

Taking a deep breath, she knocked briefly. The sound of his voice bidding her enter sent little eddies of alarm and delight through her.

He was writing in a ledger as she entered. Glancing up, Greville let his hand still and his eyes widened in surprise.

Once over the threshold, both courage and speech seemed to desert her. She halted, her feet stilling of their own accord. For a long moment, they stared silently at each other.

She made herself walk over to the desk, as he belatedly rose to acknowledge her. 'Miss Neville.'

'I'm leaving tomorrow, Mr Anders,' she blurted.

Still standing, a ledger held before him like a shield, he said, 'Yes, I know.'

As the frail illusion that he'd been ignorant of her plans crumbled, recognition of her brashness in seeking him out heated her cheeks, while something in her chest twisted painfully. 'You knew…and weren't even going to say goodbye?'

For another long moment he stared at her, his lips tight, his expression fierce, whether from anger, irritation or sorrow, she couldn't tell. She was about to turn tail in dismay and retreat when he smiled, that familiar charming, engaging smile that sent a warming gladness through her anxious heart. 'I'm much better at hello.'

'Might you be telling me that in London, perhaps?' she asked, grasping at a small morsel of hope.

'I don't know. I must talk with Lord Englemere at some point. Right now, I've got my hands fully occupied trying to keep things running smoothly for your papa who, as you know far better than I, juggles more enterprises than a circus performer. Mines! Sheep! Wool carding! Lace-making! Cattle! Grain!' He shook his head ruefully. 'I'm staying up later than

I ever did when I was a dissipated fribble, trying to sort it all out.'

His voice turned serious. 'I promise you, I *will* sort it out. I mean to make sure your father suffers no anxiety about anything involving the estate.'

'I know you will master it.'

His smile softened. 'As you will shine on a stage much grander than any offered in Devon. If ever a lady were made to be a brilliant society hostess, it's you. You mustn't spoil this opportunity fretting over your papa's health, either. Althea and I will keep a close watch over him and take immediate action if anything is required, so you may be easy.'

'Easy as I can be, separated from him.' *And you*, the unwanted thought slipped in.

He nodded. 'There will be many diversions in London to help distract you.' He paused, and she hoped he might elaborate, take that opening to prolong the conversation. But then he said simply, 'Since there's no doubt of your ultimate success, I will simply…wish you joy.'

He was dismissing her—from the room and from his life. A pain greater than anything she'd anticipated swelled in her heart, constricting her throat, hampering speech. 'As I wish it for you,' she managed after a moment.

Avoiding her eyes, he gave her a tight nod. 'I'll make sure your carriage is ready tomorrow.'

'Will you be there when I leave?' she asked, though she already knew the answer.

He gave a shake of the head. 'I'll probably be in Mr Acherman's fields by then.'

She'd promised herself she wanted only one last chance to talk with him. But need boiled up from within, a volatile combination of desire, desperation and the fear that she would never see him again, all driving her to steal one last touch.

Before she lost her nerve or sanity returned to restrain her, she closed the small distance to the desk, seized his face and kissed him.

For an instant he resisted, the shock of her unprecedented action holding him motionless. Then he pulled her to him and kissed her back in an all-out assault on her senses, his mouth devouring, his tongue ravishing hers until she felt her bones must melt, her legs went limp, and all she wanted to do was to go on kissing him like this, for ever.

She was gasping, her heart pounding with such force she thought it must leap from her chest, when he roughly pushed her away. 'I must go,' he said unsteadily, 'before I do something even more foolish than last time. God speed, Amanda.' With that, he strode from the room.

Numbly she watched his retreating back. She wanted to recall him, but a small moan of distress was the only sound she seemed able to produce. Stumbling backwards, she sat down hard on the edge of the desk he'd just abandoned, completely unprepared for the stunning strength of the sense of loss filling her chest.

She scrubbed a fist over her stinging lips and took a deep steadying breath. Dashing useless tears from her eyes, she straightened and trudged up to her chamber, chastising herself for having to learn the hard way that sometimes you are much better off not getting what you ask for.

As her carriage pulled away the next morning, Sands, Althea and Mrs Pepys stood waving from the steps. Before leaving, she'd gone to Papa's chamber to kiss him goodbye and promise to faithfully write every detail of her adventure in London.

As expected, Mr Anders had not been present, neither in breakfast room nor on the steps as the staff bid her farewell, nor anywhere along the main road that wound through the estate. Disappointed, as the carriage rolled past the boundaries of

Neville land on to the turnpike, she turned her gaze from the coach window.

So that was it; she'd not catch any further glimpses of him. With determination, she tried to bury all the confused emotions that had prompted last night's display of idiocy in the library.

Her indiscretion over that gentleman aside, though she hated to acknowledge it, for all the times she'd envisioned setting off on this journey, the reality of it fell flat. Of course, it was only natural to feel uneasy about leaving, with Papa's health still so uncertain.

Nor could she expect to be as excited as she would have been, had Mama and Grandmama been here to share it with her. Feeling an insidious sadness pulling at her, she pried her mind free.

What was wrong with her? She was embarking on the adventure of a lifetime, capitalising on an opportunity any gently bred young lady would give all her worldly goods to possess. Once she arrived in London, she'd be able to shake off this dull mood, leave behind in Devon the confusing muddle of attraction, anxiety, desire, and regret that had made her behave like someone she didn't even recognise. Thrust into the diversions of the *ton*, under Lady Parnell's careful guidance, she'd be herself again: calm, purposeful, clear-minded, ready to seize her dream and make it a reality.

However, loss and grief had tempered the idea that being on the most important social stage in England, turning heads, gathering beaux and making what was accounted a brilliant match was the most important achievement in life.

She now believed, with a painful clarity born of two years of devastating losses, that sharing her love with those who loved her was life's most essential purpose.

Was that not also her purpose in going to London? To find the one, perfect man to love her, who would replace all the dear ones lost. So she might, as the marriage service said, leave her family and cleave to her husband, in the closest and most intimate of bonds.

She'd always envisioned him as somewhat older, handsome and distinguished. A wise and thoughtful man, deeply concerned about sorting out the problems left in the wake of Napoleon's destructive march through Europe. He would want to ameliorate, as she did, the poverty of those thrown off land by enclosures, those toiling long hours for pitiful wages in the factories.

Although when she thought now of the man she wished to marry, that foggy image cleared and Greville Anders's face appeared.

She sighed. Though she supposed she ought to be appalled and ashamed of her shocking conduct with him, now that she'd escaped without dire consequences, she just…wasn't. Indeed, she only wished to repeat the experience, the sooner, the better. No longer could she imagine marriage without the deeply exciting fulfilment of the senses.

Passion was a gift of the divine, he'd seemed to suggest— and thinking back on the ecstasy of it, she could only agree. After he'd so sweetly initiated her into rapture, how could she not feel a little regret that the husband she sought could never be him?

She needed to find a *political* gentleman who inspired in her that same level of desire.

Someone like…Lord Trowbridge, perhaps? His family and position in government were everything Mama and Grandma could have hoped. Though she didn't yet know him well enough to judge his true character, she knew he was handsome, intelligent and well spoken.

Though Greville Anders had made mincemeat of his argument at their dinner that night.

She sighed as a pang of longing rippled through her. Enough—it was time, she told herself again, to put Greville

Anders out of her mind and look to the future. She owed it to Mama and herself to start over in London with a clean slate and bend every effort to bring her dream to fruition.

But despite her intention to dismiss him, deep within her rebellious heart the image of Mr Anders tucked itself away, resisting all her efforts to dislodge it.

Two days later, Amanda craned her neck, gazing out the window as the carriage finally approached London. As the Hyde Park Turnpike brought them to the last toll gate, they passed Apsley House and headed into Mayfair itself. Her heartbeat accelerating, she sat up straighter and roused the dozing maid. The knowledge that she had almost reached her destination brought a rise of the excitement she'd always expected would accompany her throughout the whole of the journey.

Her hazy recollections from her childhood visit told her they should soon arrive at Lady Parnell's town house in Upper Brook Street. A rush of warmth filled her, knowing within minutes she would be under the care of her mama's confidante.

She remembered well the elegance of the Parnell town house, the regal beauty of her mama's tall, red-haired friend, her awe of Lady Parnell's two daughters, both just beginning their Seasons and seeming to her young eyes so lovely and sophisticated. Both were now well married, busy raising families on the estates of a marquess and an earl respectively.

Would she be even half as successful as Lady Parnell's daughters? She'd never expected to be thrust under the exacting eye of the *ton* without Mama at her side, she thought, a rush of longing for her absent mother filling her.

She dashed away a prickle of tears as the carriage stopped before a smartly appointed brick town house. Then the steps were put down, a footman handed her out and she was up the steps and through the doorway, where a butler took her wrap and ushered into an elegant room done in rococo pastel plasterwork.

She'd barely seated herself when Lady Parnell swept into the room in a swish of silk and a faint scent of roses.

She found herself enveloped in a hug. 'Amanda, my dear, I'm so glad to have you with me at last! I hope your journey was not too tedious.'

'No, it was quite interesting, actually.'

Stepping back, her hostess inspected Amanda from hem to bonnet. 'What a charming young lady you've become!' she concluded. 'With such a look of your mother about you, it's almost as if I were seeing Lydia again, arriving for our début Season! But enough of that; you will be feeling her absence a hundredfold more than I,' she said, giving Amanda's hands a sympathetic squeeze. 'You didn't come here to wallow in grief, but to be diverted and to settle your future. With my girls married and breeding, I can't think of anything more delightful than finding you a husband.'

'I hope it won't prove too much of a burden.'

'With your beauty and dowry, I shall have to beat away the suitors! Although, clever girl, you have made one conquest already.'

'Conquest?' Amanda repeated, puzzled.

'Don't be coy,' Lady Parnell said, wagging a reproving finger. 'I've already heard from Jane Trowbridge that you made quite an impression on her son, Lucien. In fact, we are bid to dine with the Trowbridge family, as soon as we make you presentable.'

A purely feminine satisfaction buoyed her spirits at that confirmation of her appeal to the eligible Lord Trowbridge. With Lady Parnell's help, there was no reason she should not make exactly the sort of sterling match her mama and grandmama had always envisioned.

She only need follow her mentor's expert advice and put

her whole heart and mind into the effort, which meant burying memories of a certain gentleman and the indiscretions of the recent past.

'When do you think I will be "presentable"?'

'Naturally, you can't appear in public, certainly not at anything as important as a dinner at Ravensfell House, until you've acquired a new wardrobe. You, my dear, must set styles, not merely follow them. Fortunately, your papa can afford it!'

'You don't think society will find me…too old?'

Lady Parnell chuckled. 'My dear, you're not past your bloom yet! But here I am, chattering on, when you must be exhausted after rattling around in a coach for hours. Let me show you to your chamber. I thought you would prefer to have a tray in your room tonight and retire early.'

With the excitement of her arrival fading, Amanda found fatigue replacing it. 'Thank you, I am rather weary.'

'Ring when you're ready and Kindle will bring up a tray. I took the liberty of ordering several garments from my favourite modiste, Madame Clotilde, who will bring the gowns by tomorrow morning; keep what you like, and she'll measure you for more. I still had the copies of *La Belle Assemblée* with the designs your Mama circled.'

The memory enveloped her, vivid, piercing: sitting with Mama in the sunlit south parlour overlooking the garden, fashion periodicals spread around them as they discussed styles and colours. A sudden pang of longing for Mama swept through her, closing up her throat so she couldn't reply.

Her distress must have shown on her face, for Lady Parnell's eyes sheened with sympathetic tears. 'I'm so sorry,' she murmured, pulling Amanda into a hug. 'How unfair to be robbed of the chance to share this Season with your mama, something we'd planned since you were an infant!'

'However,' she said, setting Amanda back at a distance, 'the best remedy for distress is to fill your head with pleasant thoughts, like gowns and parties and beaux. So, enjoy this quiet evening in your chamber. After tomorrow, you will have very few such, for I mean to launch you into a full schedule of activities right from the start!'

The image of Ashton Grove, gilded in late afternoon sunlight—and a certain gentleman's golden smile—tugged at her mind again. If she wished to make a success of her Season, better to begin displacing that image as soon as possible. Firmly pushing it away, she said, 'I'm ready and eager to begin.'

And with that, Amanda was escorted by her hostess to a charming blue-and-cream bedchamber that, she was told, had been the abode of the eldest Parnell daughter—the one who'd snared a marquess. For luck, her hostess said with a conspiratorial wink, before sending in Amanda's maid and abjuring her to rest, bathe and relax.

Amanda was female enough to be excited about the prospect of spending a few hours acquiring the loveliest gowns she'd ever owned. Knowing she looked her best would help squelch the nervousness that fluttered in her stomach at the thought of meeting Lord Trowbridge again…when the stakes were no longer just an idle flirtation in the country, but perhaps the settling of her future.

Trowbridge was a handsome and extremely eligible *parti*—but he was not the only attractive single gentleman in London.

She refused to be rushed. While interested in getting to know Trowbridge better, she also wished to meet other gentleman. After all, her eventual husband must please her, as well as her pleasing him. Besides, after waiting so long, she meant to wring every ounce of enjoyment from this Season.

After helping her out of her travel-stained garments, Betsy assisted her into a steaming tub. Settling back into the scented water with a smile, Amanda turned her thoughts to browsing through street after street of shops and attending musical and theatre productions presented by the foremost performers of the age. She would make her entry into ballrooms glittering with bejewelled guests, dance every set on the arm of some charming partner, her progress across the room followed by admiring male glances and envious female ones.

And finally, one day soon, she hoped, she would find a gentleman whose ardent gaze would fill her with the same sense of desire and anticipation as Greville Anders's.

Chapter Seventeen

The next afternoon, garbed in a smart new gown of jonquil crepe, Amanda stood admiring herself in the glass, lighter of heart than she'd been in a long time. It was impossible for anyone with a particle of interest in fashion not to be delighted after having spent several hours trying on the half-dozen new gowns now hanging in her wardrobe, each one lovelier than last. Betsy was still busy putting away the accompanying gloves, bonnets, slippers, reticules, pelisses and delicate, lacy undergarments.

A knock at the door interrupted her preening. Turning to see Lady Parnell enter, impulsively she ran over and gave her a hug. 'Thank you so much for all you arranged! I feel like a fairy princess.'

'And so you look! Lord Trowbridge will be bewitched for certain,' her sponsor predicted with a smile. 'I came to carry you off for tea, so we might go over the invitations and decide which to accept.'

Amanda took that lady's arm and the two descended to the parlour. After they were seated, tea cups filled, Lady Parnell said, 'First, I've just received a note from Lady Ravensfell, Lord Trowbridge's mama, promising an invitation to dine next week. As I expect you know, the earl occupies a very prominent place in the cabinet. There are certain to be many government officials there—though perhaps not any other eligible gentlemen. If Lady Ravensfell favours her son's suit, she'll not wish to include much competition!'

'How could she have decided that already?' Amanda asked, an uncomfortable feeling of pressure settling on her chest.

'You are my protégée, of course, and she trusts my judgement.'

The discomfort eased. Naturally, all doors would be open to Lady Parnell's ward.

Her sponsor ticked off on her fingers a list of the government officials who might be in attendance, complimenting Amanda as she responded with the appropriate names and titles. 'I should hope I would be knowledgeable,' Amanda turned aside the praise. 'Papa has subscribed to all the London journals for years, so Mama, Grandmama and I would be able to follow the developments at Court and in government.'

'You shall make an excellent political wife!' Lady Parnell pronounced. 'London is still a bit thin of company, some families not arriving until after Easter, but the important society hostesses are now present. There's always the ballet or theatre if no more interesting entertainment presents itself. I think we shall start with Lady Ormsby's rout tomorrow.'

Before Amanda could respond, Kindle appeared at the door. 'My Lady, we have callers. Although I know you are not receiving, I didn't wish to turn these visitors away without consulting you.' The butler presented a card to Lady Parnell.

'Thank you, Kindle, you've done just as you ought,' she exclaimed after reading it. 'Will you see that refreshments are brought to the Blue Parlour?'

'They've already been ordered, my lady. Shall I tell the visitors you will be down directly?'

After an affirmative response, the butler bowed himself out. Lady Parnell turned to Amanda, her eyes bright with excitement.

'A conquest indeed! Our callers are none other than Lady Ravensfell and her son! Obviously Jane couldn't wait to meet the girl who so impressed Trowbridge…and he couldn't wait to see you again.'

'How did they even know I'd arrived?' Amanda asked, receiving the news with mixed emotions. Of course, she was flattered that Trowbridge had lost no time fulfilling his promise to have his mama call, but she was also a bit apprehensive to see him again—and to be subjected to his mother's appraisal.

Wasn't being sought after the point of this journey? And what better way to ensure she met all the eligible young men of the *ton*, than to have it known one of the biggest prizes on the Marriage Mart was paying her particular attention?

'Trowbridge is obviously a determined young man. I wouldn't put it past him to have tipped a groom or footman to let him know when your carriage arrived. One must admire his ingenuity.'

If Trowbridge had that strong an interest in her, she might in the next few moments be meeting her future mama-in-law. Trying to master the nervousness that observation generated, Amanda accompanied Lady Parnell to the Blue Parlour.

Their visitors rose as they walked in. Tall and blonde like her son, Lady Ravensfell had obviously been a Beauty in her youth, and was exceedingly lovely still.

After greeting Amanda's sponsor affectionately, she came to take Amanda's hands. 'I'm delighted to meet you, Miss Neville! Lucien was so eloquent in his praise of your person and character, I confess I couldn't wait to make your acquaintance.'

'You are most kind, Lady Ravensfell, though I fear Lord

Trowbridge must have exaggerated my charms most dreadfully.'

'Oh, I am sure he did not! But first, let me offer you my sympathies on the loss of your dear mama. How distressing it must be for you to make your bow without her at your side!'

Touched by her sincere sympathy, Amanda replied, 'Thank you, ma'am. It is difficult. But Lady Parnell has done everything to make me feel at home and comfortable.'

'You must count on me for assistance as well, should you ever need it. If Maria is occupied, I should be happy to act as your sponsor in her stead.'

A bit alarmed by the implications of that remark, Amanda said, 'How very generous of you.'

'Not at all. But I see Lucien glowering at me for monopolising you, so let me cede my place to my son.' That said, she settled on the sofa beside Lady Parnell, allowing Trowbridge to take the place beside Amanda.

'My mama is a lovely lady, as you can see,' Lord Trowbrdge said, bringing her gloved fingertips up for a kiss.

She waited…but felt no zing of response to his touch. Distracted by that unfortunate observation, Amanda missed his next few words before she forced her attention back to his speech.

'You see, as I assured you at Ashton,' he was saying, 'you can count upon Mama's help as well as Lady Parnell's in making you welcome to society.'

'She is being most obliging.'

'Do I not receive thanks as well? For encouraging Mama to display her natural kindness?'

She had to smile at the ingenuousness of that ploy. 'Very well. Thank you, Lord Trowbridge, for inspiring your mama to exhibit her gratifying generosity.'

He shrugged modestly. 'A wise stratagem, I hope. I'm only a man, lack-witted where ladies are concerned, but even I know enough to recognise a gentleman's access to a young maiden is strictly controlled by her chaperon. I'll have a better chance of seeing you more often if Mama makes you a frequent guest.'

'My lord, that's quite diabolical!' Amanda reproved. 'Are you already so sure you will wish to see me more often?'

'Absolutely convinced. And when I see something I want, Miss Neville, I pursue it relentlessly.'

'You make me sound like a military objective,' she protested, an uncomfortable feeling of being hunted stealing over her.

'Certainly an object I greatly desire to take,' he said in a murmur. As her eyes widened at the possible double meaning of that phrase, he continued smoothly, 'A diplomat can be as direct as a *navy man*, when the situation demands it. But you needn't fear I mean to monopolise you…too much. Particularly after the sad summer just passed, this Season should be for you to enjoy the entertainments and revel in the adulation you are sure to excite among society. Time enough later to concern yourself with more weighty matters. As long as I am one of those escorts who see to your entertainment, I shall be content…for now.'

Did he mean what she thought? she wondered, both gratified and perplexed. That though his intentions were serious, he would allow her time to enjoy herself before he pressed his suit?

She could not help but also notice his slight emphasis on the nautical, as if he were remembering without pleasure his unsuccessful verbal skirmish with Greville Anders.

A slight smile lifted her lips as she recalled it, too. While remaining perfectly polite, how cleverly Greville had deflected Trowbridge's assault!

'Why not begin at once?' he said, jolting her back to the present. 'I'd be happy to escort you and Lady Parnell to the theatre tomorrow night; there's a particularly amusing comedy at the Theatre Royal.

She had to laugh. 'For a gentleman who does not mean to monopolise me, you are certainly getting off to a quick start!'

'I did warn you I'm very determined. As I'm sure Lady Parnell has told you, the theatre is the place to see and be seen. If you accompany me tomorrow, Lady Parnell and I could point out influential members of society and tutor you on their background and interests, before you end up seated beside them at dinner or partnered with them at a ball.'

'An introduction before the introduction?' she said, impressed both by his consideration—and his cleverness. 'That would be helpful.'

He grinned. 'I'll settle for "helpful" now—and work my way towards "indispensable".'

Before she could reprove that audacious remark, he said, 'I see Mama nodding; it is time to depart.' He gave her fingertips another kiss. 'What time shall I call for you tomorrow?'

She shook her head at him. 'As you very well know, I must first consult with Lady Parnell. I will send you a note.'

Unrepentant, he bowed to her. 'I shall hope my luck is in, and I can escort you tomorrow. In any event, welcome to London, Miss Neville. I hope you will like it even half as much as it will adore you.'

After courtesies were exchanged and their callers departed, Amanda related Trowbridge's invitation to Lady Parnell. 'Obviously his lordship wants to steal a march on the other young men,' her sponsor said, 'but I've already committed us to attend a rout. Besides, it's not a bad thing for you to be unavailable. To be sure, Trowbridge is eminently eligible, but I wish you to become acquainted with many gentlemen before I allow any particular one to press his suit.'

'I would like to see more of London and society before I am pressed to bring some suitor up to snuff.'

'Of course you do, and you will. The tragedies of the last few years have made you too serious; I mean to plunge you into such a whirlwind of frivolous activity that you forget your cares and become the carefree young girl I remember. There'll be no shortage of offers when the time comes, and I have little doubt Lord Trowbridge's will be among the first. I've known him since he was in short coats, and I've never seen him make such a dead-set at anyone. You must have impressed him indeed!'

'Or the size of my dowry did,' Amanda replied drily.

Lady Parnell waved a dismissive hand. 'Naturally Trowbridge is interested in your dowry; a young man intent on a career in government must entertain, and, praise God, it will be years before he inherits. But you must not belittle the attractions of your person and lineage. So, what do *you* think of Trowbridge?'

Amanda shrugged. 'How could any girl not be flattered by the attentions of such a well-born, well-spoken and handsome young man? I'm quite happy to get to know him better. In many respects, he seems almost ideal.'

Except you feel no automatic pull to him, nor does he spark in you the immediate physical response Greville Anders does.

'I think so, too,' Lady Parnell was saying. 'Society boasts many attractive gentlemen, some with forms more attractive than their prospects. In addition to his handsome face, Trowbridge has an excellent future and a sterling character that makes him admired by all of society. Marry him and you will achieve your mama's fondest hopes!'

'Believe me, I have no intention of throwing away my dowry or my person on some unsuitable gentleman, simply because I've conceived a sudden violent passion for a handsome face.' She ignored the acerbic voice reminding her how close, during her indiscretion in the Neville Tour, she'd come to doing just that.

She'd be more circumspect in future. Starting with Lord Trowbridge. Although observing the proprieties would be easier with the earl's son, for whom she felt none of the fluttery excitement and stirring of the pulses Greville Anders's nearness inspired in her.

''Tis nearly time to dress for dinner. Come to my sitting room when you're ready, and I'll tell you about everyone you will meet at the rout.'

Watching her hostess walk out, Amanda's thoughts returned to the clever, amusing and flatteringly attentive Lord Trowbridge. She was…interested, but despite his handsome face, easy charm and undeniable eligibility, she'd not felt for him anything like the instantaneous pull of attraction she'd had to Greville Anders upon meeting *him* for the first time weeks ago.

A pull that had only strengthened with time.

But her knowledge of what happened between men and maids was so limited. Aside from the rogue at the Exeter assembly, Greville was the only man she'd ever kissed. Perhaps passion didn't always ignite immediately. Perhaps desire could grow with acquaintance, too.

As attentive as Trowbridge promised to be, she should have ample opportunity to discover the truth of that theory. In the meantime, she would look forward to all the other delights promised by the Season—and push away the lingering image of Greville Anders's smile.

Chapter Eighteen

In the early evening two weeks later, Greville glanced at the mantel clock in the estate office, then gathered up several ledgers and headed for Lord Bronning's sitting room. As the master of Ashton Grove recovered, it had become their custom before dinner each night for Greville to appraise his host about the various estate matters to which he'd attended that day.

Ever since Lord Bronning's attack, he'd been up with the sun, off to the farms after a simple breakfast, riding the land until dark, and after meeting with his host and breaking briefly for dinner, toiling in the estate office until after midnight. Scrubbing a hand over his face as he walked, Greville stretched his back to ease muscles strained from days spent in the saddle, followed by long evenings bent over the estate books.

Once again, he reflected with rueful amusement over the irony that at Ashton Grove, where he was technically a guest, he worked longer and harder tending the estate then when he'd been the hired manager of Blenhem Hill.

No time now to lounge at his ease, indulging in rich food and willing doxies.

One would think there'd not be enough time to indulge in daydreams of a sweet maiden whose innocent passion had been more arousing than the practised wiles of all those experienced seductresses. But somehow, despite the frantic busyness of his day, there was. A now-familiar pang pulsed through him.

Dragging his thoughts back before they turned, like a lodestone seeking north, once again in Amanda's direction, Greville forced himself to concentrate on the summary he was to present to Lord Bronning.

To his relief and that of the entire household, Bronning's health had been steadily improving, though as yet both his physician and the vigilant Althea had forbidden him to leave the house. But as his strength returned, Greville knew his host would soon be pressing to reclaim responsibility for the day-to-day management of the land he so dearly loved.

After knocking at Bronning's door, Greville entered and was delighted to see his host writing at his desk, rather than reclining on the couch.

'Good evening, sir,' he said. 'How good to see you up!'

'Good to be up again,' Bronning replied. 'Even better to finally be feeling more like my old self. Won't you share glass of port with me?'

'With pleasure,' Greville said, going to the sideboard to pour them each a glass.

'Now, tell me about the Smith farm. I'd been hoping the drainage we completed last autumn would permit turning over the ground earlier this spring.'

'Then you'll be happy to hear Mr Smith has just finished the initial ploughing.'

For the next half-hour, Greville answered questions and provided details about the condition of the fields, cattle and small industries that made up the mosaic of income-generating activities that kept Ashton Grove running profitably.

He'd about finished his account when a knock sounded at the door, followed by the entry of Althea Holton.

'You're not tiring Uncle James, I hope, Mr Anders,' she said. 'He's already been sitting up longer today than the doctor recommended.'

'Have to build my strength…if I am to dine at table with you tomorrow,' Bronning said, giving his niece a challenging glance.

Althea shook a finger at him. 'We'll see about that later. Time now to return to your couch for dinner.'

'No, Missy, you'll not scold me to it. I've eaten my last meal reclining like a Roman. I'll not insist—yet—on the dining room, but henceforth I shall take my dinner sitting up like a proper Englishman.'

For several seconds, the two glared a challenge at each other. Finally, Althea looked away, sighing. 'Very well, I suppose you can remain at your desk tonight. Sands will bring our dinner trays shortly. Would you like to join us for dinner?'

Since Lord Bronning's attack, Greville been taking his tray in the estate office…and during the long silent moments while he finished off his meal, he'd struggled to keep his lonely mind from dwelling on memories of the golden-haired lass whose departure had wounded him more deeply than he'd ever imagined.

Oh, he'd expected the first few days or even week would be brutal. But in his previous dire experience, after his time waiting in the hulk and the early days on the ship, his spirits had slowly risen from the edge of despair as he adjusted to the rigours of shipboard life, then came to know and eventually to master his unfamiliar environment.

In this instance, the pain hadn't lessened one whit. Quite the contrary; sometimes he thought it grew daily more acute. At least Althea's amusingly frank remarks and his host's congenial presence would keep him from lapsing once again into melancholy.

'Yes, I'd be pleased to join you.' Almost as he spoke, Sands and a footman appeared with the supper trays, his own included. After pouring everyone a glass of wine, Greville settled on the sofa beside Althea. 'Does your task go well, Mr Anders?' Althea asked.

'After working at Blenhem Hill, I had some experience at reviewing ledgers. But the income there was based primarily on fields planted in corn; Ashton Grove has a much greater range of activities. I would be rather useless indeed had your uncle not guided me and answered my many questions.'

'Guided, yes, but you've been learning quickly, Mr Anders,' Lord Bronning said. 'You have a definite aptitude for the work.'

'Thank you, my lord,' Greville said, gratified by his host's praise. Somewhat to his own amazement, Greville Anders of the expensively tailored coats and intricate cravats now wore simple country garb, got sheep dip on his trousers and good rich loam between his fingers—and enjoyed it. What an amazing transformation that represented!

'You certainly spend enough time about the business,' Althea said. 'I hardly ever see you! Off at dawn, not back until dinner. You're even worse than Uncle James,' she said, with an affectionate squeeze of her uncle's hand.

'Having nowhere near his experience, everything takes me longer to accomplish,' Greville replied.

'With cousin George off in Exeter studying with Father Bricknell to ready himself to return to university—how I wish Amanda could have remained here long enough to witness that—I've been virtually abandoned!' Althea said with a mock-tragic air.

It seemed the violent confrontation in town and the shock of his father's attack had inspired George Neville to reform his dissolute habits, Greville thought, glad for Bronning's sake that a time at sea at hard labour hadn't been required to clarify his heir's thinking.

'I apologise, my dear,' his host was saying. 'Your old uncle hasn't been a very entertaining companion. But I grow better day by day. Soon I shall be going about again with you by my side, freeing our guest to once again be our guest.'

'Assisting you has been a pleasure,' Greville said with perfect truth.

'I shall never be able to thank you enough,' Bronning said. 'Indeed, I don't know what Ashton Grove would have done, had you not been at hand! But what of your future, sir? Have you established yet what you mean to do, once the matter of your naval service is sorted out?'

'I shall seek a new position. Though it's hardly a fashionable view among our class, I've found I don't like a life of idleness. After my recent experience at sea, I was leaning towards a post in the Admiralty, which my former captain promised to help me obtain. There's much good work to be done there, working for a cause greater than oneself. However, with your wisdom and enthusiasm to inspire me, I discovered that I very much enjoying assisting as manager here. There's something profoundly…satisfying to watch fields go from rough weedy patches to rich ploughed earth to rising tender shoots, and know I had a hand in that transformation.'

'Exactly so!' Bronning nodded. 'It's why I've remained so involved at Ashton, resisting for years my friends' and family's urging that I hire a full-time manager to oversee the everyday work of the estate. I'm always driven to experiment with better techniques to manage fields and crops, or to explore new ventures to make the estate more profitable.'

'You've succeeded brilliantly. Miss Neville told me you are viewed as a model by other landowners; after the last few weeks working for you, I can readily understand why. But…'

he hesitated, not wishing to insult his host or insinuate he was angling for the position, 'I've seen first-hand what an exhausting job it is. Perhaps, while you rest and recover, you might consider that it is now time to step back and take a less active role.'

'Hire that full-time manager, you mean?'

'That's exactly what I've been urging, Mr Anders!' Althea cried. 'And not just to ease Uncle James's burdens. Though we all trust it will be many years before George takes over for him, when he does, he will need an experienced manager to assist him.'

'Much as I hate to admit it, that would be the wisest course,' Bronning said, surprising Greville. 'I probably should start searching for a good man to take over some of the responsibilities. The *right* man,' he emphasised, giving Greville a significant look.

Was Bronning thinking of him for the post? A flash of excitement ran through him. It would be a challenge to have permanent charge of so large and complex an operation as Ashton Grove… But as he considered it further, the excitement faded.

He would be considered by society as merely an employee of Amanda's father, beneath socialising with the daughter of house. Even worse, he would be here to see her come home, glowing with the success of her first Season, perhaps affianced. And later, when she returned as a bride, then a young wife, bringing her children on a visit to their grandfather.

At those images, his heart contracted with a pain so intense he almost gasped aloud. As challenging and interesting as the work was at Ashton, he could not bear to remain here and witness such moments, aching for a woman he'd deliberately sent out of his life.

Paradoxically, as much as his heart recoiled from standing by silently, watching her share her life and her bed with another man, he was equally torn by the thought of leaving Ashton, where the hills and hallways reverberated with the echo of her voice, her laughter.

Where he could ride nearly every day past the track leading to the Neville Tour, halt in the shadow of the tower, smell her perfume on the wind and hear again her ragged, panting breaths as he pleasured her...

As, soon, some other man would. No, better by far to leave here and take that government position, or enquire with cousin Nicky about finding some other property to manage.

'Ashton is so well known an estate, I'm sure you'll have no shortage of qualified applicants,' he said, tacitly answering Bronning's unspoken question.

'Well, we must wish you luck with whatever enterprise you undertake,' Bronning said, the eager light in his eyes fading. 'I shall always be grateful for your assistance, and rest assured, you will find a warm welcome whenever you visit Ashton Grove.'

'You honour me, sir,' he replied. Much as he hated to disappoint his host—and tempting as it would be to take up the challenge of running Ashton Grove—as soon as he was certain Lord Bronning was beyond danger of a relapse, he meant to visit London. He'd press Nicky about the progress of his release from naval service and consult with him and the Admiralty about what came next.

London...where Amanda was. Immediately, unbidden, a wave of longing to see her again swept through him. Should he call on her there, bring her news from home, see if she was finding London as exciting and fulfilling as she'd always hoped? A heated excitement flared within his chilled heart at the prospect.

'Well, Uncle, I see you've managed to finish your meal without collapsing into the soup,' Althea's tart tone interrupted his thoughts. 'No lingering over brandy, though! It's time for you to retire.'

'See what I must endure, Mr Anders? She scolds like a fish-wife and is as persistent as my old nanny,' Bronning grumbled, but with a twinkle in his eye. Nor did he demur as she called his valet to help him to his chamber.

'I suppose you'll be returning to your books,' Althea said a touch wistfully as they walked out.

'As you'll return to yours in the library?'

'Not if I can persuade you to a game of cards first. You've been working so hard, I think you deserve part of an evening to rest…and entertain me,' she added with a grin.

It had been many nights since he'd allowed himself any diversion. It wouldn't hurt, this once, to put off for a while his nightly wrestling with the ledgers and his seemingly incurable longing for Amanda Neville.

'Very well.'

'Excellent,' she exclaimed. 'How about piquet?' At his nod, she said, 'Let's retire to the library. I'll have Sands light the candles.'

Once they had settled there, cards dealt and lead determined, Greville said, 'You deserve a reward for all your hard work, too. Everything has continued so smoothly, I've scarcely noticed a change of mistress.'

'Thank you,' she said, pinking with pleasure. 'Managing a household is so much more complex and complicated than I'd ever imagined! There's so much to know, from how to properly clean lamps to seating guests at a dinner to getting stains out of linen. Amanda worked much harder than I ever gave her credit for. I'm sorry now I was so…resentful of her last summer.'

'I'm sure she's put it all in the past.'

'No doubt. She has so many more exciting things to occupy her now, I imagine she's forgotten all about Ashton. I really don't expect to see her again until she becomes betrothed, or maybe after she marries, when she returns to introduce her new husband to the neighbours. Lady Parnell will make sure that whoever she weds is a man of great influence and power. Except for occasional visits, I imagine they'll reside in London or Windsor. It's the life she's always wanted, and no lady could be better suited or more deserving of it.'

Althea was only repeating what he'd already told himself, but hearing it none the less revived the pain, always simmering just beneath the surface of consciousness. Amanda was in London, striving to turn all her girlhood aspirations into reality—why should she spare a thought for those she had left behind?

If she recalled him at all, probably it was only with a sense of gratitude that he'd been gentlemanly enough to conceal their indiscretion and protect her plans.

A flicker of anger stirred. Why did he continue to torture himself over the lady, however wonderful she was? They might as well exist on separate planets, she in her sphere, he in his, both determined to become master of their respective realms. He'd wished her joy before she left and meant it.

He was too isolated here, he decided, trapped in a moment of time with only his memories for company. He *should* go to London as soon as possible, remind himself of what he wanted for the future and recall all the possibilities for love and success that existed beyond Amanda Neville.

'Is something amiss?' Althea's concerned voice recalled him.

'No, no. I'm only trying to mind my cards. What do you plan to do, once your uncle recovers?' he asked, determined to steer the conversation to less painful channels.

'I've convinced Uncle James to let me stay here. Though he never complains, I know how terribly hard it must have been for him to send Amanda to London, knowing she would make her grand match and never live at Ashton again. She's the image of my Aunt Lydia, so it's like he's losing his wife all over again. I'm not as beautiful and perhaps not as clever, but I can certainly love him like a daughter. I hope we'll be a comfort to each other.'

Greville now knew something himself about the anguish of losing one's love…a precious gift he'd never known how much he'd treasure, until he let it slip away.

Shaking off the reflection, he said, 'Somehow I don't see you ending your days, knitting docilely at your uncle's side. Surely there are gentlemen in Devon shrewd enough to appreciate a lass of your keen wit and charm. That is, if they don't hear you bossing poor Lord Bronning about,' he teased. 'No man wants to live under cat's paw!'

She threw down her last card and grinned triumphantly. 'You're just being disagreeable because I beat you.'

'So you have, minx,' he said, looking at the final trick. 'Here I've listened attentively as you pour out your soul, and you, heartless scapegrace, were fleecing me. I'd best retire to the estate books before you win my last groat.'

'We'll have to play again, so you may win it back. I did enjoy the game! Thank you, and goodnight, Greville.'

'Goodnight to you, too, Althea.'

He smiled as he walked to the office. She'd be a sprightly handful for some man some day, he thought, quite certain she'd not end up living at Ashton, a comfort to her ageing uncle. Most likely she'd wed some local boy and reside in the neighbourhood, ordering her own servants about between returning to Ashton to check on her uncle and give orders to his. Unlike Bronning's brilliant daughter, who would shine like a luminous star in her far-distant universe.

From within the churning mass of loneliness, pain, regret, resentment, pride in what he was doing and sadness for what he'd leave behind emerged the fervent desire for Lord Bronning to recover quickly. It was time for Greville to leave Ashton Grove and begin carving out his own universe.

With a renewed determination in his stride, he reached the estate office and crossed to his desk. And if some inner voice warned that getting Amanda Neville out of his heart and mind would take far more than a trip to London and some solid plans for the future, he did his best to ignore it.

Chapter Nineteen

When the coveted invitation from Lady Ravensfell finally arrived early one morning two weeks later, Lady Parnell summoned Amanda to her boudoir to discuss it without even allowing her time to dress.

'Although I couldn't be more pleased at the progress we've made these last two weeks, presenting you to all the hostesses of note and many of the eligible gentlemen on my list,' she said, after inviting Amanda to seat herself and calling for fresh chocolate, 'the event I've truly been anticipating has been this dinner at Ravensfell House. Now that the invitation is here, I discover it will be even better than I expected!'

'How is that?' Amanda asked with a stir of anticipation. Though she'd found all the other candidates whom Lady Parnell had presented to her attractive, polished and gratifyingly attentive, none thus far had exceeded Lord Trowbridge in intelligence, charm or rank.

Nor, alas, had any of them elicited in her the immediate emotional pull and sensual response she'd felt for Greville Anders.

'We are to go not just for dinner, but for a ball, too, immediately following. The first great ball of the Season, sure to be attended by everyone of note in society. And though the Trowbridges give several balls each year, I find it significant that Lady Ravensfell has chosen to give her first on the same evening we are to dine with them.'

'Society will interpret this as a sort of endorsement of me as a potential bride for their son?'

Lady Parnell nodded, her face glowing with delight. 'Only intimates or important friends are invited to dine with the family before such events. Ah, how clever Trowbridge is, having you make your first appearance on society's grand stage at a ball given by his mama, rather than at Almack's or somewhere else!'

'It will be as if he's...laying claim to me?' Amanda asked, the feeling of being waltzed into a corner descending on her again.

Some of Amanda's trepidation must have shown upon her face, for Lady Parnell clasped her hand. 'Now, you mustn't refine too much upon it; Jane and I have long been friends, as all the world knows. In any event, by giving you such a clear mark of approval, Trowbridge has ensured your success, for every other young gentleman of rank will wish to vie for the hand of the lady he favours.'

Amanda recalled his earlier words to her: that this Season should be for her to enjoy entertainments and attention before she settled to the business of choosing a husband.

And she had been enjoying it. Between afternoons spent shopping, calling or receiving calls from important society matrons, and evenings attending dinners, musicales and the theatre, she found herself caught up in just the sort of giddy whirl for which she'd hoped. It occupied her from rising in the morning until she fell back into an exhausted sleep; the frenetic pace gave her no time to worry about Papa's health, feel homesick for Ashton Grove—or miss a certain auburn-haired rogue's ravishing kiss and mesmerising touch.

The sense of pressure eased, replaced by gratitude. Trowbridge was backing up his fine sentiments with action, she thought, impressed and touched by this evidence of his large-mindedness.

'It is kind of him,' she agreed.

'The ball is in four days,' Lady Parnell said, scanning the invitation again. 'As soon as Jewell has made me presentable, we must inspect your wardrobe. For such an important occasion, you may need a new gown, which means we have no time to lose!'

As it turned out, Lady Parnell pronounced Amanda's previously purchased gown of celestial-blue crape trimmed with satin ribbon and diamond crystals sufficiently grand for the Ravensfell ball, so the few days before the event were not complicated by the necessity to acquire another dress. But since the topic of the ball dominated conversation at every call they made and both dinners they attended before that event, Amanda realised that her patroness was correct in claiming it would be the first grand event of the Season—and that everyone who was anyone in London would attend.

Rather than the ball, which she contemplated with as much anxiety as anticipation, it was the dinner to which she truly looked forward. It would be her first foray into the world Grandmama, Mama and she herself had long dreamed to claim as her own, where she would encounter the leaders of government and listen as they discussed the great issues of the day.

By the night of the ball, her stomach was churning with excitement and trepidation. Though Lady Parnell would be at her side to assist and her hostess, Lady Ravensfell, had promised to make her feel at ease, she'd not yet met the formidable

Lord Ravensfell, cabinet member and intimate of the royal family. If all the expectations everyone seemed to be entertaining about her turned out to be correct, she might meet her future father-in-law this evening, within the house of which she would some day be mistress.

Assuming she ended up deciding to accept Lord Trowbridge as her master.

Nowhere close to a decision on that front, while an admiring Betsy settled a shawl of spangled gauze over her shoulders, Amanda sternly bid the sparrows that had seemed to have taken up residence in her stomach to cease flapping their wings. After inspecting herself one last time in the glass, she descended the stairs to join Lady Parnell in the carriage.

A short drive later, they had entered the Ravensfell town house and were ushered into a large handsome parlour, where her smiling hostess introduced Amanda to her husband, a tall, distinguished gentleman who looked every inch the government minister.

As they moved on past the receiving line, Lady Parnell said softly to Amanda, 'The gentleman in the corner is Lord Liverpool's secretary, Mr Thomas, the man beside him the Home Secretary, Lord Sidmouth. There are leaders from the opposition as well; the man by the hearth is Lord Holland, conversing with the Marquis of Landsdowne.'

By the time Lady Parnell had identified all the notables, Amanda's eagerness to be present had disintegrated into a terror that she might commit some verbal gaffe that would show just how unworthy she was to be included among such elevated company. Almost every gentleman present was a member of the current government or occupied a seat in the Lords or the Commons, and the ladies they escorted were equally elegant and sophisticated. All, except Lord Trowbridge and one other gentleman, were also considerably older.

She was nearly trembling in her slippers when Lord Trowbridge appeared at her side.

'Don't worry,' he murmured, offering his arm to escort into dinner. 'You need only nod, smile and look beautiful. I'll be right beside you, so you don't have to converse with anyone else unless you choose to.'

'Thank you,' she whispered back. 'The guests are rather intimidating.'

'Most occupy positions in government, as does my father. It's his world—and mine; the guests are friends as well as associates of many years' standing. Men of power and influence, of course, but in the end, only men, like your father and his neighbour, my Devon host, Mr Williams.'

'Perhaps,' she said dubiously, 'though it's kind of you to try to set me at ease. I shall attempt not to embarrass you by dropping something on the tablecloth or uttering some idiocy over the soup.'

Trowbridge chuckled. 'You are far too graceful and intelligent to do either. This is your first visit to my home; I would very much like you to simply relax and enjoy the meal and the conversation.'

At that moment, Amanda could have told him she was about as likely as relax in the company of so many notables as she was to turn into Althea's canary and fly around the room. However, she found that as time went on and she committed no social solecism, she did begin to relax. And though she remained far too on edge to do more than pick at her food, she soon became enthralled by the conversation.

To her left, Lord Liverpool's secretary, Mr Thomas, was asserting to one of Lord Holland's associates the necessity of the previous Parliament's passage of the Gag Acts suspending the right of Habeas Corpus. To her right, Lord Landsdowne insisted to the man across from him that the information obtained when the Manchester protesters were tried indicated there was no national conspiracy, and that the application of ordinary English law would have been quite sufficient to stem the unrest, without any of the extraordinary measures to which the government had resorted.

At one end of the table, their hostess was complimenting the Prime Minister, Lord Liverpool, on successfully gaining passage of the measure outlawing slavery. At the other, their host discussed with opposition leader Lord Holland the necessity to pass funding that would allow the Royal Dukes to proceed with their proposed marriages to the Princesses of Hesse and Saxe-Meinengen; after the tragic death of the Prince Regent's daughter Charlotte in childbed the previous autumn, he warned, the kingdom should waste no time ensuring the succession.

The very tenor of the words sent a thrill through her. Ah, this was the world she'd always dreamed of, the arena Mama and Grandmama had trained and encouraged her to enter! She sat raptly, hardly touching her food, trying to listen to as many of the assorted conversations as possible.

By the end of the meal, energised by the discussions around her, she'd even grown bold enough to make an enquiry here, or ask a question there, earning an approving nod from Trowbridge—and drawing upon herself so intense a scrutiny from the only other young man present that she felt a blush heat her cheeks.

Finally, to Amanda's disappointment, the covers were cleared and her hostess rose, signalling the ladies to withdraw. 'We'll grant you gentlemen one brandy,' Lady Ravensfell said, 'but with the ball soon to follow, we'll expect you shortly in the salon.'

Still glowing with enthusiasm, Amanda followed her hostess out of the dining salon. To her delight, for she hoped to hear more political discourse before the ball began, by the time the ladies returned from freshening themselves and their gowns in the retiring room, the gentlemen were filing into the parlour.

From across the room where he'd gone to greet his mother, Lord Trowbridge spied her and walked over, Lady Ravensfell on his arm.

'Miss Neville, I hope you weren't too bored by the dinner discussion,' her hostess said. 'These gentleman will talk nothing but politics.'

'On the contrary, my lady, I found it fascinating!' Amanda exclaimed. 'In fact—and I fear Lord Trowbridge must confirm this—I was so absorbed in listening to the discussions that I was a very poor dinner partner.'

'Miss Neville, you cannot believe I would be so unchivalrous as to assert any such thing!' Lord Trowbridge protested. 'Mama, she is the most charming dinner partner imaginable.'

Lady Ravensfell gazed at her for so long, Amanda felt alarm spiral in her belly. 'I believe she is,' her hostess said at last.

At that moment, the butler beckoned to their hostess. 'I hope you will enjoy the ball as well, Miss Neville. If you'll excuse me, I must attend to some matters before the other guests arrive.'

Lord Trowbridge was called away also. Unwilling to approach any of the senior officials or their wives on such slight acquaintance, Amanda stepped towards the wall, out of the flow of guests, waiting for Lady Parnell to finish conversing with a sombre-looking older gentleman she identified as Lord Melcombe.

Oh, how pleased and excited Mama and Grandmama would have been to have attended the dinner tonight! Smiling, Amanda let her mind run through again all the fascinating snippets of information she'd gained from the very lips of the men responsible for creating policy.

'Pressed into silence by all this weighty discourse, Miss Neville?' a voice at her elbow enquired.

She whirled around to find herself facing the young man who'd nearly stared her out of countenance at the dinner table.

From Lady Parnell's whispered commentary before dinner, she recalled that he was a cousin to Trowbridge.

'Not at all, Mr Hillyard. I found the discussions fascinating.'

'Ah. You've passed the test, then.'

'Test?'

'If you want to retain Lucien's favour, you must be up to snuff in the political arena. From what I saw at dinner, you performed brilliantly. Trowbridge was certainly watching you like an Oxford don with his prize pupil. I must confess, I was impressed myself. Seldom do I find a chit worthy of the hyperbole when I hear some new nonpareil praised to the skies. In this case, you may deserve the accolades.'

Some 'new nonpareil'—did he mean *her*? Amanda frowned, not sure she liked being discussed in such irreverent terms. Were the gentleman not related to her hostess, she'd give him a sharp set-down, but since that was impossible, she said coolly, 'I'd prefer the "weighty discourse", if you please.'

Hillyard merely laughed. 'Most young ladies would be thrilled to have set the *ton* buzzing even before their first appearance at a society ball. I predict the speculation will increase even more after your attendance at dinner tonight. Poised and intelligent, as well as beautiful and well dowered? I might have to enter the lists myself.'

'Please don't go to any unaccustomed trouble,' she flashed back, wishing he would leave and skirting as close to insult as she dared.

'Ah, a razor wit as well—better still. But you needn't fear I will plague you. Lucien would never have let his mama invite me if I were considered a contender for your favour. For one, I'm not a marrying man. Even should I be tempted to join the fray, Lady Parnell would never countenance your dallying with a man of my inadequate funds and…*scandalous* reputation.'

Was he trying to shock her with his unsettling conversation, as he'd tried to rattle her by staring at her during dinner? Torn between anger and exasperation, she said, 'I might be only a simple country miss, but even I know Lady Ravensfell would not have invited a man who was truly a rogue.'

'A reasonable assumption on the face of it,' he replied, 'except that, being not only kin to the Trowbridges, but wholly dependent upon them, they believe me intelligent enough not to alienate the providers of my income by trying to debauch a girl Lucien favours right under his nose.'

By now, growing more accustomed to his frank speech, she observed, 'Since when do rogues respect any boundaries?'

He raised his eyebrows. 'And what would a "simple country miss" know about rogues?'

She'd opened her mouth to deny any knowledge…until the memory of Greville Anders pleasuring her in the shadow of the Neville Tour flashed into her head, momentarily stilling her lips.

Lamentably astute, Hillyard noticed her hesitation. 'Not quite such an innocent, then!' he declared, grinning. 'Though if you're beautiful *and* naughty, I'm not so sure I shall retire from the lists. Trowbridge doesn't deserve a truly wicked miss. Too serious by half, you know.'

For a moment she teetered between amusement and anger. Humour winning out, she laughed aloud. 'Are you always this outrageous, Mr Hillyard?'

'Generally not with virginal young ladies, who either have no idea what I'm talking about or blush with horror at my candour. I'm delighted that you do neither. Perhaps we would suit.'

'Indeed! Whatever leads you to that conclusion?'

He shrugged. 'Something tells me you're more attracted to a rogue than to an upstanding gentleman like Lucien.'

Maybe not a true rogue…but she'd found one *former* rogue, now battling his way towards redemption, compelling indeed.

She returned from that reflection to find Hillyard staring at her, pure sensual assessment in his gaze.

Feeling her face flame, she protested, 'Now you are casting aspersions on my character as well! I should probably cut you completely.'

'Too late for that,' he said, having the effrontery to chuckle at her outrage. 'If you keep company with the Trowbridges for long, I'm bound to turn up, like clots in a bowl of cream. Besides, I can offer one thing Trowbridge will surely not, something you may find invaluable.'

'Indeed? And what might that be?'

'The truth. About myself and everyone else in society, including my very proper cousin. Besides…' He hesitated, burning her with another smoky, assessing look, 'you are not always prudent, are you, Miss Neville?'

Memories of when she had been far from prudent once again invaded her mind. Before she could dispel them and summon some prim rejoinder, he continued, 'In any event, Lady Parnell will shortly rescue you; I believe she's about to conclude her chat with the doleful Lord Melcombe. I'll take myself off before she has a chance to chastise me. Despite your disapproving chaperon, I hope to see much more of you, my divine Miss Neville.'

Before she could tartly reply that she was neither divine nor his, he bowed and walked away.

An inclination towards rogues, indeed! she thought, shaking her head ruefully as she watched him slip from the room. Though she was honest enough to admit, after her initial shock, she'd begun to feel a sense of ease with Hillyard that she still didn't feel with the much more proper Trowbridge.

At that moment, Lady Parnell turned back to her. 'My dear, let me present Lord Melcombe, who's most anxious to make your acquaintance.'

After an exchange of courtesies, Melcombe said, 'You

seemed quite immersed in the conversation at dinner, Miss Neville—a rather singular reaction for a lady of your tender years. Do you truly follow events in Parliament, as Lady Parnell claims?'

'Yes, my lord. My grandmother was an acquaintance of the Duchess of Devonshire, who inspired in her an abiding interest in political matters that she passed on to my mother and me. I found the discussions fascinating.'

He nodded approvingly. 'I hope you ladies will each save me a dance.'

'We would be honoured, my lord,' Lady Parnell replied for them. After Melcombe bowed and walked away, she snared Amanda by the elbow and walked her into quiet corner.

'I couldn't be more pleased,' she said in an undertone. 'Jane told me Lord Ravensfell was quite impressed and intended to convey to Lucien his hearty approval of you. And if that were not coup enough, you've attracted Lord Melcombe's interest as well!'

'Might your fondness for me have you reading too much into this?' Amanda asked, a little alarmed. She wasn't sure she wanted the powerful Ravensfells urging on their son's pursuit. 'As for Melcombe, we exchanged only a handful of sentences.'

'Trust me, my dear,' Lady Parnell said firmly. 'In all the times I've dined with Jane, I've never seen Trowbridge single out a young lady like he did you tonight. And since losing his beloved wife several years ago, Melcombe has never remained for the ball after the dinner. No, my dear, you are well on your way to being a triumph. Oh, how I wish your dear mama were here to see this! Now the dancing is about to begin, and I can't wait to see who you captivate next.'

Chapter Twenty

Two weeks after the Ravensfell ball that had launched Amanda to immediate success—a fact evident from the details Althea artlessly read to him from Lady Parnell's letters to Lord Bronning—Greville arrived in London to meet with his cousin, the Marquess of Englemere.

Over those two weeks, Bronning had improved to the point that, though still forbidden to ride out, he was well enough to manage the books and consult with Farmer Smith, whom Greville had prepared to take over as assistant and supervisor during his absence.

Eager to begin planning for his own future, Greville had set off as soon as he'd ensured all was in place. Though he'd still not made up his mind whether or not he would visit Amanda Neville, simmering under the surface, adding urgency to his desire to be away, was the titillating knowledge that, after more than a month of keenly feeling her absence, he would once again be within calling distance.

After checking his baggage at the inn, Greville headed to his cousin's home on Grosvenor Square, mentally girding himself for the interview to come.

Thinking that after his misuse of the previous opportunity the marquess had granted him, Nicky would probably leave him kicking his heels in an anteroom for some time, he was pleasantly surprised to be summoned to his cousin's library within minutes after the butler left to announce his arrival. He was further heartened by the smile with which Nicky greeted him and the warm handshake he offered.

'You're looking very well,' Englemere said, waving him to a chair. 'I understood from my Navy contacts that you had been rather badly wounded in that action off Algiers.'

'Yes, I'm much recovered. First, let me thank you for obtaining my transfer from the *Illustrious* so I might recover ashore and in comfort.' A vision of Amanda's lovely face flashed before his eyes; ah, lying in her arms would be comfort indeed! 'Life aboard a man-of-war isn't much conducive to healing.'

'You may thank your sister Joanna for that. Not even your valet seemed to know where you'd gone when you left Blenhem, and to my discredit, until she brought me evidence of foul play, I didn't take the time to investigate.'

'My mishandling of Blenhem Hill could hardly have inspired you to take much interest in what happened after you'd rid yourself of a bad bargain.'

'Haven't we all made mistakes we'd undo, if we could but go back and live through those days again? But the way you conducted yourself aboard ship wasn't one of those times, from what Captain Harrington told me. It seems a stint as a common seaman is a rather drastic medicine for curing irresponsibility.'

Greville blinked in surprise. 'You've spoken to Captain Harrington? I understood the *Illustrious* was still at sea.'

'She and the vessel she captured arrived back in British waters last week. When I expressed my desire to Admiralty to speak personally to the man who knew the details of my cousin's service at sea, their lordships summoned the captain to London.' Nicky smiled. 'Sometimes being a marquess—and a member of the Navy Board in Parliament—has its uses. Although, and I don't think you ever believed this, I truly do realise it is the quality of the man, not his title that matters.'

Greville met his gaze squarely. 'I'm pleased to hear it.'

'I believe you'll also be pleased to hear what the Navy Board has decided. After investigating the circumstances of your impressment, they informed me that you will shortly be freed of all obligations to the Navy. An official letter to that effect will be dispatched to the Coastal Brigade station, with the lieutenant in charge instructed to notify you when it arrives.'

Picturing Belcher's disapproving face, Greville thought the lieutenant would probably command Porter to deliver the letter to Ashton Grove on foot—and hide his peg leg.

Nicky chuckled, recalling Greville's wandering thoughts. 'The whole situation was a bit of an embarrassment for the Navy. Although impressments are technically legal, with the war and the necessity to maintain the blockade over, there's no real need for them. And as you know, the impressment of gentlemen was never permitted.'

'After Barksdale got through with me, I didn't much resemble a gentleman.'

Nicky's face darkened. 'For that crime and others, Sergeant Barksdale figures soon to hang. Although, it turns out, he may in the end have done you a good turn.'

'By inadvertently helping turn a lazy, arrogant bastard into something more useful?'

Nicky grinned. 'There is that. But as you know, it was Captain Harrington's anxiety to get *Illustrious* underway without delay that drove him to send the press gang ashore. He'd heard from reliable sources about the imminent sailing of several Barbary vessels said to be laden with gold and valuables, and wanted to be the first ship in the area with a chance to capture them. So, Harrington told me, some superior couldn't sail over at the last minute to claim the glory—and the lion's share of the profits—after the *Illustrious* had done all the work.'

Greville nodded. 'So the men informed me. The expectation of being able to keep all the prize money if we succeeded in capturing a ship reduced the grumbling about how hard Harrington was pushing everyone.'

'An audacious devil, Harrington.' Nicky laughed. 'Rather like a certain cousin of mine. Imagine the Fleet Admiral's chagrin when the *Illustrious* sailed into port, accompanied by the conquered vessel! I understand when the final tally is set, the value of the cargo, along with proceeds from the sale of the ship itself, is expected to make it one of the richest prizes ever captured. The captain—and his crew—should all profit handsomely.'

'I'm glad,' Greville said, thinking of Old Tom and the purser and the doctor and the others who had helped him survive his time at sea. 'I hope all the sailors will receive a comfortable retirement ashore. Perhaps with my meagre share, I will be able to refurbish my wardrobe,' he added with a grin.

'Oh, rather more than that, I expect. Harrington told me that, though initially sceptical of your claim, he came gradually to believe you were in fact a gentleman. Which made him admire all the more your endurance and strength of character, suffering the lash until your demands to speak with him were met, then working at the tasks assigned you without further complaint, once you realised nothing could be done until the ship returned to England. He admired even more your tenacity and courage in fighting off the Barbary raiders, even though you yourself were already badly wounded.'

Greville nodded, proud to have earned his captain's rare words of praise. 'I don't recall much about the action, other than trying not to get killed whilst battling alongside crewmates trying to do the same.'

'Both Harrington and First Officer Mitchell believe they would have been slain, had you not stood guard when they went down, fighting like a wild Cossack to protect them. They both agreed that, since they would not have survived to receive their share of the prize money but for your intervention, it would only be just for each of them to contribute some of their allotment into your share. Harrington estimates you stand to receive a very handsome sum, enough to allow you to live as a gentleman of leisure the rest of your life.'

As the implications of that statement penetrated, Greville was struck speechless. Then his mind began racing like a runaway colt.

'Might the sum be enough to purchase a small property?' he asked eagerly. 'A life of leisure no longer appeals to me. Though I'd tentatively planned to seek a position at Admiralty, I discovered whilst assisting Lord Bronning that I truly enjoy the challenge of managing an estate. To manage one of my very own would be marvellous.'

His spirits leapt when, after a moment, Englemere nodded thoughtfully. 'Land values have fallen since the war ended, especially with a resurgence of unrest in the countryside after the return of so many landless, unemployed former soldiers and sailors. I expect there are some good bargains to be had.'

How might he approach Amanda, if he were a gentleman of property rather than just a gentleman of leisure?

He called his rampaging imagination to a halt. Even if he was able to purchase a small estate, he would never possess a title nor occupy a high position within the political society in which she sought to belong.

But what if he stood for Parliament? If he purchased land, and there was a nearby borough needing a representative... As he knew well from listening to sailors speaking of the lot of their families back in England, the village common lands were disappearing as more fields were enclosed, throwing farm workers off their small plots and into the grinding labour of mills and factories. There was an urgent need to redress laws that increasingly placed too heavy a burden on the landless. In that cause, at least, he could share Amanda's desire to be part of forwarding the business of government.

While Greville's mind worked feverishly, Nicky said, 'At any rate, your release papers should arrive soon. What do you intend to do then?

'I've a small bequest from my aunt; with that and any prize money that comes through, I'd like to purchase a property and would appreciate your advice on a suitable one. Beyond that, I'm fully aware of the very poor job I did at Blenhem Hill. Arrogant, and, yes, resentful of you, I let a venal man lull me into ignoring my responsibilities, abusing your trust and leaving unprotected those who should have been under my care. My time at Ashton Grove has made me more painfully aware of just how difficult my negligence must have made life for the tenants. I'd like to make amends to them somehow, if I could.'

Englemere fell silent again, tapping one finger on his desk. 'I'd turn Blenhem Hill back over to you and let you make those amends, but I don't own it any longer. Always a man who relished a challenge, my friend Ned—your sister's husband, Sir Edward Greaves—bought it from me. He has considerable other property to manage, however, so he might well be willing to sell it back to you.'

Return to Blenhem Hill, face those he'd injured, earn back their trust and work the rest of his life assisting them. At Blenhem, he could take up the worthy occupation he'd been seeking while at the same time redressing the wrongs of the past.

The rightness of it settled deep within him, filling some of the emptiness Amanda Neville's departure had left at the centre of his spirit. 'I would relish the opportunity.'

'Why not talk with Ned, then? As far as I know, he and your sister are still at Blenhem Hill, completing the repairs and refurbishment Ned began when he took over the property last spring. Joanna is to present Ned with their first child shortly; I'm sure she would appreciate a visit.'

'I owe her a great deal, too,' Greville acknowledged.

'You do indeed. Had it not been for her intervention, you might still be languishing at sea. Captain Harrington was in no hurry to release such a hard-working member of the ship's company, he told me. If Ned can't give you satisfaction, come back to see me. I'll keep my eyes open; Blenhem Hill isn't the only small estate in England. I'm sure we can find a suitable challenge for a man the pirate captain called "Rage of Infidels".'

'Did he indeed?' Greville asked, a bit embarrassed.

'So Captain Harrington told me.'

Clearing his throat gruffly, Greville offered Nicky his hand. 'Thank you for all you've done.' At the words, he had to grin. 'You can't imagine how hard that would once have been for me to say! I'm sorry I spent so many years resenting you.'

Grinning back, Nicky shook it. 'I'm a rather charming bloke once you get to know me, or so my wife says. But it is hard to feel beholden. If Ned turns down your proposition, come back and I'll recommend a property in need of so much work, you'll swiftly recover from your gratitude.'

A knock sounded at the door, followed by the entrance of Englemere's wife Sarah. 'Greville, how good to see you! Will you be staying long? There's a ball tonight for the daughter of your Devon host, the protégée of my old friend Lady Parnell. Won't you accompany us?'

'A ball for…Amanda Neville?' he blurted.

At Lady Englemere's nod, he tried to sort out an immediate

torrent of conflicting feelings. He would see her again! But only as one among a great crowd, most of them London notables whose society she was endeavouring to enter. She'd have little time to spare for a man who was, and devoutly wished to remain, a simple countryman.

The political members of society led lives less devoted to idleness than the rest of the *ton*, he acknowledged, but still, the ball represented a world that no longer appealed to him. He'd already wasted far too many evenings gaming and drinking at other, admittedly much less respectable, entertainments among gentlemen of good birth. There'd be only one lady present with whom he wished to dance, and she would be besieged by admirers.

'I, ah, didn't bring evening dress with me, unfortunately,' he said at last. 'But thank you for the invitation.'

'The odds at the clubs say Trowbridge is going to snap up Miss Neville…and her excellent dowry,' Englemere was saying.

'Which only proves he's the smart lad everyone claims him to be,' Sarah replied. 'It's nearly certain he'll receive a prominent position soon, especially if Wellington ends up forming a government in the next few years.'

Trowbridge. Was she really going to accept that complaisant son of privilege? Greville's immediate flare of jealous anger was followed by an ache of desolation.

'You met Miss Neville before she left for London, did you not?' Lady Englemere asked.

He found that lady's penetrating gaze fixed on him. Afraid she might have glimpsed the pain on his face before he schooled his expression to neutrality, he replied, 'Yes. A charming young lady. It would be…pleasant to see her again, but since I would like to visit Blenhem Hill before I return to Ashton Grove, I intend to leave very early tomorrow. Lord Bronning isn't fully recovered and I wish to get back as soon as possible.'

Had he been too dismissive? Greville tried to interpret the swift glance exchanged between husband and wife.

Before he could decide whether it would be better or worse to elaborate on his refusal, Lady Englemere said, 'We won't press you, then—on this occasion, at least! But we both hope you will soon make us a longer visit. Your sister Joanna wed one of our dearest friends and we would like the opportunity to know you better, too.'

After a further expression of thanks, Greville took his leave, wanting to make a swift exit before his face or voice revealed anything further to Englemere's keen-eyed lady.

Outside the Englemere town house, he paused. It was only a short drive to Upper Brook Street. It was now mid-morning, late enough that even the newest Diamond of London society should be awake. He could make that call now and reassure Amanda her father was recovering well, something doubtless still of concern to her.

For moment, he let himself think about seeing Amanda Neville. Longing rose in him, fiercer and hotter even than his desire.

He ached to inhale the scent of her perfume, gaze into the azure depths of her eyes. See sunlight gleam in the gold of her hair. Hear the musical lilt of her laughter, so full of life and joy it made him smile just to listen.

See her…with Trowbridge at her side?

The earl's son might be there even now, if he were courting her as assiduously as Englemere said.

Though he truly hoped she would marry well and be happy, he wasn't sure he had the strength of character to witness her with the earl's son without succumbing to the impulse to smash his fist into Trowbridge's perfect nose. Knowing Amanda was happy, perhaps some day he'd be able to purge her from his heart and mind.

After a few more moments' pondering, he decided to call

244 Society's Most Disreputable Gentleman

regardless. Were their positions reversed, he'd be incensed to know someone with first-hand knowledge of a matter dear to him had not bothered to take the few minutes necessary to bring him the latest news about it.

He'd make a short call, reassure her and leave.

And shut out of his mind the fear that purging her from his heart was a task not even her marrying Trowbridge could accomplish.

Chapter Twenty-One

While Greville lingered outside Englemere House, on the other side of Mayfair, Amanda was riding in Green Park with Mr Hillyard.

'You're rather vigorous for one who was up so late,' Hillyard said, reining in his gelding beside her mare after a brisk gallop.

'If you can't keep up, stay home and sleep,' Amanda tossed back.

'Wonderful advice…as long as I'm not sleeping alone.'

'An uncommon event, I imagine,' she returned tartly, making Hillyard throw back his head and laugh.

It had become a game between them—he dropping innuendo-filled remarks to try to embarrass her, she refusing to blush and, instead, flashing back at him.

Obviously not yet conceding the point, he gave her a lascivious glance. 'Are you sure, before you trade the exhilaration of being fêted for the boredom of wedlock, I can't persuade you to be indiscreet—*again*?'

This trick went to him, for she felt her face colouring.

Brazening through, she said, 'It's never been established— beyond in your wishful thinking—that I ever *was* indiscreet.'

He gazed at her knowingly, making her feel for one panicky moment as if he could see through her mind to that passionate episode. 'Oh, I'm nearly certain of it. However, before you wed my eminently proper cousin, you might consider which man you want waiting in your bedchamber every night.'

She couldn't help it; the image flooding her mind wasn't Lucien Trowbridge or any of the other gentlemen who now filled the entryway with their floral tributes and crowded Lady Parnell's drawing room. Instead, she saw auburn hair curling over a collar, full, sensual lips curved in a crooked smile, felt fiery kisses claiming her lips, trailing up her throat while knowing fingers set her calves, her thighs aflame... Anguished longing pierced her, and for a moment, she wished she'd never left Ashton.

She pulled herself from that reverie to find Hillyard giving her a knowing look. But instead of tweaking her about her lapse, he surprised her by saying, 'Passion is a gift you don't want to squander on the wrong man.'

Hadn't Greville once said almost the same, that her 'unruly nature' would be treasured? Maybe that was why she liked Hillyard, with his rogue's smile and outrageous comments; his irreverent tone and frank speech reminded her of the unconventional Greville.

However, though she felt more at home with Hillyard than any other gentleman she'd encountered in London, she didn't wake in the morning yearning for his company. Nor was she ever tempted to seize his face and kiss him until her knees were weak and her stomach churning and her body mad for completion.

'Both of the prime contenders for your hand, my peerless cousin and the bane of his existence, Lord Melcombe, are unlikely to be as adventuresome in the bedchamber as a lady of your beauty and…spirited nature deserves.'

Refusing to blush again, she flicked him with her whip. 'Wretch! That last remark is too outrageous to deserve a reply. But why do you call Melcombe the "bane" of your cousin's existence? I thought Lord Melcombe and Trowbridge's father were allies.'

'True, but of all the suitors crowding about you like eager puppies, my cousin considers only Melcombe a true rival.'

Amanda shook her head dismissively. 'I don't believe Lord Melcombe's intentions are serious. We discuss only politics.'

'I never claimed Melcombe had finesse. But the fact remains that in the three years after his wife died, he attended not a single ball or rout; now he squires you about the dance floor at every event you grace with your presence. Society considers his attentions marked enough that it might even change the odds at Brooks's, which are now running heavily in favour of Trowbridge. Better enjoy my disreputable company while you can; if Lucien thinks Melcombe is gaining on him, he's likely to get a jump on the competition by making you an offer immediately.'

'He'd make me an offer to "get a jump on the competition"?' she echoed. 'As if I were some…game to be snared?'

'Ah, but you are, my dear. A lovely fox to be run to ground.'

She wrinkled her nose in distaste. Was that truly how Trowbridge viewed her—as a trophy to be bagged? 'Perhaps I'll just run away instead,' she replied and kicked her mare to a gallop, laughing as she left Hillyard behind.

A good gallop always cleared her mind. She'd been in London a month now, and was no closer to making up her mind about her ultimate choice. She hardly needed Hillyard's unwelcome news to alert her to the fact that Trowbridge and several others had grown so assiduous in their attentions that offers of wedlock would almost certainly be forthcoming in the near future.

She ought to be delighted. Wasn't this exactly the outcome she had dreamed of for many long years? Except…except she still hadn't quite found what she was seeking.

She absolutely loved the political dinners she'd attended. She found the exchange of ideas stimulating, and the fact that the principles discussed over the dinner table could become the policy of the nation excited her.

She liked and admired Trowbridge and respected Lord Melcombe, both men who could offer her a permanent position in that world. But no one save Hillyard amused her as Greville Anders had. And not one of them came close to engaging her heart, mind and senses with the power and immediacy of that forthright former sailor.

Damn and blast, she'd didn't have to decide this minute. She'd think no more on it now.

Hillyard caught up to her and conversation turned to Lady Parnell's upcoming ball as he escorted her home. Noting it was late enough that her sponsor might already be receiving morning callers, she rode her mare around to the mews and entered the through the garden door, not wishing to meet anyone until after she'd changed into something more presentable than her mud-spattered habit.

Crossing to the service stairs, she encountered Kindle, about to carry a tray of refreshments up to the parlour. 'A gentleman just called for you,' he told her.

'Who?' she asked idly, pulling off her gloves.

'Not a London gentleman,' the butler replied, the edge of disdain in his voice indicating the caller's appearance must not have met his exacting standards. 'A countryman. He'd come from Ashton Grove, I believe. He said he'd leave you a note.'

Greville? Her heart leapt. 'Is he still here?' she demanded.

'He might be. I left him with pen and paper in the library, composing his—'

Ignoring Kindle's startled look, she turned away from the butler in mid-sentence, picked up her skirts and practically ran up the stairs. Rushing down the hallway, she skidded to a halt outside the library door. She paused there, brushing mud off her skirts, thinking she probably should have asked Kindle to delay the gentleman until she tidied herself and changed her gown.

But, oh, if it was Greville—and who else could it be, coming from Ashton Grove?—she couldn't stand to wait an instant longer. Taking a deep breath, she pushed open the door and walked in.

Behind the desk, a lock of auburn hair falling across his forehead as he bent over, his eyes on the note he was sanding and sealing, sat Greville Anders. Her heart swelled, as effervescent with delight as if champagne rather than mere blood infused her veins, while excitement blazed through her like a dozen Congreve rockets set alight.

Since in Kindle's immaculately run household, well-oiled door hinges moved silently, she had several seconds to run her gaze fondly over his features—broad shoulders, noble profile, tempting lips—before he sensed her presence and looked up.

Surprise, then pleasure lit his face. 'Miss Neville,' he said, rising from his chair. 'I feared I'd missed you. How good it is to see you again!'

'It's wonderful to see you, too, Mr Anders.' As she'd hoped, he came around the desk…walked towards her…took her hand.

An immediate, intense zing of connection sparked between them, stronger than ever after so long an absence. Her eyes fluttering shut, she inhaled sharply, savouring the contact, feeling it in every pore.

When she opened her eyes, his vibrant gaze was fixed on

her, his lips slightly parted, as if he, too, had been struck to the core. She felt an almost overwhelming desire to seize his face and kiss him, as she had that last night at Ashton Grove, but before she could get her tingling limbs to react, he released her hand and stepped back.

Finally remembering her manners, she said, 'Won't you take a seat? Can I offer you some wine?'

To her vast disappointment, he shook his head. 'No, thank you; I mustn't keep you long. I just rode into London briefly to consult with my cousin and intend to depart first thing in the morning, but I knew you would wish to have a report about your father.'

'If you are here, he must be improving,' she said, knowing he would never have left if Papa was in any danger.

'He's doing very well. Not yet back on horseback, but moving about the house at will, able to take over the ledgers and consult with Mr Smith, whom I put in charge of overseeing the estate until I return.'

Relief filled her—and gratitude—that he had been kind enough to take time from his quick visit to give her the news in person. 'Thank you so much for stopping by to tell me.'

'And what of you? We know from Lady Parnell's reports that your début has been the resounding success everyone expected. Are you finding London to be everything you had hoped?'

'It's exciting, energising and exhausting,' she said, delighted to share her experiences. How she'd missed simply discussing daily events with him! 'It's such a thrill to attend a dinner and hear Lord Holland or Lord Liverpool or Lord Landsdowne speak about current policy! Though the balls and theatre and shopping are delightful, being able to associate with the leaders of government is by far the best part.'

Was she only imagining it, or did his pleased expression dim? Before she could decide, the momentary distress, if such it was, vanished and he smiled. 'I'm glad for you. Once again, may I wish you every success?'

He bowed, obviously about to make his exit.

'You mustn't go yet!' she cried. 'That is, I've not had a chance to enquire about your plans. Has your cousin been able to obtain your release from the Navy?'

'He has, although it will take a bit longer, I am told, for the official document to be sent to the Coastal Brigade office.'

'So you'll be at Ashton Grove for some time yet?'

'Until my release arrives, in any event. But rest assured, I shall not depart until your father is fully recovered…or until, as Althea is urging him, he hires a manager to take over the more exhausting work.'

'What will you do then?' she asked. The idea of him leaving Ashton was oddly disquieting, ridiculous as that reaction was. He was only a guest; she'd known from the first his stay would be temporary.

'I've enjoyed assisting your father with the estate. I believe I'll look to purchase a property of my own, or, failing that, find a manager's position at a large estate.' He gave her the quirk of a smile. 'Remain in the country somewhere, doing highly unfashionable but deeply satisfying work.'

'You…wouldn't consider staying on with Papa?' she asked. At Ashton, where in future, she'd at least have excuse and opportunity to chat with him.

He paused for a long moment before replying, 'I think it would be wiser for me to…go elsewhere.'

So she wouldn't tempt him to folly again? Or had her presence—or absence—nothing to do with his plans? Oh, how she wished she dared ask! But with this strange sense of disquiet squeezing her chest, she couldn't seem to recapture the warm intimacy they'd shared that night in the library, when she'd felt free to make the most personal enquiries.

He'd fallen silent, too, and now stood simply looking at her.

That intense, compelling gaze travelled from her face down to her slippers and back up, as if he were memorising her every feature. 'I'm glad you've found your heart's desire,' he said at last. 'Goodbye, Amanda.'

His tone was soft, almost like a caress, but there was a finality about it that suddenly made her fear she would never see him again. Before she could speak or call him back, with the powerful, sinuous grace with which he always moved, he walked swiftly through the door and closed it behind him.

She stood motionless, irresolute, half-wanting to follow and call him back. But what could she say? He obviously had business elsewhere. Seeing her couldn't have been that important to him, if he had planned such a short visit in London. He was moving on with his life, leaving her to move on with hers.

Was she really ready to do that? All her memories of Ashton Grove came rushing back: Papa on horseback, consulting with the tenants; the hills rising purple in the mist beyond Mama's garden; even argumentative Althea, tossing her head at Amanda. A wave of homesickness more acute than anything she'd felt so far swamped her.

Then there was Greville, walking and riding with her, advising her about Althea, diffusing the tension between Papa and George. Longing welled up, sharp enough to bring the tears to her eyes. She dare not even think about Neville Tour.

He was turning into an excellent manager, Papa had written her; the household staff had reported back compliments they'd received about his work from the tenants. He had a talent for engaging people, her father observed…hardly surprising to her, whom he'd engaged from the very first.

Praise Heaven that Papa was feeling better and might soon be able to resume his duties. After which, Greville Anders would leave to take up a new challenge at some other grand estate, perhaps even one of his own.

By the end of the Season, when she returned to visit Ashton, he might be on the other side of England. She might just have shared the last conversation she would ever have with him.

'Goodbye, Greville,' she whispered, the burn of tears at the corners of her eyes intensifying.

Her heart's desire—had she truly found it in London? Or might she just have watched it walk out the library door?

Later that evening, Amanda took her place beside Lady Parnell to greet their guests. Candles illumined the room with a golden glow, enticing odours emanated from the supper room, and every immaculate, waxed and polished inch of the public rooms was reflected a million times over by silver trays, sparkling goblets and crystal chandeliers. But as she stared across the room, a smile pinned to her lips, Amanda saw none of it.

The evening was to be the triumphant culmination of her presentation, with everyone who was anyone answering Lady Parnell's summons to honour her ward. Conscious of the honour—to say nothing of the expense and effort her hostess had expended—Amanda tried to focus on greeting each guest. But as the hour grew later, she found her smile becoming more and more automatic, her attention wandering as her eyes darted towards the entry.

Mr Anders had told her he was leaving London. There wasn't the slightest chance he would attend the ball tonight. Still, knowing he was still in town, she couldn't seem to keep herself from hoping that, just maybe, he would appear.

An urgent sense of expectation rose with each new visitor, then fell as Kindle announced a name that was not Greville's. Absently she agreed to save Lord Trowbridge and Mr Hillyard each a waltz, glad now that her duties receiving guests prevented either from being able to whisk her away for dancing or refreshments.

Midway through the evening, he still had not come. Lady Parnell had just told her she was released from her duties when a tall, dark-haired gentleman appeared, a golden-haired lady on his arm and Kindle intoned, 'The Marquess and Marchioness of Englemere.'

A shock zipping through her, Amanda jerked her gaze to the doorway. It took only an instant to ascertain that Greville had not accompanied his cousin.

Still, this was the man who had arranged for him to stay at Ashton Grove. Another bolt of excitement energised her. He'd told her he'd come to London to consult with his cousin. Perhaps the marquess might know more about his future plans.

After greetings were exchanged, Lord Englemere said, 'My heartiest thanks to you, Miss Neville, for your hospitality to my cousin, Mr Anders. He seems to have made a very good recovery, which I attribute to your family's good care.'

'You are most welcome. I understand Mr Anders just visited you.' At the marquess's look of surprise, she added hastily, 'He paid me a brief call this morning. To give me a report about my father's improving health.'

Englemere exchanged a quick glance with his wife. 'Yes, Greville visited us as well. We'd hoped to induce him to spend a few days, but he seemed quite anxious to get on with his affairs.'

Though conscious of Lady Parnell's raised eyebrow, for it was not usual to detain guests in a reception line, Amanda couldn't help asking, 'You were advising him, he said. About the possible purchase of some property?'

'My dear,' Lady Englemere said to her husband, 'other guests are waiting to speak with our hostess. Lady Parnell, would you mind if we kidnapped your lovely ward for a few moments?'

'Not at all. I was about to release her anyway,' her sponsor replied politely, her puzzled gaze following them as Amanda walked away.

'Did Mr Anders tell you anything about his service aboard the *Illustrious*?' Englemere asked.

Wondering what that had to do with Greville's future, Amanda said, 'He recounted some amusing incidents.'

'Nothing about his own service?'

'Not in detail. He told Papa most of it wasn't fit for a maiden's ears.'

Englemere laughed. 'Just as I thought. Mr Anders is quite the hero, Miss Neville! A few weeks ago, we had the opportunity to host his commanding officer, Captain Harrington. The captain sang his praises, especially his courage during the battle with privateers. He credited Mr Anders with saving both his life and that of his first officer.'

'I knew he'd been wounded in the action, but—why, he never said a word!' Amanda exclaimed.

Englemere chuckled. 'My cousin seems to have become a modest man, as well as a responsible one. For his efforts during that skirmish, he will be receiving a significant sum of prize money. He wished to have my advice on purchasing an estate to manage, an occupation for which your father has been giving him valuable experience and advice.'

'Where do you think he intends to purchase property?' she asked.

By now, Lady Englemere was looking at her as curiously as Lady Parnell had. Amanda knew she'd already passed from polite enquiry to an inquisitiveness that bordered on the ill mannered. But she couldn't seem to help herself, so driven was she to discover as much as she could about him.

'That has yet to be determined.'

'I see,' she said in a small voice. So there was no telling where in England he might end up. 'Perhaps he will settle not too far distant from Ashton Grove,' she said without much hope. As far as she knew, there weren't any properties for sale in the neighbourhood. 'I know Papa would enjoy continuing their association.'

'I'm sure your father—and you—will encounter him often,' Lady Englemere said evenly.

Amanda murmured a polite assent, but she didn't believe it. With the Navy Board releasing him, he'd leave as soon as Papa recovered, which, she devoutly hoped, would occur long before her Season ended. By the time she went back to Ashton, he would be gone.

She might well never see him again.

As desolation chilled her to the soul, Mr Hillyard appeared, claiming her for the waltz she'd promised. Repeating the familiar politenesses by rote, she took leave of Englemere and his wife, and numbly let Hillyard lead her away.

Anxious to be on his way and back at Ashton Grove, at first light Greville rode out of London. Travelling by horseback, he hoped to reach Blenhem Hill within a few days and return to Devon in no more than a week.

Leaving early also removed the temptation to call again upon Amanda Neville—senseless as that action would be. Finding her alone, a circumstance he hadn't anticipated, he'd seized the chance to ask the only question that mattered: whether the world she'd dreamed of entering had fulfilled her expectations. The enthusiasm on her face when she replied had been unmistakable.

She was well on her way to establishing herself in the position to which she'd always aspired, a hostess in a social realm that would never be his. Assured of her happiness, there'd been no need to say any more, to embarrass them both confessing a love that would make no difference. All that remained was to say goodbye, and he had.

His head understood all that. But for most of the long ride to Blenhem Hill, his heart resisted accepting it.

* * *

Other feelings surfaced as he neared the scene of his ill-fated employment. After the wrongs that had been visited upon the tenants while he sat in the manor house, arrogant self-indulgence blinding him to the abuse and embezzlement going on right under his nose, he suspected he might have been run out of Blenhen Hill, if Barksdale hadn't knocked him over the head and whisked him away in the dead of night.

He doubted anyone around the estate would be pleased to see him. It would take determined effort, probably over a long period of time, to win back the respect of the people he'd failed to serve.

Such worthwhile and necessary work would keep his mind from drifting back to memories of Amanda Neville, he thought, ignoring the little voice that reminded him hard work had not yet produced that result. Some day, he trusted, he'd be able to think of her with an affection no longer laced with the acid of anguish.

After skirting the town of Hazelwick, he took the familiar road towards Blenhem Hill, noting with recently acquired expertise that many of the cottages were newly thatched, fences had been rebuilt of timber and stone, and most all of the fields were already ploughed. He passed several farms with workers about, a few even greeting him by name.

They hadn't thrown rocks, at least.

Then he was pulling up his horse before the manor house. Somewhat to his surprise, the butler greeted him cordially, showed him to the parlour and promised to fetch his sister immediately. He barely had time to pace across the parlour, noting it was in its usual perfect order, when Joanna hurried in.

'Greville!' she cried, delight on her face. 'How good it is to see you—and looking so well!'

'All thanks to you, sister dear. I would otherwise still

be painfully crawling back to health whilst holystoning the quarterdeck.'

'Thanks to cousin Nicky as well. But, here comes Ned. I can't wait for you to meet my husband!'

Not certain the man who'd had to repair Greville's mistakes would be in any hurry to meet *him*, he prepared himself for some hard scrutiny.

Greaves had taken good care of his sister, too, Greville noted. Jo had always been a pretty lass, but now her pale skin and green eyes positively glowed. The tender look that passed between husband and wife as Sir Edward entered made him ache with longing and envy.

After the requisite introductions, Sir Edward said, 'We're delighted to see you, especially as it must mean you are feeling hale again.'

'I am. More important than that, however, I understand congratulations are in order.'

'Thank you,' Joanna replied, her glow increasing as her husband pressed her hand. Greville suppressed another pang. Would he ever have a loving wife, a son to whom he could pass down the estate he planned to acquire? Such a prospect now seemed as remote as the moon.

'Ned says Lord Englemere has sorted matters out with the Admiralty,' his sister said. 'I do hope that means the Coastal Brigade can spare you for a visit.'

'I'm afraid not. Unfortunately, my kind host, Lord Bronning, recently suffered an attack and was ordered to bed.'

'Good heavens!' Sir Edward cried. 'Is he doing better? He will recover, I trust.'

'He is making steady progress, but in the interim, I've been assisting him on the estate. Learning a great deal…about things I should have known while I was here.'

He'd given Sir Edward a perfect opening, but his sister's husband only said mildly, 'There could be no better teacher.'

Some of Greville's tension eased. Though Sir Edward was perfectly entitled to take Greville to task, apparently he did not intend to do so.

Despite Sir Edward's forbearance, Greville felt compelled to continue, 'Still, I must apologise—to you and especially the tenants. Barksdale might have inflicted the actual injuries, but I allowed it to happen.'

Sir Edward nodded. 'It sounds as if you've experienced a sea change indeed.'

Greville smiled wryly. 'After my time aboard the *Illustrious*, I'm as different now from the man who left these shores as the English Channel is from the Bay of Marrakesh.'

'What will you do when you are released?' Jo asked.

'I hope you might help with that, Sir Edward. With the prize money coming to me and a bit I inherited, I'd like to purchase a place of my own. Lord Englemere told me that, as you own a number of properties, you might be persuaded to sell me Blenhem Hill.'

Sir Edward considered him for a long moment. 'So you can make restitution to the tenants personally. I've enjoyed my time at Blenhem—how could I not, when it brought me my dear wife?' he said, giving Joanna's hand another squeeze. 'But I do have extensive properties elsewhere I need to attend.'

'Oh, my dear, having Greville take over the Blenhem would be the most marvellous solution!' Joanna inserted. 'You were saying just today that you should leave soon to tour your other holdings, and must find someone to take over here.'

'So I was. Let me think on it, Mr Anders. I'm sure we can come to an agreement.'

'You will stay a few days, Greville? For a visit, and so you and Ned can work out the details about Blenhem Hill?'

He'd intended to resume his journey the very next morning, but in the face of his sister's appeal, that resolve faltered. 'Two days, then,' he replied.

'You're looking tired, sweetheart,' Greaves said to his wife. 'Why don't you have Myles show your brother to his room, and then rest before dinner?'

Joanne tried, and failed, to stifle a yawn. 'This business of making heirs is very fatiguing,' she admitted. 'Very well, I'll go rest. Until dinner, Greville.'

Sir Edward returned to work while the butler showed Greville up to his chamber. Gazing out the window at the ploughed fields in the distance, Greville felt a glow of pride and anticipation.

It felt right, somehow, to begin anew here. He would work hard, learn well and some day soon, be able to look tenants in the eye, knowing he had made their tasks easier. He'd become a landlord like Jo's husband Ned and Amanda's father Lord Bronning, respected and admired for his expertise and his enlightened care of the land.

Maybe he'd even look for that borough to represent and serve in the Commons.

Might he some day sit down at Amanda's table as a leader of government, working to better the nation?

If enough years passed—many, many years—perhaps he might some day gaze upon her lovely face again without the agonising sense of loss now scouring his heart.

Chapter Twenty-Two

The same afternoon Greville arrived at Blenhem Hill, Amanda found herself walking in the mild spring sunshine with Lord Trowbridge, who had prevailed upon her sponsor to allow him to escort her around her ladyship's garden. Fearing she knew what he intended and desperate to avoid being forced to a decision, she'd tried to demur, only to have Lady Parnell, with a broad wink at Trowbridge, practically push her from the room.

Strolling on Trowbridge's arm down well-tended gravel paths between bare-branched shrubs and bulbs that scattered a fairy dust of whites, yellows and pinks over the beds, Amanda tried to maintain a constant flow of amusing conversation. But by the time they'd made one full circuit, she'd run out of polite chat. Her heart thumping harder than a maid beating dust from a carpet, she fell silent, a rising panic tightening her chest and preventing her from managing another syllable.

Trowbridge reached for her hand. 'I'm as nervous as you look,' he confessed. 'I've never before asked a lady to walk in the garden with me.'

She felt a little faint. 'So you didn't bring me here to discuss your concerns over the Royal Marriages?'

He laughed. 'Not royal ones,' he replied, sending another stab of anxiety through her.

Before she could try to forestall him with another light remark, he squeezed her hand. 'You can't tell me you're surprised. My attentions have been too marked. Indeed, I understand wagers are being made about our wedding date in the betting books at White's as we speak.'

Amanda felt as if the air were being squeezed out of her chest. 'Don't you think we should get to know each other better, before we have the talk I think you want to have?'

'What else is there to know? What I've observed of you and I hope what you've observed of me shows we both possess good character and high ideals. You have a strong interest in the affairs of our nation—by no means a common concern for a young lady! To that useful trait, you add every attribute a man could wish for in a wife: beauty, intelligence, skill with people. In turn, I can offer you not just wealth and ease, but an opportunity to play an important part in the political life. You'll command my respect, tenderness and devotion. I can't think of another lady in London whom I'd be prouder to have on my arm as I welcome guests to my home.'

Respect…tenderness…devotion. Pride, to have her on his arm. She thought of Hillyard's comment about trophies…and about the man she wanted coming to her at night.

'What of…warmer feelings?' she asked, her palms beginning to sweat.

He gave her a look that did not disguise his desire. 'I may not advertise it by profligate living, but I have passion enough, I assure you. Or are you referring to what is commonly called "falling in love"?'

He shook his head. 'I'm afraid I discount the emotion. Since those friends who claim to have succumbed to it generally regret the experience, it seems to me a madness best avoided. No, a successful marriage, I believe, should be founded on respect, mutual interests, and a pure and lasting affection.'

A madness best avoided. Reflecting upon the chaos into which her feelings for Greville Anders so often tossed her, perhaps he was right.

'True, we've not known each other long, so perhaps you have reason for believing you don't yet know me well enough,' he continued. 'I admit to being impatient. A lady as lovely and unique as you, my dear, attracts a great deal of notice, and I couldn't bear to have the prize I value so highly claimed by someone else.'

Is that all she was to him...a prize to be claimed, another valuable possession to embellish his home?

When she remained silent, unable to dredge out the proper words about being honoured and gratified, he continued, a bit anxiously, 'I hope you don't think badly of me for recognising what I want and pursuing it boldly. If you feel I'm being too precipitous, I'm willing to wait. I'll not press you for an answer immediately. Talk with your father first, if you want, and when you're ready, I'll call on him.'

He gave her a wry smile. 'Perhaps you're offended that I'm addressing you without first obtaining his permission. Understandably, I think, I didn't wish to make the journey to Ashton Grove unless I was certain of obtaining *your* consent. I'll not entreat you further, but simply hope we will soon come to an understanding that will make me the happiest man in England.'

Taking her numb hands, he kissed them, then looked ardently into her eyes.

Did he want to claim her lips? While she stood irresolute, torn between curiosity and a desire to flee, he bent and kissed her.

A soft, gentle brush of the mouth, made with no demands.

A shiver went through her, whether of unease or satisfaction she couldn't tell.

Then his hands clutched her shoulders and he kissed her again, his tongue tasting her lips briefly before releasing her. 'I'll show you much more passion than that, once you give me the right,' he said, his voice rough. 'Now I'd better get you back before Lady Parnell sends Kindle after us.'

He offered her his arm, resuming his discussion of the impediments the tangled finances of Royal Dukes were creating in the matter of their marriages. Her thoughts scattered, she barely heard him.

Somehow she made it through the rest of the afternoon, chatting with other guests until calling hours concluded. The moment she could, ignoring Lady Parnell's enquiring look, she fled to her room.

Too restless to sit, she stood at the window, gazing out at London streets and rooftops, feeling a pang of longing for the green fields and windswept Devon coastline whose intensity would have astonished her only a few months previous.

What was she to do, now that she'd received the declaration she'd dreaded?

Accept him, and the landscape outside her window would be her new home. She would achieve everything Mama and Grandmama had dreamed of for her: guarantee herself a life of affluence and ease, obtain an important position in society and become an active participant in helping her husband shape their nation.

He would be a husband who esteemed and admired her, who wanted her standing beside him, wanted to show her off as one more beautiful ornament in his home. One who, though he desired her, didn't believe in nor wish to experience the mad, illogical abandon of the senses that came with falling in love.

Except, she was very much afraid she had already experienced it.

She touched her lips. Trowbridge's kiss had been…pleasant. It didn't sear and burn and make her want to wrap herself around him, pull his hands to her breasts and have him bury himself deep within her.

In fact, when he'd kissed her again, she'd almost backed away, as if what he sought belonged to another.

Was she an idiot? She wasn't even sure if the man who'd created such havoc in her heart and mind spared her a thought. He'd saved only a few moments out of his visit to London to spend with her, and then spoke almost nothing of himself, as if he didn't think she needed to know much about his future.

Had their interlude at Ashton Grove been for him merely a pleasant flirtation to pass the time, and the episode in the Neville Tour just a virile man happy to oblige a maiden who'd shown herself more wanton than she should be?

Even if it had meant more, he'd made it quite plain he had no interest in London or the affairs of state. She smiled, recalling how he'd tweaked Trowbridge as his father's 'assistant' when he defended the valour of the common sailor.

Was she truly contemplating turning her back on the city, wealth and the position in the political world she'd dreamed of since childhood to run after a man who might not even want her?

And what of Papa? With his recovery still uncertain, he'd steeled himself to send her to London anyway, so she might fulfil her dream. Would he turn from her in disgust if she threw away every advantage her family and Lady Parnell had worked to give her to choose a man who wished only to be a simple country gentleman?

Her stubborn heart insisted what they'd shared had been more than flirtation, more than obliging lust. Insisted, before she made the irrevocable decision to choose esteem over love and satisfaction over passion, she must find out for certain how Greville Anders felt about her.

By now, her head was throbbing. In the midst of the turmoil, she knew only one thing for certain. Some time tonight, she would tell Lady Parnell that she wanted to go home.

After greeting her hostess in the parlour before their dinner guests arrived, Amanda fell silent, not sure how to tell Lady Parnell she wished to leave at the height of the Season without seeming ungrateful for all that lady had done for her.

'You seem pensive, my dear.'

'Lord Trowbridge told me he intends to make a formal offer,' she blurted out.

'Wonderful!' Lady Parnell exclaimed. 'I'm so happy for you! It's what you've always wanted, isn't it? Oh, your dear mama would be so pleased!'

'Except…I'm not so sure it's still what I want,' she admitted. 'Oh, I have enjoyed London, especially the political evenings here and at Lady Ravensfell's and Lady Holland's. They were stimulating, exciting and I loved every minute.'

'That's a foretaste of what your life would be, if you married Trowbridge. His character and understanding are excellent, and it's clear he cares for you. My dear, you can hardly do better than an earl's son. Why the hesitation?'

'It's just…my heart is not totally engaged. He seemed to say that love would come later, a deepening of mutual respect and affection. Can that be true?'

Lady Parnell frowned, clearly not pleased by Amanda's unexpected indecision. 'Not everyone experiences falling in love. My own marriage was arranged by my family, but I came to esteem my husband very much, and miss him still. Besides, quite frankly, "love" may be well and good, but there are much more important considerations in wedlock. Money. Property. Family connections.'

Amanda knew so little of the world. Would mutual respect and admiration last longer, be more likely to make her happy, than the extremes of passionate emotion Greville evoked in her?

'Is there…someone else?'

Startled out of her musing, Amanda jerked her head up to find Lady Parnell's thoughtful gaze resting on her.

'The fact that you are not falling for the charms of Lucien Trowbridge makes me wonder if you left a beau in the country, someone who still holds a claim upon your heart.'

After a moment's hesitation, Amanda confessed, 'Yes, there is someone.' *Ah, how good it felt to finally admit that!* 'I hoped to meet a gentleman in London I could like just as well, but I haven't.' She gave a pained laugh. 'To make it worse, I don't even know if he really wants me. Or if Papa would approve the match if he did.'

Lady Parnell's frown deepened. 'Is he that ineligible?'

'He's a gentleman's son, but cannot boast the wealth or title of Lord Trowbridge. Nor has he any aspirations to play a role in the political arena.'

Lady Parnell shook her head. 'Be very careful, my dear. I've seen a handful of misses make the mistake of believing passion a sufficient substitute for a substantial income and a secure future. I assure you, it is not.'

She took a restless turn about the room, while Amanda stood silent, anguished at having displeased the lady whose approval meant so much to her.

Lady Parnell stopped and turned back to her. 'Amanda, if you turn down Trowbridge, society will be astounded. The Ravensfells will not take a refusal of their son's suit kindly, and their influence is substantial. There's no guarantee you would ever receive so advantageous an offer again, or one that would gain you entrée into the political world you enjoy. Meaning no disrespect to your father, who is a most estimable gentleman,

I none the less sometimes think your mama regretted settling for a simple country gentleman.'

Not trusting herself to speak, Amanda merely nodded. Then, with a shuddering breath, she said, 'Would it inconvenience you terribly if I went home to Ashton Grove to talk with Papa?'

'It's only natural you want to consult him on so important a decision. I'm sure he will advise you to be sensible. Very well, my dear, make your plans. Enough of this, now. Our guests will be arriving any minute.'

'I'm sorry to have disappointed you,' Amanda said softly, feeling tears sting her eyes.

Lady Parnell sighed and gave her a quick hug. 'You know I only want the best for you. I just hope you'll temper emotion with prudence. And remember—such opportunities as you have been blessed with occur only once in a lifetime.'

Before Amanda could add more than a thank you, Kindle entered to usher in their first dinner guest, and social duties left her no more time to worry over her future.

As soon as their guests departed, though, she would set Betsy to packing. Greville Anders would be returning to Ashton Grove, and before she distressed Papa by announcing a choice that might pain and disappoint him, she must see Mr Anders again.

In the morning three days later, home again in her own chamber, Amanda stood gazing at her reflection in the glass, nervously smoothing her gown before going in to speak with Papa.

To her great disappointment, when she arrived late the previous evening, she'd discovered Greville Anders was not in residence. He'd gone to visit his sister, Sands told her, and hadn't yet returned.

So she would have to talk with Papa without seeing him first. Smoothing the lace of her gown one more time, she began to pace, wondering just what she should tell him. If she confessed her partiality for Greville, how would Papa react? With disappointment…anger…disgust?

`Her thoughts still swung wildly back and forth between putting her feelings aside and meeting everyone's expectations by accepting Trowbridge, and abandoning the secure future he represented to offer herself to Greville Anders.

Her practical side said she was a fool even to contemplate doing something so risky—what if Papa disapproved and threatened to disown her for throwing away her grand prospects? She didn't think she could bear to forfeit his love and support. But if he didn't approve, what was she to do about her passion for Greville Anders?

She simply didn't know…and the prospect of having to make a choice between them was devastating.

On the other hand, she didn't want to finish her days a successful hostess and esteemed wife…whose heart ached with longing for the man she'd never stopped loving.

Oh, if only Greville were here! She just knew that if she could see him again, confess her feelings and watch his face, she'd be able to tell if her powerful, tempestuous emotions were returned. Or discover she'd been building a castle of dreams about his love that was completely devoid of reality.

In that case, she could always go back to London and accept Trowbridge's offer.

A sudden, powerful conviction seized her, freezing her in mid-step. For the first time, with brilliant clarity, she realised that accepting Trowbridge—accepting any other man—was no longer possible. Regardless of how he felt about her, she loved Greville Anders and no one else would do.

She didn't want to settle for mutual respect and tepid affection, or insult Trowbridge by living a lie, pledging her hand to him while her heart belonged to another.

Along with that surety came the knowledge that she had no choice but to take the risk of confessing everything to Papa.

If she was about to put her whole future in the balance, she might as well get straight to it. Her heartbeat accelerating like a bird taking flight, she headed for her father's study.

He gave a delighted smile as she entered and came over to embrace her. 'Sands told me you'd arrived home last night! How good to see you, my child!'

'I suppose you can guess why I came home.'

'To see if Althea was taking proper care not to let me slip out of the house in defiance of doctor's orders? To discover whether Cook was nipping at the sherry or the underbutler nabbing the silver?' he teased. 'Althea is doing a wonderful job, by the way.'

'I knew she would. And, yes, I did want to check on you and all those things. Oh, how I've missed you, Papa!' she exclaimed, giving him another hug.

'I must confess, I didn't expect to see you again so soon. Is…is everything going well in London?'

'Oh, yes, Papa! I've loved becoming better acquainted with Lady Parnell. The parties and dancing and theatre, the shops and entertainments have been marvellous.'

'The handsome escorts, too, if London gentlemen have eyes in their heads. But if nothing is amiss, I'm guessing you've come about one in particular. Am I right, puss?'

Amanda nodded. 'Lord Trowbridge told me he intends to ask you for my hand. Unless I tell him not to.'

Her father raised an eyebrow. 'And why would you do that? Is Trowbridge not exactly the sort of husband you've been seeking?'

'His character and position are everything admirable. Except…he doesn't really love me.' When her father started to protest, she halted him with a wave. 'No, he admitted as much. He believes admiration and affection to be a better basis for marriage. But…there is someone else who *has* engaged my heart, more deeply than I ever thought possible.'

She gave her head an agitated shake. 'Oh, Papa, I've tried and tried to talk myself out of it, but in the end, I can no longer deny how I feel. I hate to break the promise I made to Mama and disappoint you and Lady Parnell, but somehow, against all my better judgement, I…I've fallen in love with Greville Anders.'

There, she'd said it. Now she held her breath, watching her father anxiously.

'I see,' he said non-committally.

At least he hadn't leapt to his feet in anger, or called Sands to have her expelled from the house. But then, she should have known her gentle father would not chastise, but instead seek to understand before reacting to her confession.

'I suspected there was some…partiality between you,' he said at length. 'Does he return your feelings?'

Her laughter had an hysterical edge. 'I'm such a fool, Papa, I don't even know! I *think* he returns my feelings and kept silent to let me have my Season, unimpeded by any other commitments. But even not knowing what he wishes, I can't marry Trowbridge. Or Lord Melcombe or any of the other gentleman Lady Parnell expects to offer for me. I must marry the man I love…or no one.'

'Anders is a gentleman, too, and will make excellent estate manager. But will being a mere country gentleman's wife make you happy? Since you were a little girl, you've thought of nothing but becoming a grand society hostess. Are you sure you can abandon that vision?'

'I can't blame you for doubting it. I've enjoyed the Season, but more and more lately, aside from the dinners at which political matters are debated, the endless rounds of parties and pleasures and entertainments, shopping and gossiping, just seems so…trivial. It is like existing on a never-ending diet of sweetmeats.'

She laughed ruefully. 'After all that time spent thinking I couldn't wait to leave the country and live in London, I found I missed it. The rustle of wind in the trees and across the grass, the soft low of cattle in the fields, the scent of meadow-fresh air untainted by smoke and street refuse. I missed the rhythm of country life, people tending fields and flocks, their days spent in hard, useful, necessary labour. Missed tending to them and the household, activities focused on more than just gratifying my own desires. When I arrived home yesterday, nothing had ever looked more beautiful to me than the fields and manor at Ashton Grove. I guess I'm a countrywoman at heart after all.'

'You are sure this is what you want?' he said again. 'If you abandon your Season now, you will most likely forfeit for ever any chance of making a great society match.'

'Lady Parnell already warned me as much.' She smiled tremulously. 'I never thought I would choose woods and fields and cottages over the excitement of the city, but it seems I have.' She came over to kneel before him, looking up anxiously into his eyes. 'I'm sorry I've turned out to be such a disappointment. You…you won't cast me off, will you?'

He leaned forwards to envelop her in a hug. 'How could you even ask such a thing? Surely you know your happiness is always, ever what counts most with me.' He chuckled. 'How could you imagine I would be *disappointed* for you to eschew London in favour of the country, when I'm sure to spend more time with my eventual grandchildren if I don't have to visit the city to see them?'

Sobering, he continued, 'Greville Anders is a good man of sound principles. He may not be titled, or as rich as Trowbridge, but he's a gentleman, with connections to some of the highest families in the land. If you want him and he asks for your hand, I'll not deny him permission.'

An enormous feeling of relief flooding her, she squeezed her father's hand. 'Thank you, Papa.'

'So, how do we proceed now? Do you wish me to speak with Mr Anders when he returns?'

'N-no. If I end up making a fool of myself, I'd rather he not know I'd discussed my feelings with anyone else.'

Papa gazed down at her, tenderness in his smile. 'If my daughter loves him, 'tis Anders who'd be the fool not to love her back. And Mr Anders, Puss, does not strike me as foolish.'

She exhaled a shaky breath. 'Well, if he doesn't want me, I can stay here and keep house for you, can't I?'

Papa chuckled. 'Oh, I don't foresee so dull a future.'

The very notion of becoming Greville's wife, waking with him at her side, greeting him with a kiss every day when he returned from his tasks—and spending every night in his bed—brought an upswell of joy within her. 'I think I would love becoming mistress of a small estate somewhere.'

'Just make sure you're the *wife* of the master, not just his mistress,' Papa warned, a twinkle in eye.

'Papa!' she protested, blushing as she recalled what she let Greville Anders do to and for her. What she couldn't wait to do again.

'Come talk with me after you've spoken with Mr Anders. And don't worry so much about his reaction. I may be a dried-up old man, but even I noticed how he's moped about since you left, looking like his last friend had abandoned him. I'm betting his reaction to discovering you are willing to turn your back on London will be everything you hope.'

'Oh, I hope so, too, Papa!' she cried, throwing her arms around him again and hugging so tightly that he protested he was hardly able to draw breath. But with Papa's blessing on her choice, her happiness was complete.

As long as Greville Anders loved her.

How long was she going to have to wait to find out?

Chapter Twenty-Three

Late that evening, mud-spattered and weary, Greville rode in from Blenhem Hill. He'd pushed his tired mount on until they reached Ashton, not wanting to spend another night on the road, so he might be ready to resume his duties first thing in morning.

His excessive fatigue might have one benefit; perhaps tonight he wouldn't dream of Amanda Neville, waking with delight that turned to bleak desolation as he discovered the image of her in his arms, her passionate panting breaths filling his ears and exulting his heart, was only an illusion.

After walking up from the stables, he encountered Sands in the hall. Stopping short, the butler said, 'Welcome back, Mr Anders! I wish you'd sent word that you'd be arriving tonight; I could have had some supper waiting. Shall I have Cook prepare you a tray?'

'I'd be most grateful. Please, don't disturb Lord Bronning or Miss Althea to inform them I've returned; I expect they've both already retired. I'll greet them tomorrow.'

Sands hesitated, as if he were about to add something, then nodded. 'Very well. Shall I send the tray to your chamber?'

'Yes, please. And make it just a cold collation. Before I retire, I wish to review the accounts, so I may discuss them with Lord Bronning first thing tomorrow.'

Sands bowed. 'Very well, Mr Anders.'

Greville thought longingly of a hot meal, a warm bath and a soft bed. He could scarcely wait to wash off the grit of the road, but Lord Bronning was an early riser, and he wanted to greet his host already in possession of the latest details on the status of the estate.

The allure of sleep did prompt him to quicken his step. Half-an-hour's inspection of Lord Bronning's well-organised ledgers should be sufficient to bring him up to date, and then he'd rest.

Greville checked in surprise at the threshold of the estate office. It must be fatigue, for he didn't recall asking Sands to illumine the candles, but golden light was spilling out into the hallway. He was through the door and halfway across the room before he realised it wasn't empty.

Sitting at his desk, her face angled pensively towards the window, was Amanda Neville.

Greville blinked once, then twice. Memories of her had ridden on his shoulder, whispered in his ear all the way back from Blenhem. After discussing details of purchasing the estate with Greaves, he'd argued with himself over whether to go immediately to London before returning to Ashton Grove. Asking her, this time point-blank and directly, whether the emotion he knew they shared was strong enough for her to consider giving up London and her dreams of a life there.

Had having her fill his heart and mind for so many hours made him conjure up her very image?

Before he could decide whether his wits had been addled by some pleasant madness, she looked up, saw him and gasped.

In one graceful movement, she leapt up from the chair, flew across room and into his arms.

Greville bound her to him, pressing his face into the silken warmth of her hair. If this were an illusion, he wanted it never to end. It took several minutes of contact—and his body's inevitable response to her nearness—before he decided he wasn't hallucinating and it really was Amanda he held in his arms.

In which case, he needed to put her at a distance before his hungry body tempted him to bring her closer still.

He was, with difficulty, forcing himself to release her when, apparently realising the impropriety of her actions, she disentangled herself from his arms, blushing.

Though thrilled by the spontaneous warmth of her greeting, he tried to rein in his stampeding hopes. 'What are you doing at Ashton?' He recalled Sands's hesitation when speaking about the family, and sudden alarm pulsed through him. 'Nothing has happened to—'

'No, no, Papa is fine. I…just needed to come home.'

Alarm of a different sort filled him as the *other* matter she would have felt compelled to see her father about flashed into his mind. 'For…some particular reason?'

She stepped away from him. 'If there was, how would you feel about it?'

Hoping she wasn't referring to an engagement with Trowbridge, but afraid she might be, he asked, 'About your connection with a certain…gentleman?'

'Precisely.'

Panic whipped through him and he felt a searing pain, as if his heart were shattering. For a moment he couldn't summon even thoughts, much less speech.

The new Greville, noble gentleman that he was, would want only the best for her. He'd congratulate her on achieving her fondest desire and wish her every happiness.

Greville opened his lips to say just that. But before those

syllables emerged, the old Greville wrested away control and he heard himself cry, 'Do you really love Trowbridge? Do you want to give yourself to him? Do you want his hands, his mouth, on you every night for the rest of your life? Will he worship you with his heart and all the passion within him… as I would?'

While her eyes widened and her lips parted, Greville found himself on one knee before her, rushing on, 'I know he can offer you the brilliant future and position you've always wanted. But I can't let you go to him without telling you how I feel. I think I started loving you the moment you frowned at that disreputable specimen besmirching your pristine entryway—but made him welcome anyway. I tried to conceal my feelings, even from myself, but by the time you left for London, I could no longer deny the truth, though I kept it from you. I said nothing because I wanted you to arrive in London unencumbered by any previous attachment, free to pursue your dreams.

'Though my wealth will never match Trowbridge's,' he rushed on, desperate to get it all out before she stopped him with a flat refusal, 'you would be mistress of Blenhem Hill, filling the role of a country gentleman's wife, a task you would perform as expertly as you would that of society hostess. One I think you enjoy. There's even a seat in Parliament in a nearby borough I might stand for. If you would consider, my darling, making me the happiest man alive by agreeing to marry me, no one could love you or desire you more than I do and always will.'

She shook her head wonderingly. 'You truly love me, then?'

'"Love" isn't large enough to encompass all I feel. For weeks I tried to forget you, mourned losing you, pined for you, tried to convince myself that I could build a life without you. The misery I experienced only proved to convince me of the depth of my emotions. I…I know you care for me. Can I dare hope you could love me even half so well, and marry me, and be content as the wife of a country gentleman and member of Parliament, rather than lady to some great leader of the Lords?'

'As long as I am *your* wife, that's all that matters,' she murmured, pulling him up from his kneeling stance and leaning in to his kiss.

His dazzled mind could scarcely comprehend her assent, for the instant her lips met his, all his thoughts dissolved. Greville harnessed every iota of the joy and wonder coursing through him and put it into that kiss.

After a reverent, gentle brush of his mouth against hers, he deepened the pressure, using a sweep of his tongue to trace and caress the outline of her lips. Moaning, she swayed into his chest, opening to him.

Fired by her invitation, he plunged within the sweet warmth of her mouth, sought out her tongue, teased and traced it, sucked and nibbled gently. Then harder, faster, deeper, until desire pulsed in his head and the sweet sound of her gasping breaths filled his ears.

Not until one hand began to creep towards her breast and his arm moved to pull her closer against his turgid length did prudence break the hold of need, and he realised he must stop before he was beyond caring that the butler waited outside and her father and cousin slept somewhere down the hall.

Gently he broke the kiss, setting her at arm's length, while both of them tried to catch their breath. Wonder and elation and desire filled him until he was so effervescent with happiness, he felt he might float to the moon and shout his happiness from the skies. 'Shall I speak to your father? Tomorrow, of course, 'tis too late tonight! Shall we have the banns called this Sunday? But, no, you'll want to finish your Season.'

Shaking her head in the negative, she trailed loving fingers over his face, his lips. He sighed with bliss and angled his face into her hands, eddies of delight coursing through every nerve.

Fortunately, since he hardly could string two words together when she touched him thus, she said, 'I've learned all I needed to know from London. I don't need to go back.'

Some other imperative tickled at the back of his mesmerised mind. 'Lady Parnell?' he mumbled.

'I think she will understand. And if she doesn't...having you in my life, my love, will more than compensate for her disapproval and anything else I leave behind in London.'

She brought his face down to hers and kissed him again. This time, he let her take the lead,

By the time she stepped back, the new Greville's brain had ceased to function. Old Greville instincts were taking over, suggesting he urgently needed a bed, a sofa, a soft pile of hay, or any other reasonably comfortable horizontal surface.

But as he reached up to pull her back to him, a small clod of mud fell from his bespattered coat, breaking into dust on the fabric of her gown, and reality returned in a rush.

With a groan, he made himself release her again, finding it even harder this time, now that he knew he had her love. 'You inflame me so, I should like to devour you whole, now where we stand. Perhaps I should ask your papa to lock you up until the wedding day! I've wanted you so long, I'm not sure how I will endure waiting until all the banns are read. But forgive me, I'm covered in dirt from the road. Let me bid you goodnight, my sweet, and meet you tomorrow when I'm more presentable.'

He would have bowed and left her, but she stayed him with a hand to his arm—and gave him that siren's smile that sent a rush of sensation pulsing through his member. 'Then you need to be bathed, do you not?'

His mind flew to an image of warm water, naked bodies, Amanda's full breasts floating atop the surface, pink nipples peeking at him, while she soaped...

Heat blasted through him, searing any reply he might have intended right off his lips.

Before he could get his tongue untangled, she continued, 'It was the custom in medieval times, was it not? The lady of the manor bathed guests. Imagine what wicked nights those knights must have experienced after such a ritual. Why not order a tub sent to your chamber…and let me show you?'

Trying to keep that seductive vision from overwhelming his senses again, he replied, a bit desperately, 'If I allow you to do that, I'll never survive waiting until after the wedding.'

'I don't want you to wait,' she said. 'Oh, my love, I have struggled and denied and tried to will away my feelings even more strenuously than you! Now that we have found each other again despite all the obligations and expectations meant to keep us apart, all I want to do is surrender…and revel in that love. I want *your* kiss…*your* hands…*your* mouth on me.' She paused and slid her hand slowly down his trouser front, smiling as he gasped. 'I want *everything* you can give me.'

Dimly, in the far corner of his brain, the new Greville was nattering on about sleeping fathers and inquisitive cousins and gossiping servants. Snuffing out the sound, the deliriously happy old Greville murmured, 'Tonight and ever after, I'll give my lady all she desires.'

'Then kiss me again.' Placing his hand over her breast, she pulled his mouth back to hers.

* * * * *

COMING NEXT MONTH FROM

HARLEQUIN®
HISTORICAL

Available February 22, 2011

- **THE WIDOWED BRIDE**
  by **Elizabeth Lane**
  (Western)

- **THE SHY DUCHESS**
  by **Amanda McCabe**
  (Regency)
  spin-off from *The Diamonds of Welbourne Manor* anthology

- **BOUGHT: THE PENNILESS LADY**
  by **Deborah Hale**
  (Regency)
  Gentlemen of Fortune

- **HIS ENEMY'S DAUGHTER**
  by **Terri Brisbin**
  (Medieval)
  The Knights of Brittany

REQUEST YOUR FREE BOOKS!

HARLEQUIN® HISTORICAL:
Where love is timeless

2 FREE NOVELS PLUS 2 FREE GIFTS!

YES! Please send me 2 FREE Harlequin® Historical novels and my 2 FREE gifts (gifts are worth about $10). After receiving them, if I don't wish to receive any more books, I can return the shipping statement marked "cancel." If I don't cancel, I will receive 6 brand-new novels every month and be billed just $4.94 per book in the U.S. or $5.49 per book in Canada. That's a savings of at least 18% off the cover price! It's quite a bargain! Shipping and handling is just 50¢ per book in the U.S. and 75¢ per book in Canada.* I understand that accepting the 2 free books and gifts places me under no obligation to buy anything. I can always return a shipment and cancel at any time. Even if I never buy another book from the Reader Service, the two free books and gifts are mine to keep forever.

246/349 HDN FC45

Name _____ (PLEASE PRINT) _____

Address _____ Apt. # _____

City _____ State/Prov. _____ Zip/Postal Code _____

Signature (if under 18, a parent or guardian must sign)

Mail to the **Reader Service:**
IN U.S.A.: P.O. Box 1867, Buffalo, NY 14240-1867
IN CANADA: P.O. Box 609, Fort Erie, Ontario L2A 5X3
Not valid for current subscribers to Harlequin Historical books.

**Want to try two free books from another line?
Call 1-800-873-8635 or visit www.ReaderService.com.**

* Terms and prices subject to change without notice. Prices do not include applicable taxes. N.Y. residents add applicable sales tax. Canadian residents will be charged applicable taxes. Offer not valid in Quebec. This offer is limited to one order per household. All orders subject to credit approval. Credit or debit balances in a customer's account(s) may be offset by any other outstanding balance owed by or to the customer. Please allow 4 to 6 weeks for delivery. Offer available while quantities last.

Your Privacy—The Reader Service is committed to protecting your privacy. Our Privacy Policy is available online at www.ReaderService.com or upon request from the Reader Service.

We make a portion of our mailing list available to reputable third parties that offer products we believe may interest you. If you prefer that we not exchange your name with third parties, or if you wish to clarify or modify your communication preferences, please visit us at www.ReaderService.com/consumerschoice or write to us at Reader Service Preference Service, P.O. Box 9062, Buffalo, NY 14269. Include your complete name and address.

HH11

USA TODAY *bestselling author Lynne Graham*
is back with a thrilling new trilogy
SECRETLY PREGNANT, CONVENIENTLY WED

Three heroines must marry alpha males to keep
their dreams…but Alejandro, Angelo and Cesario
are not about to be tamed!

Book 1—JEMIMA'S SECRET
Available March 2011 from Harlequin Presents®.

JEMIMA yanked open a drawer in the sideboard to find
Alfie's birth certificate. Her son was her husband's child.
It was a question of telling the truth whether she liked it or
not. She extended the certificate to Alejandro.

"This has to be nonsense," Alejandro asserted.

"Well, if you can find some other way of explaining how
I managed to give birth by that date and Alfie not be yours,
I'd like to hear it," Jemima challenged.

Alejandro glanced up, golden eyes bright as blades and
as dangerous. "All this proves is that you must still have
been pregnant when you walked out on our marriage. It
does not automatically follow that the child is mine."

"'I know it doesn't suit you to hear this news now and I
really didn't want to tell you. But I can't lie to you about it.
Someday Alfie may want to look you up and get acquainted."

"If what you have just told me is the truth, if that little
boy does prove to be mine, it was vindictive and extremely
selfish of you to leave me in ignorance!"

Jemima paled. "When I left you, I had no idea that I was
still pregnant."

"Two years is a long period of time, yet you made no
attempt to inform me that I might be a father. I will want
DNA tests to confirm your claim before I make any deci-

sion about what I want to do."

"Do as you like," she told him curtly. "*I* know who Alfie's father is and there has never been any doubt of his identity."

"I will make arrangements for the tests to be carried out and I will see you again when the result is available," Alejandro drawled with lashings of dark Spanish masculine reserve.

"I'll contact a solicitor and start the divorce," Jemima proffered in turn.

Alejandro's eyes narrowed in a piercing scrutiny that made her uncomfortable. "It would be foolish to do anything before we have that DNA result."

"I disagree," Jemima flashed back. "I should have applied for a divorce the minute I left you!"

Alejandro quirked an ebony brow. "And why didn't you?"

Jemima dealt him a fulminating glance but said nothing, merely moving past him to open her front door in a blunt invitation for him to leave.

"I'll be in touch," he delivered on the doorstep.

What is Alejandro's next move? Perhaps rekindling their marriage is the only solution! But will Jemima agree?

Find out in Lynne Graham's
exciting new romance
JEMIMA'S SECRET

Available March 2011
from Harlequin Presents®.

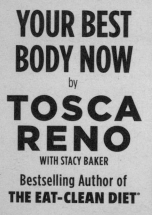

Top author
Janice Kay Johnson
brings readers a riveting new romance
with
Bone Deep

Kathryn Riley is the prime suspect in
the case of her husband's disappearance
four years ago—that is, until someone tries
to make her disappear…forever. Now
handsome police chief Grant Haller must
stop suspecting Kathryn and instead begin
to protect her. But can Grant put aside the
growing feelings for Kathryn long enough
to catch the real criminal?

Find out in March.

*Available wherever
books are sold.*

HARLEQUIN *Presents*

USA TODAY *Bestselling Author*

Lynne Graham

is back with her most exciting trilogy yet!

SECRETLY PREGNANT
CONVENIENTLY WED

Jemima, Flora and Jess aren't looking for love,
but all have babies very much in mind...and they may
just get their wish and more with the wealthiest, most
handsome and impossibly arrogant men in Europe!

Coming March 2011

JEMIMA'S SECRET

Alejandro Navarro Vasquez has long desired vengeance after
his wife, Jemima, betrayed him. When he discovers the
whereabouts of his runaway wife—and that she has a two-
year-old son—Alejandro is determined to settle the score....

FLORA'S DEFIANCE (April 2011)
JESS'S PROMISE (May 2011)

Available exclusively from Harlequin Presents.